The
Money-Whipped
Steer-Job Three-Jack
Give-Up Artist

The
Money-Whipped
Steer-Job Three-Jack
Give-Up Artist

A Novel

Dan Jenkins

DOUBLEDAY

New York   London   Toronto   Sydney   Auckland

PUBLISHED BY DOUBLEDAY
a division of Random House, Inc.
1540 Broadway, New York, New York 10036

DOUBLEDAY and the portrayal of an anchor with a dolphin are
trademarks of Doubleday, a division of Random House, Inc.

Book Design by Nicola Ferguson

Library of Congress Cataloging-in-Publication Data
Jenkins, Dan.
The money-whipped steer-job three-jack give-up artist :
a novel / Dan Jenkins.— 1st ed,
p. cm.
I. Title.
PS3560.E48 M66 2001
813'.54—dc21   2001028602

ISBN 0-385-49723-7

Printed in the United States of America

June 2001

FIRST EDITION

1 3 5 7 9 10 8 6 4 2

Once more for June Jenkins.

Only you.

Not to write a song or anything.

Hell, I should have worn my ball gown

the way y'all waltzed me around today.

—old Texas golf lament

The

Money-Whipped

Steer-Job Three-Jack

Give-Up Artist

1

SAY HELLO TO YOUR LIGHT-RUN-
ning money-whipped steer-job three-jack
give-up artist.

This is pretty good. Man talking to
himself. But it's me, all right. Your no-
heart Mother Goose who blowed about
$80,000 in the last round of the Hawaiian
Open today.

Lost my swing, lost my tempo. Tempo
Retardo. Also, I played too fast. I mean
shit, the way I raced around out there
you'd have thought I was a pickup truck
on the way to happy hour.

You don't have to stick a thermometer
up my ass to find out I shot a fever-
running 73. Just look at the scores in

tomorrow's paper and you'll find a dunce named Bobby Joe Grooves tied for nineteenth over here at Waialae Country Club in Honolulu.

"Over here," by the way, don't get it done. Not when you're talking about Hawaii. The first time I came over here I didn't think much about it. I just hopped on a plane, flew to Honolulu, got off, inhaled a bottle of perfume, golfed my ball, hauled ass. Perfume is what the air in Hawaii smells like when it don't smell like suntan lotion.

Then one day I looked at Hawaii on a globe, and whoa—it ain't near nothing. There's about six thousand miles of lateral hazard on all sides of it. You're seriously off the fairway when you're over here, and I think that's one reason nobody in Hawaii knows anything about what's going on anywhere else in the world, especially in America.

Your basic Hawaiian wears shorts, sandals, and a shirt that looks like Granddad ate dinner in it six times. He'll light a torch, paddle a canoe, and grill a fish for you. And at the drop of a mai tai, he'll sing to you about a Waikiki moon, which, for my money, don't look much different than the one that comes up over Fort Worth, Texas. But he's nice and sweet-natured and wants to take you to see his fern grotto and his slippery slide and his Killykooky Canyon.

Yeah, right, Punchbowl. Wait till I get this lei around my neck and I'll go with you.

One thing they have over here is good souvenirs, though. I say you need to remember where you been in your travels. Souvenirs do that. Souvenirs and photos of yourself with movie stars who've since shrunk up.

The other day was I was poking around in one of those Waikiki gift shops and I bought me this old dinner menu. It was from the Royal Hawaiian Hotel and dated December 7, 1941. Not exactly an incidental date in your history of mankind.

Dinner that evening at the Royal Hawaiian consisted of a fruit cocktail, consommé soup, hearts of lettuce salad with French dressing, chicken casserole with glazed carrots, string beans, and fig fritters, and coconut layer cake for dessert—all for $1.25.

The menu also says that the EVENTS OF THE DAY are going to be a sunset serenade by the Royal Hawaiian glee club, a modern hula exhibition by Annie Annini and her Six Hula Maids, and music by Rollie Beelby's Royal Terrace Orchestra.

That was all canceled, of course, when the Yellow Peril showed up for breakfast. Too bad. Those glazed carrots and fig fritters might have knocked down some Zeros.

You can't talk to most haoles over here either. A haole is your white guy dropout from the Mainland. He's generally too stoned to talk at all. Or he has a surfboard under his arm and the only thing he can say is "Grab your stick, dude, there's a swell at Pipeline."

You hear that the Tahitians discovered Hawaii. Okay, I've looked at Tahiti on a globe too, and I'll tell you what—it was uphill all the way.

I was talking about it the other night with this haole bartender, name of Denny. A scruffy kid with a far-off gaze. Looked like he was working his way through dopefiend school.

I was in a waterfall joint on Kalacomma Boulevard, hydrant water washing down from the ceiling behind the bar indoors, make you think it's raining outside. Tropical shit.

These types of bars are all over Hawaii, and to be honest, they're what I like best about the place, being a fan of old flicks on TV. Sit there in my blue Sahara golf shirt and khaki pants and loafers and play like I'm a South Seas drunk. Play like I'm a guy in a grimy white suit who needs a shave, sitting there smoking under a ceiling fan, waiting for some kind of Rita Hayworth to walk in the door.

I asked Denny, "You get a lot of South Seas drunks in here?"

"Get you what?" he said.

I said, "I put the over-and-under on the Tahitians trying to get to Hawaii at five hundred years, what do you think? If they'd taken a little longer a Shrine convention would have gotten here first."

Didn't hear me or didn't get it. He was busy sticking umbrellas in everybody's drink but mine. A Junior and water don't do umbrellas, I told him. When I'd asked him for a Junior, he'd only squinted, puzzled.

"Mr. Justerini," I said.

"Who?" he said.

"If you don't have J and B, I can do Curtis—they taste the same."

"Curtis?"

"Cutty," I said. "You been over here a long time, huh?"

Fucking San Diego burnout.

There's more to Hawaii than Honolulu, of course. I've whapped it around pretty much everywhere over here, so I'm able to drop some geography on you.

You've got your Oahu. That's where they invented Honolulu, Pearl Harbor, and surfers. You've got the "Big Island" of Hawaii, where they invented volcanoes. You've got Lanai, where they invented pineapples. You've got Molokai, where they used to keep the lepers back when people caught leprosy. You've got Maui. That's where movie stars or people trying to look like movie stars go to hibernate in public. You might see dueling Sharon Stones standing in a snack bar line on Kapalooey. Last, you've got your Kauai. That's the prettiest of the islands, I believe. It's where you can scare up Grand Canyons and waterfalls and enchanted beaches, and it's never bothered me any that Kauai is where they manufacture most of the rain that goes to Seattle and Portland.

No question Hawaii has more paradise scattered around than your rural Oklahoma. But in my case it's hard to appreciate paradise when your golf game sticks a fork in you.

I know what people think. They think the $40,000 I won in Hawaii beats a young dose any day, and they're right. But take away my four three-jacks on the last nine and I'd have been up there in the $150,000 neighborhood.

Or take away those four three-jacks plus the steer-job tee ball that was so low and thin it would have made skid marks on I-20. It left me where I couldn't reach the par-five thirteenth in two and grab a gimme birdie. I don't piss those five drops and I'm up there in contention for the whole deal.

But no. What I come up with is a 73, which is an okay number if you're an offensive lineman, but it don't do squat for a man who dons his Softspikes for a living.

I can't play a track like Waialae anyhow. It's too easy. I know I'm supposed to like it because one of those respected architects designed it. Seth Raynor is who it was. I know about Seth Raynor because I like to read golf history. I like golf history, as a matter of fact, better than any other kind of history, including wars I've heard of.

Other than Ben Crenshaw, who lives in the past and wishes his balls were gutta-percha, nobody else on the tour can jack with me on golf history. Ask me who was runner-up to Bobby Jones in the 1926 U.S. Open at Scioto and I'll hit you with Joe Turnesa. Ask me where Johnny Revolta won the 1935 PGA and I'll hit you with Twin Hills in Oklahoma City. Or ask me who Seth Raynor was and I'll tell you he was a man who got his start working with Charles Blair Macdonald, the legendary architect who designed the National Gold Links and everything else out on Long Island except the stock portfolios.

To me, Seth Raynor's best work is the Country Club of Fairfield in Connecticut. I once did an outing up there for socialites. It's short but covered up with charm. But you can't join Fairfield, I hear, unless you've got a photo of your granddaddy sitting on Queen Victoria's knee.

Waialae's another story. Not even interesting. A diddy-bump layout with a bunch of tall skinny palms on every hole and pineapples for tee markers. Somebody's idea of atmosphere.

Waialae is out past Diamond Head in a residential area for people who've got big-time stroke. The Beverly Hills of Honolulu. Guys shoot fifteen and twenty under on it for four rounds. Somebody's always coming in with a 63 when I've played my ass off to get in with a 68. Hell, Julius Claudius even shot 60 on it a few years ago. Julius Claudius is what some of us call Davis Love III, that Roman numeral chasing his name around.

I'll probably skip Honolulu next year unless I can tie in an outing, rob some corporate sponges. Round of golf, dinner, Q-and-A, scoop twenty-five grand—*Buenos noches*, coaches.

SO WHAT it is, the tournament's history and I'm in my room at the Kalahammer Hotel, which is near Waialae. I was in a lagoon room where I could step out on the balcony and tell the pet dolphins about my birdies and bogeys. They bob up and look at you like they think they're one of you or you're one of them. I could have gone out and sought some nighttime entertainment but I've had about all the hooky-wooky I can take.

I could have been over here even longer if I'd been eligible for the Mercedes on Kapalooey. The Mercedes is our first stop on the tour every year. It's the old Tournament of Champions. You have to win a tournament to qualify for it, and I didn't. I won't comment on why I didn't win anything last year, except to say it was obviously a plot on the part of your left-wing liberal nutbags to give America away to the sorry folks.

If I'd been over here for *two* weeks I'd have really been up to my overlapping grip in raw fish, pineapples, grass skirts, little grass shacks, ukuleles, and poi.

Poi. There's a deal for you. It's something they eat in Hawaii and pretend it don't look like putty and don't taste like rubber cement.

I'd been warned to avoid poi. I'd succeeded for three years. But I finally got hold of some two nights ago. I was having a cocktail and letting this Hawaiian babe work me at the bar under the banyan tree at the Moana. She was wearing a painted-on blue T-shirt and tight jeans and possessed all the physical attributes that could make a man with no moral code fall deeply in love for twenty-four hours.

She wasn't a brown midget either, although you could tell she had some tan blood in her. Off-duty cocktail waitress is what she was. Had a name I couldn't say without grinning. Louleenie is close.

I was patient enough to listen to her tell me a bunch of Hawaiian lore, like I'm supposed to give a shit about Prince Kamookymocky and outrigger canoes and lava rocks.

Somewhere along the way she got me to take a bite of poi. Just try it, she said. Man, you want to talk about a gag. I might as well have been standing over a three-foot putt to win the Masters.

"You like?" she said.

I couldn't speak. I was busy trying to swallow that crap. It took me two or three minutes.

I finally got it down, and I was so hot at her for even suggesting I taste it in the first place, I said, "You stupid wahine bitch, I wouldn't fuck you with a Samoan's dick."

I probably should have said bubble-head driver. It would have been more "politically correct" in case she was some kind of bleeding-heart clown. But that poi had me out the door. I left her sitting there, rack and all.

I figured her not getting to *hukilau* a big-time PGA touring pro was punishment enough.

2

WHILE I WAS THREE-JACKING
around the pineapples, the tournament
got itself won by the crowd-pleasing
Knut Thorssun, friend of the stars, bulge
of the shapely adorables, Sweden's gift to
morons in the galleries.

Everybody knows Knut. Next to Tiger
Woods and maybe Cheetah Farmer, our
newest child star, you have to say Knut is
golf's most popular fellow. Him and his
long tee ball and long blond hair and
tight-fitting pants that often show off his
bulge, the kind you see on a ballet
dancer.

I know for a fact the phony asshole
pads his bulge, and I'd guess more than

one bimbo has discovered it. This doesn't matter to Knut, though. All he cares about is his image with the public. Mr. Golden Boy Long Ball Wagon Tongue.

Knut swamped all of us at Waialae. He set a tournament record of 270 when the cup wouldn't get out of the way of his ball. In his third-round 64 he only took twenty-three putts, which can sometimes get your ass kicked if it don't get you sent to prison.

Knut used to be a good friend. That was when he first came on our tour. He was just a simple Swede who never said much and laughed out loud at all the wrong things. If you've ever known any Swedes, you know their idea of humor is somebody pee-peed in the hot tub. Laugh *har, har*, bang fist on table. That's Knut Thorssun for you.

I started playing practice rounds with him when nobody else would, and when I found out he knew how to play bridge I invited him into our regular Tuesday night bridge game.

Talk about gin all you want to, but bridge is the best card game to gamble at. Gin's nothing but pick up the cards and hit the silk. Bridge is about half-cerebral.

We traveled together for a while, and Knut being a tall, broad-shouldered, trim-waisted, blue-eyed guy with his blond mane, I have to confess he helped me get laid a few times—I swooped his culls.

But all that was before Knut won himself the PGA at Oak Hill and the British Open at Birkdale—two majors to his credit—and became a European Ryder Cup star and therefore a favorite of the idiots among the sportswriters and the morons among the fans.

Suddenly he's Knut the Cute, Knut the Nuke. His all-time favorite headline in a moron Florida paper was *THOR MORE NUCLEAR!* Morons in the galleries started wearing buttons that said *Knut's Brutes,* and no-slack dirty legs started showing up in T-shirts that said *Thor's Whores.*

I'm often asked to explain the difference between a no-slack dirty leg and a cut-slack dirty leg. It's easy. Your cut-slack dirty leg is classier—you cut her some slack—whereas your no-slack dirty leg may well have a safety pin in her navel. But like they say about any dirty leg, stand close enough to her and you can hear the ocean.

Knut loves all his nicknames. When you're paired with him, you can see him light up, flash a big smile, every time he hears a moron holler, "Nuke 'em, Knut!" or "Let Thor eat!"

All of which means he eventually got to send off for the arrogant kit. Shows you how to turn yourself into an arrogant prick overnight. I think you can order one from a Neiman Marcus catalog.

Knut started to lose me the day we shared a cab from JFK to our hotel in New York City, the Four Seasons. Knut picked it for us. As far as I could tell it was conveniently located in the heart of the money funnel.

This was after he'd won the British Open at Birkdale, four years ago. Cynthia, his wife, the ex-stew, wasn't with him. She was minding the mansion back in Palm Beach, taking care of Sven and Matti, the unruly little shits they call sons. Knut rarely takes Cynthia and the little shits on the road with him. Puts a damper on his side gash.

We both had commerce in New York. His agent at IMG, Killer Tom McBride, had scheduled a commercial for him to do—part of his ten million dollar golf ball contract—and had him a fifty million dollar apparel deal to discuss. My agent at Dotted Line, Inc., Smokey Barwood, had arranged an outing for me with meat distributors at Baltusrol in New Jersey.

I'd never been successful enough to be represented by IMG, the powerhouse International Management Group, handlers of Tiger Woods and all other Babe Ruths that come along.

So we're unloading our things from the cab, and this was before the slow-moving doorman had decided to help us after I hit him in the palm. Knut's got nothing but his briefcase in one hand while I'm loaded down with my own gear, things slung over my shoulders, but Knut casually tells me to grab one of his bags.

"Grab your bag?" I said, looking almost practically dismayed.

"Yes, the green one there," Knut said, nodding at this vinyl-type carry-on deal sitting on the sidewalk.

I said, "Grab *this*, man. I don't grab the bag for *Jack Nicklaus!*"

He'd started in the door of the hotel but turned around.

"I am sorry, pal, I did not mean to insult you," he said.

"Of course not, *pal*," I said. "You were just saying, hey, you no-major, somewhere-down-the-money-list crudball, pick up my bag and be happy you know me."

He said, "I do not think in such a way of you, Bobby Joe. You are an excellent player. You have very many fine attributes. You are a good driver and are quite adequate with the long irons. . . . Still, it is in my honest opinion, now that the subject has come up, that you need to work harder on your short game, particularly around the greens."

I could only stare at him.

"I have been meaning to say this to you," he said. "When you putt from off the edge of the green, you are not accelerating your putter at impact. You should use a firmer stroke. You must try to make your follow-through as long as your backswing. Do you understand?"

"This is great," I said. "A golf lesson. I'm standing on the sidewalk in New York City getting a fucking golf lesson from a fucking Swede. Maybe a Turk or a Serb'll come by in a minute and gimme a swing tip. Do they play golf in Turkey? Serbs play?"

"I am only trying to help you," he said, and went inside.

He didn't hear me say to a lady entering the hotel, "Let Thor eat."

IT WAS the bridge game that did it for me.

There are six of us who like to play on Tuesday nights on the road. I'm the game's secretary. This means I find out which four are playing ahead of time. It will usually be me, Buddy Stark, Jerry Grimes, and somebody else. Buddy and Jerry are my two best friends out here. They're easy to tell apart. Buddy is tall, a neat dresser, reads books. Jerry is short and stocky, reads *USA Today*.

In the bridge game we cut for partners. It's the honor system. I don't believe any two guys have ever developed signals. One of us will have a suite so there'll be a room to play in. We deal the first hand at seven, the last hand at midnight. It's a long-established nickel-a-point game. Enough to hold your interest, but not enough to strap a serious hurt on you.

I arrange for the food. Everybody chips in to pay for it. I see that the cuisine varies. Maybe I'll pick up Kentucky Fried, or maybe I'll go to Wendy's, which has the best fast-food cheeseburgers, or maybe I'll go to Sonic for country fried steak sandwiches and shakes. I have a crucial rule for going to the drive-through window. Never get behind a woman in a minivan. She's there to order food for the whole little league team.

Most guys wanted me to go to Kentucky Fried when Knut was still in the game—they liked to watch him eat.

He'd hold the cards in one hand, lift a piece of chicken out of the barrel with his other hand—didn't matter what piece, big or small—and you'd see him sort of run it across his mouth like a harmonica. You'd hear a sound that would remind you of a woodpecker, or more like a woodpecker with a muffler, and about five seconds later you wouldn't see anything left but a slick bone, which he'd flip into a wastebasket.

Buddy Stark once said, "Knut eating fried chicken would be at the top of the charts if a rapper did it."

Knut was my partner on this night at The Players Championship in Ponte Vedra. We were in a suite at the Sawgrass Marriott. Buddy and Jerry had been getting all the hair all night—the face cards—and we were losing pretty good, but suddenly I was dealt a scorpion.

It's the best hand I've ever picked up, or ever will. I was holding the the ace, king, queen, jack, ten of spades, and four other spades—nine in all—and the ace-king of hearts, the ace-king of diamonds, and a void in clubs. That's a lay-down seven spades. A grand slam.

In case you're a bridge know-nothing, my hand was like picking up a royal straight flush in poker. Or better still, it was like holing out a three-wood for a double eagle in golf. My hand said nobody could take a trick but me if the bid was spades. I could trump a club lead, if somebody led a club, because I was void in clubs. That's how it works in bridge.

I played it cool and opened the bidding at two spades. I knew I'd wind up at seven spades, bid and made, but if I bid it up gradually there'd be a good chance Buddy or Jerry would double. None of us are master players and we were all likely to double a seven bid just on the chance that whoever was playing it would screw it up. A double meant heap big more points—more money—if you made the bid. Which was to take all thirteen tricks.

Buddy passed and Knut bid three hearts. Well, I didn't need his help in hearts. I didn't need anything. I had more hair in my hand than the sixties. So I bid seven spades, close out, telling my partner I had a lock.

But I didn't get to lay it down and tell jokes. That's because my old podnoo's arrogance kicked in. He bid seven no-trump over my spades.

This meant *he* would play the hand, not me, and he would play it in no trump, which, for you bridge know-nothings, means that the card led is the suit to be played for that trick. I was stunned. But I thought, oh, okay, Knut must have the ace of clubs, so it's a lay-down seven no-trump. He has the ace of clubs and I've got everything else with my scorpion. Seven no-trump, bid and made, would score even more points than seven spades.

Buddy routinely doubled, so I naturally redoubled, knowing we were going to take every trick, kick some serious ass.

What then happened was, Buddy Stark, with an evil grin, led the ace of clubs. If the bid had been in spades, I could have trumped it with a low spade, taken the trick. But we were in no trump, thanks to Knut. When you're in no trump, the highest card in whatever suit is led takes the trick. And in no trump, if everyone else is out of clubs, for example, you can lead a lowly, homeless, forlorn deuce of clubs and take the trick.

I was shot in the heart. We were down one. I glared at Knut. He was staring at the ace of clubs like he didn't know there was one in the deck. Then Buddy played the king of clubs. I was shot in the heart again. We were down two.

"Are you *kidding* me!" I shouted at Knut, who was now looking at the king of clubs as if he wondered where *that* came from.

Now Buddy led a small club to Jerry, who took yet another trick with the queen.

"Jee-zus . . . fucking . . . Christ!" I yelled at Knut.

Bim, bam, blooey. Having no stoppers in high clubs, we were down three before we hit a lick, and it was going to cost us a wing of the Taj Mahal, and all because the Swedish asshole took me out of spades, outbid his own partner—he knew best.

And me with a once-in-a-lifetime hand.

"Hmm," said Knut. That's all. While he looked bewildered that those clubs have killed us.

"Gee, I'm sorry, Knut," I now said, standing up. "It's my fault. I should have just opened seven spades and laid it down . . . you igno-rant . . . arrogant . . . no ace of clubs . . . Swedish . . . smorgasbord . . . subtitled . . . shit for brains . . . seven no-trump *motherfucker!*"

It's all part of Tour lore now. I did turn the table over and I did break out a Marriott window with a chair.

I think any bridge player would understand my actions completely.

3

I'VE BEEN OUT HERE SIXTEEN
years. I grab me a W every year or so. I
swoop close to a million a year in official
money now. But I'm pleased to report
that my head's never swoll up so much
that I refer to myself in third person.
Saying shit to interviewers like "Knut
Thorssun knows the kind of golf Knut
Thorssun is capable of playing."

I'm embarrassed for athletes who talk
like that. Sounds like they're not talking
about themselves but some stud on the
cover of *Golf Digest* or *Sports Illustrated*.
It's a cringe deal around my house.

Not that it can't be funny sometimes.
Like the night I came out of this tourna-

ment party in Atlanta and found Rickey Padgett, one of our top money winners, looking pissed and mumbling, "Rickey don't like it when Rickey can't find Rickey's limo."

I'm proud to say I'm a native Texan. I'm even prouder that I come from Fort Worth, the city that gave you Ben Hogan and Byron Nelson—not that I've ever been drunk enough to compare myself with those immortals.

When I was a kid trying to learn the game I was disappointed that I didn't have a chance to play some of the courses Hogan and Nelson did. Public courses like Worth Hills, Katy Lake, and Oakhurst. They were gone by then. Worth Hills, the first 18-hole muny in town, became part of the TCU campus. Katy Lake, a 9-hole layout with sand greens, where Hogan used to win long-driving contests, has long since been part of a shopping plaza on Seminary Drive off I-35. And Oakhurst, a course where Hogan worked as a young assistant pro, has long since been nothing but a playground by the same name down below the cliffs of the Riverside neighborhood.

Those courses were all designed by a man named John Bredemus. He was once a well-known track and field athlete. He ran and threw things against Jim Thorpe. Bredemus did courses all over Texas and he was the original designer of Colonial Country Club in Fort Worth, the course that was host to the 1941 United States Open Championship, an event which helped make my hometown famous for something besides the cattle drives and gunfights of the old Chisholm Trail days.

A chain-smoking fellow named Craig Wood won that National Open, hitting shots with a cigarette in his lips and wearing a corset for his bad back. He's the only man who ever started a U.S. Open double bogey, bogey on the first two holes, then went on to win it.

Every time I'm home and drive past Worth Hills, Katy Lake, and Oakhurst, I can't help but think about Bantam Ben and Lord Byron being out there honing their wedges as youngsters.

Those places are historical landmarks, is what I say. There ought to be plaques. You know, like the kind you see on an old three-story house where some rich guy lived when he was president of a biscuit company.

Glen Garden is still around. That's the country club over on the southeast side of town where Hogan and Nelson caddied as kids and played that match for the caddie championship. This was while they were going to different high schools. Hogan went to my old school, R. L. Paschal, fight for the purple, which was called Central High in his day, and Nelson went to Poly, a school on the east side of town that was better known in my day for turning out street fighters with shaved heads whose idea of a conversation was "Hit him, Aubrey!"

The straight lore on Ben and Byron's caddie match is this: Hogan was one up at the end of nine and thought he'd won, but some members said, naw, you boys play eighteen holes. So they went nine more and Nelson was one up at the end of that—he was the champion. First prize was a two-iron and second prize was a five-iron, but Byron already had a two-iron, and Ben didn't, and Ben already had a five-iron, and Byron didn't, so they swapped prizes.

I won two hunks of silver at Glen Garden in my amateur youth. It's where I dusted Puny Reece, who weighed 250, to win the Cowtown Invitational, and where a year later I won the Men's City when I dusted Greasy Waddell, who worked at a Texaco on University Drive.

Greasy Waddell is the man who told me how to get out of jury duty one day. By chance the two of us were standing in line at the courthouse, waiting for the mean-looking women in charge to tell us when we had to serve, which would be a pain in the ass, or excuse us for now, which would be a win. There in line, Greasy said, "I'm gonna beat this deal."

"You are?" I said. "How you plan to do that?"

He said, "It says here on this form that you have to be of good moral character and I don't meet that."

"You don't *meet* that?" I chuckled.

Greasy said, "Why hell no. Like I'm gonna tell this lady, my whole married life I've always had a girlfriend on the side."

I stood there and watched him say that to the lady in charge, and I'm a sumbitch if she didn't let him off, after she stopped laughing.

I'm saving that up to use if I ever get called again.

As far as Glen Garden goes, I can speak to the fact that it's the goofiest layout in all of golf captivity. Glen Garden plays to a par of 37-34-71, and you can bust me if there's a funnier back nine anywhere. It goes 4-4-5-5-3-3-4-3-3. That's back-to-back par fives once and back-to-back par threes twice. There are other courses that have back-to-back par threes once—Cypress Point may be the best known—but back-to-back par threes *twice*? That's just plain silly, although I never gave it any thought when I was a kid trying to make pars on the sumbitches.

Glen Garden was designed in 1912 by Tom Bendelow, one of the early pioneers of golf architecture. He was a fellow from Scotland who came to America at the turn of the century and decided America needed more golf courses, even though he wasn't a real estate developer.

All this history comes in handy for me, of course, when I'm on the road and dining alone in a Courtyard Marriott.

GROWING UP, I don't know how I ever became interested in any kind of history, other than the part my granddad played in World War II. He flew thirty B-17 missions over Germany. He was a granddad I never knew, but I still heard about him every time my own dad didn't like something some foreign country was doing on TV. He'd say, "Send G. T. Grooves back over there—he'll straighten them scogies out."

I should have been interested in coat hangers and pot plants. George and Louise Grooves, my folks, owned and operated Purple Cleaners and later they owned and operated Horned Frog Florists.

Both establishments were on Bluebonnet Circle in the general area of the TCU campus. My dad was a slow-death TCU football fan and his names for the establishments won out over Louise's names, Bluebonnet Cleaners and God Loves Flowers. The stores were close to the little one-story cream brick house on Worth Hills Drive where I was raised.

George Grooves never wanted to own a business where he couldn't be the deliveryman. He liked to leave the place so he could stop somewhere and hit golf balls, or even sneak in a few holes while out on delivery. He kept his golf clubs in his blue '68 El Camino. My mama drove the green '65 Plymouth four-door, ran the businesses, and prayed for him.

That Plymouth was the car I inherited when I entered Paschal High. Even though a lot of other students drove Corvettes and Mustangs, I have fond memories of the Plymouth, particularly those evenings in the backseat with Susan Evelyn Blanton, cheerleader and junior favorite. She didn't invent the high school blowjob, but she made all-district in it.

The dry cleaning business fell on hard times when customers found other cleaners in the neighborhood that didn't burn holes in shirts and coats as often. My folks finally closed it down and opened up the florist shop in a location only three doors away. This put the florist shop even closer to the Oui Lounge, a TCU frat hangout where my dad could slip off for a beer.

George was a tall, heavyset fellow, sort of a grump. Louise was a considerate, ladylike woman who wore glasses but came without a sense of humor. Her only enjoyment was going to Bible study at the Travis Avenue Baptist Church, and going to weekly meetings of the South Side Business & Professional Women. The B&PW was a group of ladies who were either divorced or widowed, or wanted to be divorced or widowed. Louise liked to remind me that life wasn't funny—life was hard, save all your receipts, and "Please close those drapes, I have another migraine."

The florist business did okay during holidays, but at normal times my dad complained that not enough white people died every week. White people funerals meant flowers.

At the breakfast table one morning I remember him turning to the obituaries in the *Light & Shopper* and saying, "Here we go again—four pepperbellies and three stove lids. . . . That's it for today."

Louise said, "Mexicans and colored people buy flowers, too."

George said, "Not like they buy dope."

I was helping my dad deliver flowers by the time I was in McLean Junior High. That's when he started me playing golf. He said I had a "natural swing." He wouldn't let me work at the shop in the summers—he wanted me to work at golf. He'd drop me off at a public course and say, "Hit it hard, compete hard, don't get outbet."

He must have figured I'd learn enough that someday I'd be able to buy my folks the condo inside the gates at Mira Vista Country Club where they now live amid the rows of ungodly mansions, which causes Louise to gaze at them and say, "My Lord, the upkeep."

My dad's seventy-five years old now and plays golf by his own rules—hit till you're happy off No. 1, roll it over everywhere, mulligan every three holes, free throw every six holes, use one ladies tee on each nine.

"Recreational golf ain't meant to be agony," he says.

4

A LITTLE KNOWN FACT ABOUT the PGA Tour is that several of your big names out here would rather spend a week in a cage with squealing lunatics than play in the Bob Hope Desert Classic.

That's why they skip it every year. They like Palm Springs as a place. We all do. Great winter climate. But most of our "stars" hate the tournament. When you get right down to it, the only people who really like the tournament are the amateur slugs who clutter it up.

You play five rounds on four different courses—Indian Wells, Bermuda Dunes, Tamarisk, PGA West. You're scattered across the desert like Apaches looking for wagon trains to fuck with.

The first four days you're paired with three amateurs who come from all over. They're either big-shot assholes or they have a letter that says they get to act like big-shot assholes all week.

Only good thing is, the seventy pros who make the 72-hole cut get to play the last 18 among themselves, like a regular tournament.

Incidentally, I don't like the format either, and I don't like desert golf, but I play there for one reason. All those big names who don't enter open up good money spots.

And let me make myself clear about desert golf. I don't just not like it. I despise it. The courses are all the same. Fairways meandering through phony mounds and airlifted boulders, papier mâché mountains in the distance, slow greens, fake waterfalls, decorator palm groves, Brooke Shields lagoons, reptile exhibits, and how much cactus can you do?

The Hope is the only desert golf I play. I duck Phoenix and Tucson and don't even do outings that would be lucrative in the Scottsdale area. Not in years. Not since I read this story in an in-flight magazine. It pointed out that there are seventeen different kinds of esses—your rattle esses—in North America and sixteen of the sumbitches live in Arizona.

That info must be a great sales tool for real estate agents. In my wildest dreams I can't imagine a sane man naming a major league team the Diamondbacks, although I guess it speeds up baseball.

I played good that week. Swooped $108,000 for sixth place. I shot 67, 70, 65, 67, 70 for a total of 339. That didn't exactly threaten Cheetah Farmer's winning 332, but I liked the way I hit the ball, tee to green, plus I drove it off the planet.

I realized on the practice range why I'd been losing distance lately. I was taking the club away too fast, straining. That's a natural mistake you can slip into. First thing I did was tee it up higher so it would stay in the air longer. Next thing I did was widen my stance so my heels were about even with my shoulders. Better for balance. The last thing I did was the hardest part, and one of the hardest things to do in golf.

Make yourself swing slow. You might as well try to teach a dog to stop barking. So every time I got over the ball on the tee I made myself think s-l-o-w, very s-l-o-w. Sometimes I even whispered it out loud to myself. Got some looks.

It all worked, but you could still call it a minor miracle that I played as well as I did considering the amateur slugs I was paired with.

The first day at Bermuda Dunes I drew geezer, codger, and gramp.

The second day at Indian Wells I got Ed, Fred, and Dead.

The third day at Tamarisk I had dot.com, dot.dumb, and dot.dick.

The fourth day at PGA West I was even luckier. I found myself with the Chance brothers—Slim, Slight, and No.

It made me think how just one time I'd like to draw me a six-handicapper who can play to a six, or a ten who can play to a ten. But what I always catch are guys who have the clothes, the big bag, and the newest mallets, but they couldn't hit water if they fell out of a boat.

It was No Chance who kept apologizing to me Saturday. One thing I pressed into my memory book was him saying, "I can play a lot better than this . . . but I never do."

THE PERMANENT residents of Palm Springs are every bit as scenic as the petrified forest.

Most are skinny as one-irons and have better tans than beef jerky. They don't walk, they shuffle. Which is why the place suffers its share of ridicule. It's called the Official California Wax Museum, Heaven's Parking Lot, God's Waiting Room, and other endearing things. I figure somebody's bound to come up with a drive-through funeral parlor there someday.

But it wasn't all golf in Palm Springs. If you know where to look, there are these fun-loving ladies out there. I'm talking about your rebuilt, over-forty, glitzed-up dolls. Your ladies who usually have a rich husband that's crawled off and died, or he's stone drunk at home, or he's gone somewhere to seek relief from a light hook. I'm talking about your gold-plated sparklers in skimpy outfits who consider the evenings to be their playtime.

They can be found in the hot-ticket hotel bars around the desert, but closer to old original Palm Springs than Indio. The best joints are *White Cargo, Gilda's, Hit or Mrs.*, and *The Pre-Nup Lounge*.

I should caution that you need to steer-job your way clear of a joint called *Fresh Horses*. The name alone ought to be a tip-off, but it didn't stop Jerry Grimes one night last year.

Jerry said he'd never seen so many beautiful women under one roof in his whole life. The only trouble was, if you delved deeper into the subject, you found out they all had a dick and balls. Still, he confessed, there was this one blonde so gorgeous he almost went for it anyhow.

On Wednesday night after the first round of the Hope, Buddy Stark and I investigated *White Cargo*.

I wanted to find out if the name had anything to do with the old flick, see if it looked like a rubber plantation in the jungle with Hedy Lamarr hanging around.

It didn't look like that at all—the name must have meant something else. It was up to the brim with sequins and low-cut implants and bronze guys in pink blazers. Grown-ups. Two or three couples were dancing to music from the piano bar. People were jabbering around tables. The long stand-up bar was crowded. We nudged our way into the bar and ordered drinks while the jovial fat lady at the piano sang about how she guessed she'd travel on to Avalon, and then how you were nobody till somebody loved you, and then she launched into "I don't know why I love you like I do . . . I don't know why, I just do."

Next thing we knew we were being brushed up against by these two sequined stoves with store-bought racks, eye jobs, cocktail glasses in their hands, and hair that was still trying to be blonde in places.

The one pressed against me said, "Me Tondelayo. Want to fuck?"

She let out a big whiskey laugh.

I looked at Buddy. He looked at me. We weren't really in there hoping to get fixed up, we just wanted some laughs.

I said to the doll, "You may have said that to the only person in here who knows who Tondelayo was. It was Hedy Lamarr's name in the movie."

"That's right," she said. "I love that name. The owner of this dive has no idea there was ever a movie called *White Cargo*. The asshole thinks he made it up . . . Tondelayo wants vodka."

I waved to the bartender, who came across like a shot with a vodka-rocks—the national drink of your stoves.

With a nod my way, Buddy said, "Me Clarence, him Larry. We're meeting Jeffrey and Dexter here."

"You're full of shit," mine said, turning to her running mate. "He's full of shit. They're pro golfers. This is Billy Bob Grooves."

"Bobby Joe," I corrected her with a smile.

"Whatever," she said. "And you're Buddy Stark."

"I try to be," Buddy said.

She said, "I'm Camilla . . . this is Gretchen."

Camilla handed me a huge emerald ring to shake.

"You ladies follow golf?" I said.

"Golf is my life," Camilla said, and roared laughing again. "Actually, golf is my husband's life. Jim would *kill* to be here with you two right now, the suck-up asshole. He has a business dinner tonight—ho, ho, ho. I do play some, and I usually go to the tournament. We're members at Eldorado and Indian Wells. Oh . . . and Tamarisk. Jim plays with Jews there. We're only here four months in the winter—never in the summer, thank God! We live in Saddle River, New Jersey. We're members at Ridgewood."

"Nice course," I said. "Tillinghast."

"Who has?"

"The golf architect," I said. "A. W. Tillinghast."

"Never met him."

"That's probably because he died in 1942," I said.

"Terrific," Camilla said, looking around the room.

"He was one of the greats," I said. "He did Winged Foot, where the Open is this year. Quaker Ridge, Somerset Hills . . . Brook Hollow."

She said, "Christ. Ask a question . . ."

Buddy said, "What about you, Gretchen?"

Gretchen said, "What about me *what*?"

"Is golf your life?"

"Yeah, right," she said. Buddy might as well have asked her if she liked poor people.

"Gretchen shops," Camilla explained.

Buddy said, "Well, it's been a little bit of heaven, but me and Billy Bob were just leaving."

"Early tee time," I said.

Camilla said, "You can't leave till you dance with me."

"Camilla!"

That came from Gretchen, with a look that said they could do better than us in a homeless shelter.

But Camilla tugged me onto the dance floor, where I was reminded that you never make contact with a glitzed-up doll in Palm Springs without first doing the feel-around test.

I didn't dance as much as I just stood there with my arm around her back, listening to "When You're Smiling," while Camilla humped my leg and pretended to moan.

That's when I was presented with the opportunity to feel the iron-works inside her dress. Some kind of heavy, skintight elastic deal that held everything in—her waist, hips, butt. It was obvious that if you were crazy enough to unhinge that elastic thing, there'd be this great whooshing sound and suddenly you'd have an inflated raft on your hands.

Call it a tourist tip.

I led Camilla back to her vodka-rocks at the bar, gave Buddy a head signal, and we ran for our lives.

5

FLYING OVER ARIZONA AS HIGH
up as the airline could take me—and
being thankful the Skipper didn't put
wings on esses—I went home to enjoy a
week off. Except I didn't get to enjoy a
week off because I wound up in a jackpot
with women.

The first thing that happened, Cheryl
Haney, my current honey and possibly
my next ex-wife-to-be, picked me up at
DFW in a gold four-door Lexus I'd never
seen before.

Cheryl was a top real estate agent at
Donald Hooper Realty, and she allowed
that it had become too embarrassing to
drive her clients around town to look

at houses in her old '84 Mercury. The Mercury had developed a recent tendency not to heat or cool very well, and it was starting to go *clickity-clickity* on occasion, not a good sign at all.

So she'd put $500 and the Mercury down on the Lexus. Got a good deal on it, she said. The balance was only $52,000 and the dealer was carrying the note. The car was fully loaded—a sunroof and CD player were essential for her clients, people looking for houses to buy. It would be best if the balance on the Lexus was paid off as soon as possible, she informed me, because if she kept paying it off by the month it would cost $450,000 before she was done. That was based on the contract she'd signed with the dealer.

I said $450,000 was an exaggeration, surely.

It was, she said, but not by much.

I said, "I wish your car dealer was my agent."

She said she'd looked several places for a practically new car and this was the best deal she'd found.

"It'll be a happy day for me," she said, "when every car dealer is in Huntsville."

"On death row."

"No, I don't want them to die. That lets them off too easy. I want them to live indoors for forty-five years with Big Leroy for a housewife."

I said, "What's in it for me if I pay this thing off for you?"

"What you *been* gettin', baby," she said with a little smile and a pat on my thigh.

Cheryl is a smokin' babe. She's a spunky, blue-eyed divorcée in her middle thirties with a major championship body that's all hers. She has long, dark blonde hair that she can wear different ways—piled up, swept back, ponytailed, Farrah Fawcetted.

We'd been together two years, ever since I scooped her up during the Colonial because of what she was wearing, which was close to nothing, on a hot, sultry day—it was humid as everybody's armpits.

I liked the round button pinned next to her tournament badge on her flimsy top. It read **MAKE AMERICA SAFE FOR ADUL-TERY.** I liked her sophisticated manner of speaking at a table in the clubhouse with a group of people having cocktails. She managed to turn everything anybody said into a reference to fucking and sucking.

She scored big with me with her aw-hell, go-anywhere, do-anything attitude, and the fact that she came with no kids, which is a huge plus today where your divorcees are concerned.

We weren't living together. Well, we did some when I was in town or when she made a rare appearance on the road with me, but we kept separate places in Fort Worth for various reasons of convenience.

Her white stucco garden home was out in Ridglea on the West Side, the one she was awarded in her divorce from the stockbroker, "Talk Big Burt"—her name for him. Her place was in a cluster of other garden homes with shade trees and crawling vines and little ponds all around, but it was sort of dark and I felt like I was down in a hole when I was there. And besides that I'm a South Side person, born and raised, as I've mentioned.

I've always had friends from every side of town, but it was an established social rule in Fort Worth that if you didn't come from the West Side or South Side, or didn't live on the West Side or South Side or Southwest Side of town, you'd probably be better off if you just went ahead and killed yourself.

My speckled brick townhouse—two stories, two bedrooms, two and a half baths, fireplace—was on Bellaire Drive South. It's well located if you want to play golf at Mira Vista or Colonial, or drive around the TCU campus to look at shapely adorables out walking or jogging, or go buy a stack of Swanson's frozen chicken pot pies at Tom Thumb, a combination food emporium and soccer moms jamboree. The Tom Thumb is on Hulen, a drag strip that used to be a city street.

Cheryl's favorite thing about my place was cable TV in every room, including the master bath. When I was home I didn't want to miss any old movies, and Cheryl never met a talk show she didn't like. She very much liked the talk shows where the guests were fat and loud white trash—they made her proud to be a Republican.

MY TOWNHOUSE was the one I'd wound up with eight years ago in my divorce from Terri Adams, my second ex-wife. Terri was a receptionist in a bank when we met. She was sitting at her desk in the lobby with nothing to do but wait for some guy to ask her out to lunch. I was the guy.

The lunch lasted so long we both got drunk and she got fired. I was also drunk enough to decide that she looked like Meg Ryan's long-lost twin sister. I suspect that even in Terri's drunken state she thought I looked like Son of Meal Ticket.

We were married about a year and Terri even took up golf herself out at Mira Vista, but one day she decided to start looking around bars and clubs for someone who didn't travel as much as I did and somebody who might even look more like the Marlboro Man's younger brother. That's when she met Cowboy Leon. She was so taken with him, she believed him when he boasted that he was a wealthy rancher out around Weatherford.

But after a year Terri was greatly saddened to find out that Cowboy Leon wasn't the wealthy rancher himself—he was the wealthy rancher's ranchhouse sitter and caretaker. Terri found this out one day when the real rancher showed up and sold the ranch out from under them and they were forced to move out.

They tried to stay on with the new owner but the new owner said he didn't need Cowboy Leon and Terri to ride herd on the condominiums he planned to build on the property as far as the eye could see. Cowboy Leon couldn't find anything better to do than start selling used cars, and Terri said, "I didn't sign up for this shit." She divorced him and moved back to Fort Worth and went to work for Red Taggert, the jake-leg criminal lawyer downtown who likes to keep killers and armed robbers out of jail. That's where she still is.

It's been my good fortune that Terri not only kept the Mira Vista club membership with me paying the monthly bills, but occasionally she needs a loan because Cliff Doggett, the muscled-up slug who now lives with her in the apartment she rents on Sunset Terrace, doesn't do much but drink beer at Hooters. I was only home long enough to buy the Lexus for Cheryl and throw away a load of junk mail and catalogs when I heard from Terri.

"I figured I'd catch you at home this week," she said on the phone, "knowing how you feel about the esses in Arizona."

"How are you, Terri? How many murderers did Red put back on the street this week?"

"That's not fair. Red Taggert believes every person has a right to the best legal defense available. I really hate to ask you for this, you've always been so generous . . ."

"How much this time, Terri—and what for?" I said.

"I really feel bad about having to ask you for money, Bobby Joe."

"No, you don't."

"I do too. I wish I had somebody else to turn to, but Cliff keeps having the darndest luck with jobs . . ."

"He sure seems to," I said.

"He's up for a job right now with the fire department."

"Good," I said. "He'll be real valuable to the fire department if a blaze ever breaks out at Hooters."

"That's not nice, Bobby Joe. Cliff's a good person. He's just looking for his proper niche in life—and you ought to be glad he's a gentle soul who don't beat me up or anything."

I said, "I *am* glad he doesn't beat you up, Terri, because if he did, I'd have to bury a five-iron in his forehead—and trust Red Taggert to get me off. How much this time?"

"They say it'll cost $4,000."

"What will?"

"The surgery."

"What surgery?"

"My mother has to have to her appendix out."

When I stopped snickering, I said, "Terri, you need to be more creative. I paid for your mother's appendix operation four years ago."

"It's come back."

"It's what?" I snickered again.

"This is not funny," she said. "Either it's come back or they took out the wrong thing the first time, I don't know. All I know is, she has a problem with her insurance, and she has these x-rays that show she still has her appendix, and her doctor says it has to come out before it grows a head and four legs."

"You're making this up, Terri. Tell the truth."

"Bobby Joe, if I wanted to con you out of money, don't you think I could come up with something better than my mother needs to have her goddamn appendix out *twice*? Jesus!"

"I'm not sure," I said. "This is awful good."

She said, "I'll be happy to show you the x-rays!"

I told her not to bother, the check was in the mail.

A DAY later I received an urgent phone call from Alleene Simmons, my first ex-wife. Cheryl answered the phone that time and said she'd clean forgotten it must be Ex-Wives Week in Fort Worth—we ought to be flying a flag or some fucking thing.

Alleene was my sweetheart the two years I was in TCU on a golf scholarship. I dropped out because the professors made college so boring. That should be against the law for professors to do, is what I say. It's an easy thing to fix. All you have to do is make the professors talk a lot less about socialism and amoeba and a lot more about dinosaurs and Napoleon and the Civil War and Geronimo and Hitler.

Alleene wasn't a TCU student. When I met her she was the hostess in a blackeyed-chili-Fridays joint called Bodobber's. Two giant-screen TVs showed football and other clashes, and the owner, Bodobber Roberts, could play the TCU fight song on his armpit.

Alleene's exposed belly button in her hip-hugger jeans and the rack that supported her haltertop were certainly an attraction for most customers, but there was a lot of that going around. Her body was only part of what made me fall in love with her and propose marriage.

What really did it was, the more Juniors I drank in there every night for a week, the more she started to look like Sigourney Weaver's long-lost twin sister.

Alleene married me thinking I wasn't serious about golf—she hated golf then. The sex was good. She particularly liked to play Warden's Daughter and Escaped Convict. Matter of fact, when I think back on it, the sex was extraordinary.

But she thought after I quit school I'd do something responsible, like sell office supplies or carpet or some other foolishness. But I kept playing golf, making a living at $5 Nassaus—press when you get lonesome. So no hard feelings, she said one day, and dumped me.

I hardly blamed her. I did like hitting golf balls better than being married. We've stayed friends. She's never married again, afraid it would piss off the Pope, but she's had her share of live-ins, which I guess the Pope overlooks. Her current live-in is Phil Murcer, a pretty good old boy, near as I can tell. He helps her in the catering business I financed.

The first business I put Alleene in was her pastry shop. She made good cinnamon rolls, no dreaded raisins, and worked hard at it for five years but the health craze killed it. She particularly blamed drugstores for starting to sell those little gadgets you can take your own blood sugar with.

Her catering business was doing real good, according to the last financial report I received. Good enough to help her buy a nice house over on Hilltop, not far from where I live, and a Toyota delivery van.

I was skeptical about the catering business because Alleene wanted to cater herb-crusted salmon to people in a place where folks mainly eat barbecue, chicken fried steak, and Tex-Mex.

But she's developed a clientele of thin West Side ladies in blue and pink pastel dresses who like to have herb-crusted salmon served when they entertain their friends, who by a strange coincidence happen to be other thin West Side ladies in blue and pink pastel dresses.

Cheryl Haney says Alleene's customers keep reminding her of a country song—"New Tits and Old Money."

Funny thing. Alleene stopped hating golf a few years ago and took up the game. Then she got fairly decent at it. Then she started working at it even harder and now she wins the occasional tournament.

Mind-boggling, is what it is. To see somebody take up the game they used to throw cold cream jars at. She's a member at Mira Vista, where I paid her initiation fee, and she pays her own dues and bills. She and Terri know one another but I don't believe they have a regular game together.

Cheryl once asked me what I thought about having two ex-wives who decided to take up golf. "Anything for the betterment of the game" was all I could say about it.

When I returned Alleene's phone call I was afraid I might hear that her catering business had suffered a setback and she needed money, but that wasn't it—she wanted to discuss a serious matter with me in person.

We met at Herb's Café, an old restaurant-bar on the South Side where TCU professors like to hunker down over mugs of coffee all day and talk about dead Russians who wrote thick books.

It was still January in Fort Worth, as it was most everywhere, even as far away as Argentina. I mention this only because I was surprised to find Alleene with a neat tan.

It turned out she'd just come back from a long week in Florida, down around Boca, where she'd taken a vacation to play golf every day. She still looked plenty okay for a babe right at forty, same age as me. Even with her hair too short for my taste.

"Your hair is short," I said.

"Yes," she said. "Simple but elegant . . . hip but classic."

"Exactly how I was going to describe it," I said.

She congratulated me on my sixth-place finish in the Hope, which in reality meant the $108,000 I won. Nobody in pro golf reads the money list closer than ex-wives.

We made small talk for a few minutes, then she said, "You have to cure my slice, Bobby Joe."

"That's why I'm here?" I said.

She shook her head. I smiled.

"This slice came on me my last three days in Florida," she moaned. "Out of nowhere. It's terrible. I went out this morning and hit some balls, chilly as it was, and it's still there. This contemptible . . . diseased . . . *thing*. I'm not talking about a fade here, Bobby Joe. I'm talking about a *slice*. I'm talking about I swing the club like normal, but what happens? Every stinking time? Here comes this godawful banana ball, and I'm like, Hit a *house*, for Christ sake!"

"A slice don't know who's talking to it," I said.

"Deep, Bobby Joe. Thanks."

I said, "If it was possible to cure a slice for good, Alleene, all the golf magazines, instruction books, and gurus would be out of business."

She said, "Don't fool around with me, Bobby Joe. This is serious."

"Loosen up your grip a little," I said. "Relax. That ought to do it."

"I did," she said. "It doesn't."

"Aim to the right side of the fairway," I suggested.

"That's idiotic. If I aim to the right on No. 1 at Mira Vista, you know where my drive will wind up? In somebody's living room."

"No it won't," I said. "Try aiming more to the right of your target. You'll mentally correct without realizing it. Probably pull the ball."

"You have to do better than that."

"Did you try closing your stance, shifting more weight to your left leg when you come through the ball?"

"Yes," she said.

"And . . . ?"

"Horror movie."

I said, "Okay. Here's the key to the vault—we'll cure it at the address. First, make sure your right shoulder is lower than your left . . ."

She gripped an imaginary club, lowering her shoulder.

"That's critical," I said. "Now . . . make sure your right arm is closer to your body than your left arm before you take it back. Those two things should make you swing inside out, which is what you want to do."

"What if that doesn't do it? I need a fallback position . . . the last desperate measure, before suicide."

I thought about it a minute and said, "Try to hit it on the toe."

"That's a golf tip?"

I said, "You're obviously coming over the top with the face open. So . . . when you swing at it, try to hit the ball with the toe of the club. You won't be able to do it, but it'll automatically force you to square up the face when you come through the ball."

"One of these things better work, Bobby Joe. I can't live like this."

"You're all set," I said. "Let me know which one does it for you."

Two hours later Cheryl and I were watching fat and loud white trash yell at each other on the living room TV. The fat wife was accusing the fat husband of swapping their three-year-old daughter for a beachfront cabin on the Gulf Coast in Mississippi, and the fat husband was telling the fat wife to mark her lip or he'd punch her in the gravy tub.

Alleene's phone call tore me away from that drama.

She wanted to tell me how happy she was with my golf instruction. She'd gone back out and hit more practice balls, and every tip I'd given her worked to some degree, but dropping the right shoulder was the biggie. Slice cured, for now.

"Happy to be of service," I said. "I hope I can be as much help to the amateur slug I'll be paired with at Pebble Beach next week."

Soon as I hung up, Cheryl Haney, wiseguy, had a word for me.

"I think I'll take up golf," she said. "We'll have more time together."

6

WOMEN AND GOLF HAVE ALWAYS
been a tight fit for me, but I guess I'd
rather see women play golf than, say, go
shopping.

Women don't shop, they browse. Like
dopeheads. Me? Either the store has what
I want or I go somewhere else. I know
what I want. A 44 long. Maybe socks and
underwear. But not your women or your
dopeheads. They want to peruse, be intrigued, see something they like, talk it
over with their inner selves or their
friends. What I say is, you like the lamp,
buy the sumbitch, take it to the cabin.

Also, I'd rather see women play golf
than pay for groceries. It seems like every

woman I stand behind in the checkout line at a supermarket invariably waits until Conchita totals everything up before going one-on-one with her purse.

Then out comes the checkbook, or the coupons, or the coins, and sometimes all three. And there goes ten more minutes. Coins are the real killer.

About then it's all I can do to keep from telling the clerk, "Yo, Conchita, just put all that on my bill so I can get the fuck outta here."

So here's my position: women should be able to play all the golf they want to play, and not only on Ladies Day but all through the week, whenever they can get a tee time. But not with me.

I've played my last round of golf with women. At least I have until a gang of feminists pins me down and threatens to stick forks in my eyes. My last round with women was two years ago in the JCPenney Classic.

This tournament's been around since the early '60s. It's usually played in early December somewhere in Florida after both tours are over. It's an end of the year thing. Unofficial money. It pairs up a guy from our tour with a lady pro from the LPGA. It's seventy-two holes of best-ball. The women seek out their male partners, and the lady pros generally take the event more seriously than the guys.

I'd always avoided playing in the JCPenney, but two years ago they held it at Black Diamond Ranch, over near Ocala, and I wanted to see that Tom Fazio golf course. I'd heard how distinctive it was—the quarry and all that. So I said yeah, sure, when Cora Beth Kenny called up and asked me to be her partner.

A rogue might suggest that I agreed to play only because I knew from photos in *Golf World* and *Golf Digest* that Cora Beth Kenny was one of the cutest young players on the LPGA Tour.

Cora Beth's handlers at IMG were energetically marketing her as "the Anna Kournikova of golf."

It was Buddy Stark's opinion that I was only in the JCPenney because Cora Beth was my partner. What he said was "If one of those hags had invited you, you'd have said piss on Black Diamond."

This gave me a chance to remind Buddy that if he hadn't been asked to be partners with Perkie Haskins, he'd have bagged the deal, too. Perkie Haskins, in her late twenties, an older woman compared to Cora Beth, was one of the LPGA's better lookers.

Cora Beth and Perkie could both play in the shapely adorable league, sports division. Tan legs, healthy racks. Cora Beth came with a blonde ponytail, Perkie with brunette bangs.

They were almost as good-looking as Black Diamond. Cora Beth and I played one practice round with Buddy and Perkie, and I was truly impressed with the course.

The five holes that Tom Fazio designed around the deep dolomite quarry—the thirteenth through the seventeenth—was a stretch of holes you'd want to take pictures of, they're so original. They're as unusual and memorable as any stretch of holes anywhere.

I don't keep up with the LPGA, in case anybody's wondering. I'm not steeped in LPGA history. I know their three greatest players were Babe Zaharias, Mickey Wright, and Kathy Whitworth, and I guess I'm aware that they've got a bunch of Annikas and Yellow Peril and Australians out there today, but that about covers it for me.

My lack of knowledge helped me make a big hit with my partner the first day. Cora Beth Kenny and I were on the putting green, and in an effort to instigate a friendly conversation I said to Cora Beth, "I guess you played golf in college, huh?"

"Yes," she said, with a strange look.

"Where?" I asked.

"*Where?*" she said, looking more strange. "I played at the University of Florida."

"Oh?" I said. "Did y'all do any good while you were there?"

"We won the NCAA twice," she said coldly.

"Hey, that's great," I said. "Did you do any good individually?"

She said, "You mean aside from winning the individual title three times and making All-America four years?"

All I could do was laugh. "I can't tell you how happy I am I brought it up," I said.

I didn't give it any thought when I noticed that Cora Beth and Perkie Haskins were a little cool toward each other during our practice round. I figured they were just grinding, getting ready for the tournament.

As luck would have it, then, our teams were paired together in the first round, and that's when things became a little clearer.

First of all, they tried to outslow each other. Cora Beth was Queen of the Waggle. Perkie was Princess of the Plumb Bob. Most women golfers are slow to start with. But these ladies wore my ass out doing Slow-Play Fay and Play-Slow Flo.

Now I don't believe you ought to play golf like you're double-parked, like it only takes you thirty minutes to watch *60 Minutes*, but I do think you ought to move it along.

Next thing I realized, we'd gone six holes without the girls even speaking to each other. Each one hit some good shots, but the other one acted like she didn't see it happen.

Competitors, I wrote it off. Well, wrong.

It was on the seventh green that Perkie directed her first remark of the day to Cora Beth. This was after Cora Beth sank a ten-foot birdie putt and was taking the ball out of the cup. Perkie said, "Nice putt, bitch."

"What did you call me?" Cora Beth said.

"Just a bitch, that's all," said Perkie. "*Bitch.*"

"You're hopeless," Cora Beth replied.

Buddy Stark and I exchanged glances, and Roy Mitchell, my caddy, mumbled to me, "We fixin' to have us a spat."

On the eighth tee, a good par four, Cora Beth laced a big drive down the fairway. She admired her tee shot for an instant, and when she walked back to her bag to put her club away, she gave Perkie a nasty look and said:

"Chase that one, *cunt.*"

Buddy and I exchanged glances again.

They then struck out down the fairway together, saying things to each other we couldn't hear. Heated. They rushed their second shots onto the green, but before we reached the green, and to our astonishment, we saw Perkie suddenly grab Cora Beth by the arm and pull her over into a thicket of trees and shrubs.

I might mention that we didn't have a gallery, luckily. All of the spectators were elsewhere, following the marquee teams—Davis Love III, or Julius Claudius, with Beth Daniel, John Daly with Laura Davies, Knut Thorssun with Helen Alfredson, Rickey Padgett with Juli Inkster.

We gave the ladies a little time by themselves to settle the issue, whatever it was. But when Perkie slapped Cora Beth in the face and Cora Beth quickly slapped her back and they started pushing and shoving and scratching at each other, Buddy and I rushed over, me hollering, "Hey, hey, whoa!"

We got there as Perkie was spitting out, "You never cared a thing for me, you devious little shit! I gave you all the love I had and all you did was use me to get close to Phyllis!"

"Oh, *really?*" Cora Beth said. "And you and Phyllis didn't have anything going behind my back? Like I don't *know* that?"

They were both in tears.

"It was *over* with Phyllis," Perkie said. "It was over with Phyllis the minute I laid eyes on you—and you know it! God, what a fool I've been!"

I said, "Uh . . . ladies . . ."

"Fuck you!" Perkie snarled at me.

"This doesn't concern you," Cora Beth said in my direction, dabbing at a tear.

"People are going to be coming along here," I said, "and I was wondering if . . ."

They ignored me.

I looked at Buddy Stark.

"How 'bout this?" he said. "Is this any good?"

Perkie was then saying to Cora Beth, "If you think I'm going to spend another minute on this golf course with a deceitful little bitch like you, forget it!"

Cora Beth said, "You don't need to worry about *that*, you fucking whore! I'm outta here quicker than you are!"

They hurried off in different directions.

"That's it?" I called after them. "We're done here?"

Neither one looked back.

That was it. We WD'd, both teams.

Trudging back to the clubhouse with our caddies, Buddy Stark said, "I don't know about you, man, but I've got to find out who Phyllis is."

Phyllis, it turned out, was Phyllis Atkins, a somewhat attractive LPGA player who, the last I heard, was the "companion" of another LPGA player named Sarah Velma Thompson.

I've also heard lately that Cora Beth Kenny and Perkie Haskins are back together—and have been back together for more than a year. Not only that but they're pretty darn excited about becoming parents. Tell me Perkie is carrying a sperm baby.

Women's golf. Hell of a deal.

7

SOMEDAY IF YOU FEEL LIKE YOU'RE
in bad need of an idiot, I'll give you Knut
Thorssun.

We played a practice round together at
Pebble Beach today—me and him and
our two amateur slugs—and Knut spent
the whole time talking about what a bad
course it is.

He didn't used to make statements
about anything, or even *think* about anything, aside from pussy. But this was before he took rich and famous. Now he
confuses rich and famous with smart,
which is a disease, I've observed, that in-
fects numerous professional athletes and
Hollywood actors.

Here's how totally Hall of Fame ignorant Knut is: he thinks No. 8, No. 9, and No. 10 at Pebble are the three worst holes on the course.

"They should dig them up and start over," he said. "Put the tees where the greens are . . . put the greens where the tees are."

That statement went beyond dumb. It climbed over idiotic, raced through stupid, and did a hook slide into the insane asylum.

I didn't say anything during the round while he bitched about the course, but our amateur slugs were impressed. They listened eagerly to everything he said, laughed when they thought they should, and shook their heads in agreement with this and that. Amateur slugs do this. They nod, giggle, agree with everything any "celebrity" says, no matter how ridiculous. That's why they're slugs.

We'd finished the round and were on the putting green across from the Lodge before I said anything to Knut.

I said, "You know, Knut, if I were you, I wouldn't talk about what a bad course Pebble is to anybody who doesn't know you're a Swede."

He stared at me and blinked once or twice before he said, "You are meaning to be humorous?"

"No, not completely," I said. "People who know golf and know you're a Swede, they'll understand you just don't know any better. But if they *don't* know you're a Swede, they'll think you're totally fucking stupid."

In a matter of words then, I'm afraid I launched into a lecture and let him in on the following:

No. 8 at Pebble is without a doubt the greatest single par four in the world. Even Jack Nicklaus has said the two-hundred-yard second shot over the Pacific Ocean to the small green is the greatest second shot in golf—only Tiger Woods has ever brought the hole to its knees.

And those three holes in a row—eight, nine, and ten—all of them built along the cliffs above Carmel Bay, make up one of the great stretches in golf.

"Abalone Corner," some golf scribe once named it.

There aren't even that many stretches to compare with this one at Pebble. You've got your Amen Corner at the Masters, which is the eleventh, twelveth, and thirteenth at Augusta National, and you've got the last three at Merion in Philadelphia, the quarry holes.

Only a couple of others ever get mentioned when the subject comes up among non-idiots. One is those quarry holes at Black Diamond Ranch, where I resigned from ladies golf, and the other is the three-hole finish on TPC Stadium in Ponte Vedra Beach, Florida, where we contest The Players Championship every spring.

What's even more interesting about Pebble, I informed Knut, is that it was designed by two California amateurs, Jack Neville and Douglas Grant. They never designed another golf course. And here was another little-known fact: when the place opened in 1918, it was known as the Del Monte Golf and Country Club.

When I was done with all that, I said, "The only reason you don't like Pebble is because it's so tough. You can't tear it up like Tiger did in the Open. You can't score on it unless there's no wind and the greens are soft."

He said, "That is being exactly the point, Bobby Joe. People want to see Thor make birdies."

"Damn, I don't know why I keep forgetting that," I said. "It's always about you. Let me get out of the way and let Thor putt."

MY SUITE was among the smaller ones in the Pebble Beach Lodge. On the enchanting Monterey Peninsula. Postcard Overdose.

The night before the tournament I partook of a room service dinner with a cozy fire going. Lentil soup and club sandwich, pot of coffee.

I guessed there was more than one golf nut in the country who would have cut off his left Titleist to be where I was.

Like most golf fans, I still call it the Crosby instead of the AT&T Pebble Beach National Pro-Am. I wish I'd been fortunate enough to compete in it when it was known as "the Clambake," or the Bing Crosby National Pro-Am.

My first Crosby was in 1988, a few years after Der Bingle, the Old

Groaner, died—took up residence with the Heavenly Host Pro, as they say. The briefcases were running things by then. It's still the glamour event on the Winter Tour, but it doesn't seem as glamorous to me as the Crosby I used to watch on TV.

A lot of the old movie stars and amateur regulars are no longer around. They've been replaced by briefcases, friends and neighbors of briefcases, and celebrities like Bumpy Weems, a popular comedian, who's about as funny to me as a terrorist with a gun pointed at my head.

Bumpy Weems is Rickey Padgett's partner every year and he delights the gallery by rolling around in bunkers, throwing his driver down the fairway like a javelin, and howling like a wolf when he makes a putt.

Sadly enough, we don't play Cypress Point anymore. Now we play two rounds at Pebble, the last round and one earlier, and one round each at Spyglass Hill and Poppy Hills, a new course that took the place of Cypress Point in '91.

I started making it to the Crosby in time to play Cypress my first three years. Even though it's not that difficult, Cypress might be the most wildly scenic course in America. Windbent. Weird trees and plantlife everywhere. Boulders. Mounds. And the ocean's always close by.

Golf on the Discovery Channel.

Cypress Point is best known for its sixteenth hole. It's one of the toughest par threes in the world. You have to hit from a ledge on 17-Mile Drive across the Pacific to a green that looks about the size of a pool table, and down below are the jagged rocks and crashing waves that Joan Fontaine in *Suspicion* was afraid she'd be tossed down on.

The course is the artwork of Dr. Alister Mackenzie, the Englishman who gets a lot of votes as the best golf architect who ever lived or died. Among his other classic designs are Augusta National, Royal Melbourne, and Crystal Downs, a jewel located up in a part of Michigan you can't get to without a chopper, a boat you paddle, and an Indian guide.

Cypress Point is one of the most exclusive clubs in America and yet it was a part of the Crosby for more than forty years. It withdrew from being a host course because it's a private club and its members didn't feel like they ought to told what they *can* do and *can't* do by any outside swinging dick.

The Shoal Creek "racial incident" at the PGA in Birmingham, Alabama, in '90 is what did it. After all that commotion, it was ordered by the PGA Tour and the USGA that no private club could host a tournament that sold tickets to the public unless its membership included your African-Americans for sure, and if possible even your Hebrew-Americans, your Yellow Peril-Americans, your A-rab-Americans, your Illegal Alien-Americans, and your Women-Americans.

That was when Cypress Point said something on the order of "Where's my hat?"

MY AMATEUR slug in the Crosby was J. Rodney Hemorrhoids.

Well, ought to be. Real name was Harrison. Chunky guy in his early fifties. I could swear he wore makeup. I know he wore a dark red rug.

He was one of those guys whose voice got bigger off the golf course. Like now he was in charge of the world, not you.

He quickly let me in on the fact that he had sold his bank in Atlanta to "the Nazis" for $140 million. I gathered this was why he could afford to own the mansion in Buckhead and the mansion in Highlands, North Carolina, "up there in the mountains," and the mansion in Sea Island, Georgia, "down there on the coast," and was a member of so many clubs I lost track of the names, except for Highlands Country Club. I remembered that one because Bobby Jones helped Donald Ross design it.

J. Rodney said with a big laugh, "Anne Frank might have hid from them Nazis, but I didn't. Man, I jumped right out there and hollered at 'em. Here I am! Over this way! Come get me!"

That called for more of his own laughter.

His thin and snooty wife and her thin and snooty sister, both brunettes in their late thirties, were accompanying Rod. Nonnie the wife, Neenie the sister. They weren't altogether bad-looking if you liked your non-smilers.

J. Rodney had all the mallets. A big leather bag of Callaways with a few Tight Lies thrown in. But that's where it stopped. When he swung you'd get your pop-ups, your thins, your stabs. Which he blamed on the equipment.

"These darn new clubs," he kept complaining, like I'd never heard *that* before.

It was his first time in the Crosby and he was a bundle of nerves. Not because he drew me as his pro or anything, although he did believe he'd heard of me. He was afraid forty thousand people were going to be watching every move he made.

"What if we get paired with Clint Eastwood?" he asked.

"Then you really don't have to worry, Rod," I said. "You can pull down your pants and shit on the eighteenth fairway and the crowd will still be looking at Clint."

J. Rodney had the kind of swing that started off looking like he was trying to scoop something up and finished looking like a photograph of Mickey Mantle swinging for the fence. You know what I mean. Feet wide apart, one knee almost touching the dirt, the bat wrapped around his neck.

I didn't fool with him much during the practice round. I didn't want to confuse him, make matters worse. But later in the day I took him over to the range and worked with him a while.

I didn't know whether I helped him or not, but I did get his attention after he hit a few balls and I studied his swing closely.

"Doesn't that hurt?" I said.

8

THE CROSBY ANNUALLY OFFERS you a Luby's Cafeteria of weather. Although it's a little short on butter beans and cornbread, it gives you wind, cold, rain, mud, fog, and mist. Bring a rubber suit and two umbrellas.

I was here in '90 when the wind blew so hard they had to suspend play in the third round because your Titleist wouldn't stay still long enough on the green for you to take the putter back. That year I was in third place at 140 after two rounds but the three-club wind on Saturday turned me into a tight end—old 84—and I even missed the 54-hole cut.

This time we were given a full buffet of "Crosby weather."

We attracted another wind on Thursday at Pebble—not like '90 but strong enough to jack with J. Rodney's hairpiece—and it rained on Friday when we were at Poppy Hills, and on Saturday, the day we were at Spyglass Hill, that's when the light snow fell on all three courses, which you know about if you were watching TV.

The weather didn't bother J. Rodney's game—nothing could have. Our pro-am team missed the cut from Carmel to Salinas. On every hole he pledged the IPCB fraternity—Ice Plant Claims Ball.

But through all the elements I kept it in my mind that the place owed me one. I think my mental attitude is what helped me tag Pebble for a 72 on Thursday, sculpt my 68 at Poppy on Friday, salvage a 74 at Spyglass on Saturday—one of the low rounds in the snow—and finish up with a light-running 70 in a stiff breeze at Pebble on Sunday.

Totaled up, that gave me 284, a tie for fourth, and $165,00 to put in the kick. Not a bad week's work for playing through J. Rodney, a cyclone, a rain forest, and Stalingrad.

I was only five shots out of first. Two better than Knut Thorssun, I'm pleased to say. He started out hot on Sunday. Birdies on the first four holes. But he did a Clark Gable—gone with the wind—when he got to the real golf course, which starts at No. 5. That's the only criticism of Pebble. The first four holes are inland and don't look anything like the other fourteen. But this doesn't keep it from being one of my favorite courses.

I have to confess that I wasn't as upset as everybody else about what happened to Bumpy Weems on Saturday. I wish I'd seen it live instead of on the replay is all.

Bumpy was confronted with this pitch shot out of the rough to the right of No. 8 green, and while he was waiting his turn to play he started to entertain the gallery by doing calisthenics. He did push-ups, he did sit-ups, and then he did side-straddle hops. Real funny.

It was when he was doing the side-straddle hops that he misjudged where he was and disappeared down the cliff. He tumbled all the way to the beach at the bottom. Down there with the rocks and seals and abalone.

Got himself a broken arm, two cracked ribs, multiple scars, and a concussion. Only funny thing he ever did is what I say.

Jerry Grimes played well enough to win it, but on Sunday he lost out by a stroke to Salu Kinda, one of our new foreign players from Borneo or maybe it's Bali. Salu became the first foreigner ever to win the Crosby.

He's a tall, dark-skinned, nice-looking, well-spoken guy. Nobody's real sure what his nationality is—I'm told he's half this, half that—but he could pass for an officer in your local branch of the NAACP.

We can always use new stars out here, but I suppose I was a little happier about Salu Kinda's victory than Jerry Grimes was.

Jerry said to me later, "Hell, I don't mind him being low cannibal, but he don't have to win the whole deal."

YOU COULD say I had my share of social life at the Crosby.

One afternoon after we finished the round J. Rodney hired a long white limo and we went into Carmel. Me and him and Nonnie and Neenie. We strolled around town where I was privileged to watch Nonnie and Neenie buy suede and scoff at paintings of seals in the art galleries.

J. Rodney insisted I join them for dinner three straight nights in the Lodge, his tickets. Twice in the main dining room and once downstairs in Club XIX, which is where you often find your celebrities.

It was on Friday night that Neenie, a recent divorcee, picked up a handsome guy at the bar in Club XIX. She was sure he was a movie star she'd seen in something or other, and I didn't have the heart to spoil her fun, or his, by telling her he was Rickey Padgett's caddy.

Nonnie wasn't interested in celebrities. She mostly occupied her time before dinner, during dinner, and after dinner by sneering at the clothes the other ladies in the room were wearing.

"You certainly know you're in tasteless California," she said.

This was the night J. Rodney Harrison turned in early. Said his ass was wore out from the rain and the ice plant and the bunkers. He wanted to go to his room and put his feet up.

"I'm not tired," Nonnie announced. Snappish.

Signing the check, J. Rodney said, "Hey, no problem. You and Bobby Joe finish off the rest of this Chateau $97.50."

He walked away, waving to other rich turds on the way out.

I stood up and got as far as saying, "Actually, I'm a little . . ."

But Nonnie rudely pulled me back down in my chair beside her and said with a glare, "You *are* a gentleman, aren't you?"

It was the first time in the whole three days that she had even acknowledged my presence as someone other than a day laborer her husband had hired to make pars and birdies for him.

"Rod is a golf nut," she said. "Pathetic, really."

I said it was getting to be an epidemic in many places.

She hoisted her wine and gazed around the room, as if looking at fools on parade. Then she turned to me.

"Married with children, I assume?"

I said, "Nope. I've been married twice, but no kids. I *am* pretty much involved right now in Texas with a real estate agent. Her name's Cheryl Haney. She works for Donald Hooper Realty in Fort Worth."

"Looks? Body? Got all that?"

"She's a great American," I said. "It could be love."

A few minutes passed while Nonnie drank wine and I drank coffee.

Finally she said, "Let's go outside. I'm dying for a cigarette."

She filled up a glass of wine and took it with her. Outside, she handed me the glass to hold while she dug a long cigarette out of the pack in her purse and lit it and inhaled deeply and sighed in ecstasy.

"California," she said with disgust. "I'm sure it will soon be against the law to smoke outdoors in your own *yard* in this stupid state."

"That's right, you're from North Carolina," I said. "Tobacco state."

"I rather think I'm from a *sane* state, if you don't mind," she said. "Which way is your room?"

I said, "Which . . . what . . . ?"

"You heard me," she said.

Next, while I was saying are you serious?, and I don't think it's a great idea, and what about J. Rodney?, and I'm sort of tired myself, Nonnie was moving up against me and putting her hand where I believe almost any man under the circumstances would have suddenly gotten untired.

When we reached my room, I took off my sport coat and turned on the TV while she went straight to the john. I wasn't sure what to expect.

I was standing in the room, flipping around on the TV, looking for a movie, when she came out of the john with nothing on but her white bikini panties. She stood there, hands on her hips, no expression.

I could only stare at her like an idiot. At a curvy body from the rack on down that I hadn't expected her to have. A body that looked "quite useful," as an Australian would describe it.

Now she came walking slowly toward me. And took my hand and pulled me to the bed. Pull might be too strong a word.

All I could think of to mutter was "Rocky Sullivan dies yellow."

"What's that supposed to mean?" she said.

"Nothing," I said, easing onto the bed with her. "It was just something I thought of from an old movie."

"Why don't we not talk for a while?" she whispered.

I suppose you could say Nonnie was my Pebble Beach souvenir.

I might mention that before she went back to her own room an hour or so later, she finally smiled.

9

MY NICKNAME ON THE TOUR IS Spin. Not many golf writers or radio and TV broadcasters know this, which is fine with me. My longtime caddy, Roy Mitchell, came up with it, and it stuck to me like latex sticks to a dirty leg at the mall.

It stems from my last name, Grooves. I never liked my name much as a kid—it would have made me happier to have a normal name. Anderson, Johnson, Smith. Hogan wouldn't have been bad. That's a joke.

The nickname attached itself to me back in '89 when this big controversy came up concerning the grooves on the Ping Eye2 irons. Back when the officials

of the USGA and the PGA Tour put on their braid, saluted themselves, and declared the grooves on those clubs to be illegal.

A lot of players on the tour agreed. They said those "square"
grooves give you a greater "spin rate" on shots—more control, in
other words—particularly when you hit a shot out of damp rough.

All kinds of tests were made, pro and con, but tests are like surveys.
They prove whatever the test-givers or the survey-takers want to
prove.

I didn't have a strong opinion one way or another—I play Hogans.
However, from time to time I did observe that a guy with a Ping could
occasionally hit a pitch shot that danced like Fred Astaire.

The debate raged in the newspapers and magazines, and in locker
rooms and on putting greens, but it struck me as silly for the simple
reason that the difference between the spacing in the Ping Eye2
grooves and the grooves in other irons was about the width of a gray
hair on a geezer's head.

The pros who argued that it made a difference are the same pros
who think that what they do on the golf course is brain surgery. Like
a single blade of grass on a fairway can cause a flyer. Like they can
read the grain on a bent green from as far away as Istanbul.

The Ping people finally made the controversy disappear. They sued
the USGA and the PGA Tour and vowed to spend five hundred bil-
lion dollars on legal fees, whatever it took, to make those organizations feel like they'd been fucked like tied-up sheep. That's when the
USGA and the PGA Tour folded their tents.

Nicknames in golf go way back. I suspect they go all the way back
to Harry Vardon. Most likely there was this wit in Vardon's day who
nicknamed him Grip, seeing as how he invented the overlapping grip.

"Yo, Grip, how's it lapping?"

It's even money the Scots may have nicknamed him something
else. The Bloody Prick is a good guess. That's because Vardon was an
Englishman and had a habit of kicking Scottish butts in the game the
Scots invented. Near as I can tell, your Scots don't really like anybody

who's not a Scot, except maybe Ben Hogan and Bobby Jones and Tiger Woods.

Sportswriters popularized nicknames in the 1920s.

If you didn't have a nickname back then, you couldn't hit a home run, knock anybody out, scamper for a touchdown, or win a golf tournament—you might as well buy a monkey wrench and crawl under somebody's sink.

It was in the '20s that the golf world saw Bobby Jones become The Emperor Jones, Walter Hagen become The Haig, Gene Sarazen become The Squire, Tommy Armour become The Silver Scot, and Horton Smith become The Joplin Ghost, apparently because Smith came from Missouri and was tall and thin and could outputt a preacher. Made sense to Grantland Rice and Damon Runyon and them.

After that, here came Slammin' Sam Snead, Bantam Ben Hogan, who was also the Hawk and the Wee Icemon. Lord Byron Nelson, Golf's Mechanical Man, Mustachioed Lloyd Mangrum, the Riverboat Gambler, Dutch Harrison, the Arkansas Traveler, Methodical Dr. Cary Middlecoff, the Golfing Dentist, Jaunty Jimmy Demaret, Golf's Goodwill Ambassador, and Tempestuous Tommy (Thunder) Bolt.

Then here came Arnie's Army, Buffalo Billy Casper, Gene the Machine Littler, Chi Chi Rodriguez, Super Mex Trevino, Craig (The Walrus) Stadler, Greg Norman, the Great White Shark, and Ohio Fats, alias Jack Nicklaus, who trimmed down to turn into the Golden Bear.

On up to Tiger Woods and Cheetah Farmer, who, if they went by Eldrick and Chandler, probably couldn't win doodad.

But of course none of that has anything to do with how I've come to be known to some people as Spin, as in spin rate, as in Grooves.

ALL THIS came up when I was standing in the parking lot at Torrey Pines, rearranging the luggage in the trunk of my rented Lincoln, preparing to risk my life on the freeway to LA.

Since my performance hadn't been exactly splendid at Torrey Pines, I'd already cussed all twelve names the tournament's had, a tour record. And it's been proved for whip-out that I'm the only guy in the locker room who can name them all. The tournament started in 1952 as the San Diego Open, and since then it's been the Convair–San Diego Open, the San Diego Open Invitational, the Andy Williams–San Diego Open Invitational, the Wickes/Andy Williams San Diego Open, the Isuzu/Andy Williams San Diego Open, the Shearson Lehman Brothers Andy Williams Open, the Shearson Lehman Hutton Andy Williams Open, the Shearson Lehman Hutton Open, the Shearson Lehman Brothers Open, the Buick Invitational of California, and now it's the Buick Invitational, where I shot straight up.

Behind my back, the voice came out of the sky. Or off the Pacific Ocean, about a hundred feet down from the cliffs of Torrey Pines, where some of my putts had tried to go.

"Hey, Spin, how's it going?"

I turned around to find a young punk in baggy shorts, hairy legs, sneakers with no socks, faded golf shirt, soiled baseball cap, bottle of water in his hand. I didn't need to notice his "working press" badge to know he was with the media.

"It was okay until now," I said, going for wit.

If I hadn't already calmed down from playing so bad, I would have said, "Aw, I'm doing all right, I guess, for a lockwrist cage-case who didn't make a putt in four rounds, only broke 70 once, finished tied for fifty-second, and leaves this bungee jump with only $7,000 for the week."

But I'd cooled off, like I said.

The punk introduced himself as Irv Klar and said he worked for a paper "in the LA area," but he expected to be offered a job with the *Los Angeles Times* or *Sports Illustrated* pretty soon, or possibly he'd go in the movie business, be a studio executive. He stated that he was way too good for the dead-end paper where he now worked. He added that this had been his first golf tournament to cover.

"Kind of cool," he said. "But not like, you know, a real sports event. Too much whispering . . . standing around."

"I agree," I said. "More guys out here ought to get high-sticked . . . chop-blocked . . ."

Ignoring that, he said, "I've never played golf. I might take it up, though. It doesn't look so hard. I have a good baseball swing."

"That'll help," I said. "But in your case, I'd say the hardest part might be getting into a country club."

Missed him completely. He was swinging an invisible bat.

He said, "Buddy Stark . . . I was interviewing him earlier . . . he told me to talk to you, call you Spin. That's your nickname, right? Cool."

"Buddy's a thoughtful guy," I said.

"I want to do a piece on nicknames," he went on. "Buddy says you're a good source. I tried to talk to Cheetah Farmer on the practice range yesterday. He said, 'This is my office, do you have an appointment?' Can you believe that? He never said anything else . . . and he knew I was with the press. Fucking asshole."

"Asshole gets a lot of votes," I said.

"So where'd he get the name Cheetah?"

"Tiger was already taken," I shrugged.

"Hey, that's good. I can use that," he said, and made a note.

Irv Klar looked like he planned to hang around awhile, so I figured the only way to get rid of him was drop all that nickname lore on him. After I finished off the immortals, him taking notes as fast as he could, I moved into the present.

I said Buddy Stark's nickname is Austin Memorial. Austin is Buddy's home. He still lives there, loves it, but mourns the fact that it's being ruined by developers who are succeeding in making it as big and congested as Atlanta. I said that Buddy and I first met on the Texas amateur golf circuit, but we didn't become close friends until we wriggled through the Q-school together. Back then, we'd discovered we shared mutual interests in things other than golf—ladies, bridge, dimly lit corner taverns.

There aren't many close friendships on the tour like Buddy Stark and myself. Guys don't hang out anymore. The closest they come is watching their children turn over glasses of milk in a motel dining room.

Buddy averages one win a year, same as me, he's majorless, same as me, and he's had the same luck in marriage as I have. He's been involved with a variety of women over the years, ranging from local news anchors to aerobics instructors. Not long ago he said he was thinking of zeroing in on chicks who wore glasses—he was totally exhausted from crawling around looking for contacts.

I passed along to Irv that the nickname for Jerry Grimes, my other good friend out there, is Cloyd Highway. Jerry's from Cloyd, Tennessee, which is basically a highway going past Cloyd.

Knut Thorssun's nicknames might be Thor and Nuke to the morons in the gallery, I said, but the players have other names for him. Mule Dick, for one. Wagon Tongue, for another. And Woodrow. Woodrow was inspired by Knut himself, bragging that a lingerie ad was all it took for him to produce "a woodie a cat can't scratch." This was after he'd heard that old expression for the first time—*har-har*, bang fist on table.

Irv said, "If I wrote for *Playboy* I could get Mule Dick in the piece."

I said the name Buddy Stark and I preferred for Knut didn't have anything to do with his hard-ons. We called him Better Deal.

Having not gone to Harvard, I said, I couldn't begin to count the number of times Knut had better-dealed me on dinner plans. I'd almost come to expect it if I saw in the paper that a "celebrity" was in town. Could be a movie star, rock star, sports star, United States senator, or some kind of Arafat. Didn't matter. I'd learned the hard way that good old Knut would be with that celeb at dinner somewhere when he was supposed to be having dinner with me or with Buddy and me.

It was a joy to remember the night I went to meet Knut for dinner at this tough-ticket joint called *Piece of the Gross* in Santa Monica. He'd told me to get there early to grab a table, which I did. I stood in line for thirty minutes before I was finally seated by this snotty little bitch I wanted to strangle. She had sunflowers for eyes.

I sat there nursing a Junior and feeling foolish for thirty more minutes, and when Knut eventually came in he glided right past my table, didn't even nod, and went on to another table—him and Wayne Gretzky.

Another fond memory was the evening during the Doral in Miami when Knut arranged for Buddy Stark and I to meet him for dinner at Joe's Stone Crab. We arrived first and waited an awkward forty-five minutes before he waltzed in with this couple. Ignoring us completely, he went to another table with his good friends Michael Douglas and Catherine Zeta-Jones.

Knut's never embarrassed when he does shit like that. He thinks everybody's supposed to understand how he has these social obligations, being a supercelebrity himself. On the other hand, Mitch, my caddie, says when Knut does that kind of thing, somebody ought to "bitch-slap the motherfucker upside the head."

"What do you think about the ruling Thor got today?" Irv Klar asked.

That was the first I'd heard of it. I knew Knut was the Mother Goose who won the tournament. He shot four rounds in the 60s, closed with a 66, nipped Phil Mickelson by a stroke. But that's all I was aware of. Ever since I'd finished my own round I'd been alone out in a corner of the range, working on some things. "What ruling?" I inquired.

"They're still showing the replay in the press room," Irv said. "I don't know anything about golf rules. Some guys in the press room are trying to turn it into a scandal. What's the big deal about a drop off a cart-path?"

I gradually pulled the story out of him.

It seemed that a TV viewer had phoned the tournament office Saturday night to report what Knut did. The viewer was one of those rules junkies—every country club has one. The rules junkie said for the officials to go back and look at the telecast of Knut at the sixteenth hole on Saturday.

They did that, and what they saw on TV was Knut lift his ball off a cart-path, where it had come to rest, and take a free drop of one club-length, no nearer the hole. All well and good, perfectly legal—you're allowed a free drop from an immovable obstruction.

But then when Knut played the shot, he'd kept one foot on the cart-path. Clearly a violation. Should have been a two-stroke penalty. Thus, Knut didn't win the tournament. In fact, he'd signed a score-card with a lower total than he should have had Saturday. He should be disqualified. Not even collect second-place money. He should get zippo, Circle O Ranch, Xerox.

Knut was shown the videotape of his infraction before the prize-giving ceremony and was even reminded that Craig Stadler had been disqualified in the same tournament in '87 for placing a towel under his knee before he hit a shot—you can't "build a stance." Some rules junkie watching TV had called that one in, too.

According to Irv Klar, Knut insisted that there was a very good rea-son involving "crowd safety" for his keeping one foot on the cart-path. Had he kept that foot *off* the cart-path, he'd have been forced to change his aim more toward a pack of spectators, and a mis-hit shot, he argued, might have seriously injured or even killed someone.

Bullshit. I was willing to bet my stack that Knut had obviously liked his lie where it was, knowing he had a better shot at the flag with one foot on the cart-path. But since Knut Thorssun was a foreign star, the gutless tour officials and tournament committee hadn't wanted to cause an "international incident" by disqualifying him, so they ac-cepted his explanation. He was still the winner.

Nevertheless, I grinned all the way to LA, knowing that Knut had garnered another nickname for himself. Cheater.

10

YOU CAN FALL INTO A BAD PUTT-
ing streak out here that's so frustrating, it
makes you cuss Mary Queen of Scots for
inventing the game. Her and everything
she stands for. Kilts. Bagpipes. Blood
pudding. I've suffered bad putting
streaks that lasted longer than a tune on
a bagpipe.

Change putters is the first thing you
do. The second thing you do is change
putters again. There've been guys on the
tour who've changed putters five times in
one month. There've been guys so desperate they've changed the kind of underwear they wear. Changed caddies.
Changed cars. Grown beards. Studied

Zen shit. Buddy Stark likes to say he even changed wives one time, but there was a little more to it than that.

Buddy's first wife was Laura, a frisky Dallas stew. After three years of what he thought was a happy marriage, he fell into a bad putting streak when he found out that Laura was sleeping with various major league baseball studs and NBA stalwarts.

That's when he canceled out Laura in a divorce and married Trudy, the frisky nurse. Buddy and Trudy stayed happily married for about a year, until Buddy fell into another bad putting streak when he found out Trudy was sleeping with Todd Everett, another tour player. Buddy divorced Trudy and Todd Everett divorced his wife, and Trudy and Todd got married and now Todd has his own putting problems.

For over a year now, Buddy's been going with Emily, a well-packaged young chick in Austin. Emily doesn't travel with him much, preferring to complete her education. Once an aerobics instructor, she's taking classes in English literature at the University of Texas. "Far as I know," Buddy says, "she's not fucking anybody but me and Hamlet."

I was in a lethal putting funk when I suited up for the LA Open at Riviera. Inconvenient, is what it was. Inconvenient because it's a tournament and a golf course I hold in high regard—lot of history involved. I'd never won it, but I'd always played well in it. Finished in the top 5 once, the top 10 four times.

Riviera was designed by George C. Thomas, a wealthy aristocrat from Philadelphia. First architect to put a pot bunker in the middle of a green. It's still there at Riviera's sixth, a par three. He also did Bel-Air, the course with the best elevator in golf—it gets you from the holes down in the bottom to the holes up on top. And he did the North Course at Los Angeles Country Club, the finest course that's never held a major. Also a club you can't join if you've ever been in the movies. Bing Crosby once lived across the street from the course but could only play there once a month as a guest. Randolph Scott did become a member after he retired from Hollywood, although some would argue that Randolph Scott was never an actor in the first place.

George C. Thomas was originally a banker and a gardener and was led to golf course design by what he called the landscaping possibilities. Today's millionaire designers might find it astounding that Thomas designed those three wonderful courses—Riviera, Bel-Air, and LA Country Club—and never accepted a fee for his work. He quit golf course design in the late 1920s. Went back to growing roses.

It's part of Riviera lore that it held the first big-money golf tournament in history, which was the inaugural LA Open in 1926. All the Grantland Rices rode trains out to cover it. All the Walter Hagens played in it. All the Mary Pickfords galleried it. "Lighthorse Harry" Cooper won the thing and received a whopping $3,500 check. At the time, that amount was seven times more than any pro tournament had ever paid for first place. Harry Cooper once said in an interview, "Don't tell me I never won a major. All the boys would have traded a U.S. Open for that kind of dough."

Riviera is in Pacific Palisades, another rich-guy residential area you run into on Sunset Boulevard after you leave Beverly Hills and you're going west toward the ocean.

Turn in a lush tropical drive and you come to a clubhouse that's almost as big as a TV producer's home. The course is down in the canyon below, down there with the barranca running through it, with the towering eucalyptus trees that line and darken the fairways, and the weird kikuya grass that sits the ball up pretty good in the fairway but hugs it like a bear in the rough.

I always like walking around in the clubhouse, peeking into all the alcoves and dining rooms and nooks and crannies. It's easy to imagine the time when Riviera was the "home of the stars," when such Hollywood figures roamed the premises and took divots on the course as your Mary Pickford, Will Rogers, W. C. Fields, Katharine Hepburn, Spencer Tracy, Clark Gable, Humphrey Bogart, and Johnny Weissmuller. That crowd.

Ben Hogan gave the place even more stature when he turned it

into "Hogan's Alley" by winning the LA Opens of '47 and '48, and returning later in '48 to win the U.S. Open with a record 72-hole score
of eight under par that stood for fifty-two years—until Tiger Woods.

WHAT MADE matters worse about my tragic putting stroke at
Riviera, I was playing jam-up, lights-out tee to green. Smoking my
driver, wearing out the clubface on my irons.

"Hello, Golf."

Mitch said that over and over when I pulled the trigger in the first
two rounds. But all I got out of it was a 71, even par, on Thursday, and
a one-under 70 on Friday.

Pured everything but came up empty. Putter disease.

On Friday afternoon after the round, while I was experimenting
with my grip and stance on the practice green, Mitch said, "Spin, we
fixin' to change putters. Where that old Armour of ours?"

The old Armour was my Tommy Armour Iron Master, a bit of a
MacGregor antique, a putter I once loved until it betrayed me and
had to be sent to the museum, which is the storeroom in my garage.
The Armour was a rear-shafted putter, too, a model that didn't look
much different from the Wilson 8802 I'd been using for three years.
The one that was deeply into betrayal right now.

I said the Armour was back in Fort Worth, in a storeroom at my
townhouse, with about a hundred other clubs.

Mitch said, "The Armour a little heavier, tad shorter blade. We better send for that Mother Goose . . . get us a new feel . . . change our
outlook on this and that."

The next thing I knew Mitch had taken my cellphone out of his
pocket and reached Cheryl Haney at her office in Fort Worth, telling
her she needed to get on an airplane tonight—her and that putter—
or else put the putter on an airplane tonight so we'd have it for the
last two rounds of the LA Open.

She must have said something about being busy in her real estate career, because Mitch said, "Girl, this is serious. The man not rollin' his rock. You can be jackin' with them houses some other time."

Mitch was only doing his job. Sometimes the caddy has to be your good friend. A tour caddy's job is not just lugging your fifty pounds of mallets around. He has to know the yardages and pin positions and help read the greens on all the courses you play. He's expected to be on time everywhere and keep the clubs clean and always be a positive influence and make sure your bag has all the necessary ingredients inside.

My necessary ingredients consist of four new gloves at all times, two dozen Titleists, rainsuit, umbrella, rain cover, sleeveless sweater, slipover sweater, windshirt, a new Sahara golf shirt, two pairs of socks, spare towels, extra cap, hand warmers, Swiss Army knife, Advil, Mylanta tablets, GenTeal eyedrops, Alka-Seltzer Plus cold tablets, toilet paper, Band-Aids, tees, pencils, a bottle of Evian, two packs of Juicy Fruit, box of Milk Duds, and a box of Caramel Nips.

A couple of years ago there would have been three packs of Marlboros in the bag as well. But I hauled off and quit one day after I saw myself in a taped replay of a tournament. There I was, me and my Marlboro, staring at the lighthouse on the eighteenth at Harbour Town. Mitch had to nudge me to remind me it was my shot.

Right then I realized I didn't look like Ben Hogan smoking—the cigarette was part of Hogan's personality. I looked more like Bette Davis.

Mitch does a great job and I'm lucky to have him. Which is why I pay him better than he could make if he bargained through the TBLA, the Tour Bag Luggers Association, although the TBLA has given us some balance out here. Before them, we didn't have any Commies.

I keep Mitch on a yearly contract of $80,000, but he pockets a piece of the prize money when I do good. He earns 7 percent of my winnings if I finish in the top ten, and 10 percent if I win the whole deal.

There on the putting green at Riviera, with the big old Spanish-style clubhouse behind us, looking like something Teddy Roosevelt and the Rough Riders had ridden up and shot at, I took the cellphone from my caddy.

"Hey, Cheryl, what's up, babe?" I said jovially.

Then I listened.

First she related how she'd checked the phone messages at my house and thought I'd be pleased to learn that the surgery on Terri's mother had gone well—they'd found an extra appendix. But the operation was costing $2,000 more than Terri had expected, so please mail a check. Then I heard how the business Cheryl was in was as important to her as my business was to me—and how come I didn't understand that? I learned she was on the brink of unloading a "cur dog" on El Campo for $700,000. No pool, no fireplace, no terrace. She was about to unload it on a red-faced couple from Atoka, Oklahoma, who'd just moved to Fort Worth—what did they know? The house was on a "tear-down" street in "Eastover Hills." All the other houses on the block, most of them frame, would be torn down someday, and the "cur dog" was on the wrong side of Horne Street, on the east side of it. "Not by any stretch of the imagination is it in Westover Hills," she said. The Atokas didn't know Westover Hills from a Red Lobster. Didn't know it was the city's ritziest neighborhood. But they did know they could walk from the "cur dog" to Roy Pope Grocery and get the chicken and dumplings, like she'd bought them for lunch today. This would be a nice fee for her, in case I didn't realize it. Naturally she wouldn't receive the whole 6 percent commission, or $42,000. She'd have to split the fee with the broker, her boss, the prick Donald Hooper. He didn't do anything but pay the office rent and take half of what his agents sold—his hardworking, drive-all-over-hell-and-back, deal-with-dumbass-clients, sweating, laboring, scrambling agents. That's what being a Donald Hooper real estate broker-prick was all about. But the $21,000 she'd make wasn't to be laughed at. All that aside, assuming she could even find the Armour putter in my storeroom, she wasn't sure she could make a plane tonight—it was already three in the afternoon, Fort Worth time. And why would she want to come out to California, anyhow, with nothing to do but sit around in a Holiday Inn on some LA freeway?

"I've moved to the Beverly Hills Hotel," I told her.

She said she could be there by nine o'clock—hold dinner.

11

I WASN'T AS RICH, TAN, FAT-
bellied, baldheaded, and goateed as the
old boy I had fun looking at across the
way, but that didn't mean I couldn't have
my own poolside cabana at the Beverly
Hills Hotel. Fast-paced whip-out handled it nicely.

Cheryl Haney and I had devoured our
eggs Benedict for breakfast, our newspapers, and our McCarthy salads for lunch
while the fat boy had about a hundred
phone calls and visits from three briefcases and two shapely adorables.

The briefcases stood at attention and
took shit, then left. The shapelies talked
on the phone themselves, wriggled out of

their snug jeans and flimsy tops to reveal they were wearing bikinis and store-bought racks. They sunned themselves for a while, gave him lingering kisses, and left.

The scene reminded Cheryl of another country song—"Get Your Tongue Out of My Mouth 'Cause I'm Kissin' You Goodbye."

Cheryl spent most of the day in the sun on a recliner. Earlier, she'd wondered whether the plump gent across the pool was a gangster or a movie producer. I'd said I was sure there wasn't much difference in the two, based on everything I'd ever heard about Hollywood. I said he did look rich enough to own a spare prostate.

The handsome pool kid, in charge of spreading towels on reclining chairs for twenty dollars a pop until he got an acting job, straightened us out. The plump gent was president of Earthquake Records, we learned.

I asked the pool kid what artists recorded for Earthquake Records. Figured he'd know, and I was right. He excitedly ran off the names of five rock groups I'd never heard of, but that was no surprise to me. If Patsy Cline or Louis Armstrong hadn't sung it, I probably hadn't heard it.

Cheryl thought maybe she'd heard of Glow Dopers, but she confessed to being totally unfamiliar with Liver Transplant, Four Vaginas, Dripping Shit, and Piss on Mom and Dad.

This was Monday. What we were doing at poolside was relaxing and resting and unwinding from my heart-stirring performance in the Los Angeles Open.

We would be flying home tomorrow, where I was awarding myself two weeks off before I hit the Florida swing.

I was dropping a bypass on the Sominex Match Play Championship at La Costa, even though I was among the sixty-four players eligible for it in the world rankings. While I was grateful to be in those rankings, I'll never understand how they work. They're based on some chink's homework.

I couldn't see taking the trouble to go down to La Costa and unpack, settle in, play a practice round, then get dusted in an early round by some no-name chip-shot magician from Taiwan. The week after that, it went without saying, I'd be skipping the Tucson Open, leaving it to Mr. and Mrs. R. Ess and all the little esses in their complete Arizona family, may a goat stomp on all their heads.

Cheryl and the Armour arrived safely Friday night, but not without the kind of difficulty that's typical of your air travel today.

First class was full on the American flight she took at 6 P.M., but she braved it in coach. Turns out it was duty beyond the call. The only good thing was, she had an aisle seat, 24-C.

This was good because the passenger next to her in 24-B was Big Girl, a young woman in a straw hat, tank top, and shorts who was holding a pot plant with artificial flowers in it. Furthermore, Big Girl was so gigantically overweight, she removed the armrest in order to make room for all of herself.

What this did in turn was permit Big Girl's all-points flab to spill over onto Cheryl's left side. Which meant that Cheryl's left arm was rendered unusable, more or less buried, whenever she needed it for anything, like trying to put cream and sugar in her coffee or trying to dine on the cardboard deli snack that was served.

Trapped in the flab, Cheryl found it equally difficult to turn the pages of the John Sandford paperback she was reading. She solved this problem by sticking one side of the book between her teeth each time she wanted to turn the page, then turning it with her free hand, then quickly clamping the book back down on the tray table. She said she got pretty good at it.

The flight landed at LAX on time but Cheryl didn't arrive at the hotel for four more hours, not until almost midnight.

The reason was, she couldn't claim her luggage, or my Armour putter, because none of the passengers on the plane could claim their luggage for three hours. Somewhat inconceivably in this age when people have been known to go to the moon, land on it, and hit golf balls on it, the airline couldn't get the cargo door open on the aircraft.

Every forty-five minutes, Cheryl said, the airline would make an announcement about the problem, say they were working on it, and loud cries of agony could be heard throughout the terminal.

Cheryl eventually endeared herself to an American employee by saying, "You know what? I'll bet we can find a terrorist around here somewhere who can get the goddamn door open in about thirty seconds."

The American employee told Cheryl she shouldn't talk like that, she could get in trouble, and Cheryl told her what she could do with her airline.

12

I WAS SIX STROKES OFF THE
lead after thirty-six holes at Riviera. Six
back of Cheetah Farmer, child star, with
three lurkers between him and me.

Lurkers are your basic nobodies.
They've never won a tournament. A magazine writer I know, Jim Tom Pinch,
named them lurkers one time and
it caught on with the rest of the
media. As Jim Tom explained it, your
lurker will lurk around the top of the
leaderboard where big names are involved and occasionally win a tournament, thereby screwing up everybody's
story.

I was once a lurker myself, of course,

but I hauled off and won me a Milwaukee Open twelve years ago and became a non-lurker.

The ever-popular Knut Thorssun was taking the week off. Oh, he was in the tournament, all right, but he was still taking the week off, slopping it around the course, out of contention, but enjoying himself.

Every time I saw Knut out on a terrace or around the putting green or in one of the dining rooms, he'd be in the company of his Hollywood friends—a gathering of midgets smoking cigars and miniskirted, perfect-legged, rack-jiggling, hair-tossing shapely adorables who might even be actresses.

The midgets, I assumed, made laser-beam and monster movies. The shapelies looked like they were primarily in the business of cockdiving. They'd do that for a few years—until they snared a rich husband—after which they'd shop their way into middle age and spend most of their time worrying about what to wear to parties.

I happened to overhear one of Knut's Hollywood midgets complain about how exhausting "the cotillion season" was. I nodded at him sympathetically and said, "Those damn cotillion seasons have worn my ass out a time or two. Have to drive in from the ranch."

That afternoon I'd been moving gingerly through the crowded clubhouse when Knut waved at me to come over to a table where he was sitting with his midgets and shapelies. I knew the only reason he wanted me over there because I was among the leaders on the scoreboard and he wanted to show me off.

What the hell, I stopped by the table for a moment and Knut made introductions. In my whole life, even though I'm a fan of old movies, I'd never heard of any of the famous people he introduced me to.

I stood there while Knut told a joke. He asked all of his friends if they knew the definition of making love. They all looked at him inquisitively.

Knut grinned and said, "Making love is what a woman does when you are fucking her!"

Har, har. Bang fist on table.

I walked away amid the roars and screams of laughter.

Six off the lead with two rounds to go is no big hurdle if you can make a few putts, and thanks to Cheryl and air travel I had the old Armour putter in my hands. As Mitch had predicted, the Armour gave me a whole new outlook. Putting is all mental anyhow. That's the rumor.

Saturday I went out and holed almost everything I looked at, and shot me an Amarillo, Route 66, Upside Down 9's. I waltzed past the three lurkers. It pulled me up to within two shots of Cheetah, who posted a 70 but still led. My round put me in the final pairing with Cheetah on Sunday.

Cheetah's size gives him a big advantage normally. He's 6-3, 190, and only twenty years old. No wonder when you put him together with today's technology, he can drive it 340. He's longer than Tiger on the average—the morons love his length—but he's not nearly as good a guy as Tiger, and not nearly the player, but who ever has been, or ever was, or is?

Chandler (Cheetah) Farmer came to us from California as a three-time NCAA champion at Southern Cal, a U.S. Amateur champion to boot, and he's already won three times on the tour in a year and a half. If he was ever a lurker, it only lasted five minutes.

Cocky shitass doesn't quite describe him accurately enough, and I'm not sure arrogant prick does either. Maybe if you combine the two.

Buddy Stark says, what Cheetah is missing in personality he makes up for with his lack of humility.

SUNDAY WAS one of those ideal sunny days that people who live in Southern California like to brag about, call your attention to, even take credit for—in the sense that they're so smart to live out here and you're not.

I was standing on the first tee Sunday when Cheetah's daddy, Hank, the burly crew-cut jerk who caddies for him, came over to me and said, "You're in deep shit today, Bobby Joe. Cheetah brought his 'A' game."

I said, "I'll try to stay out of his way, not hold you up too much."

Cheetah and I shook hands without smiling.

While we were waiting to hit our tee shots, Mitch, looking serious, held out a piece of paper and a pen to Cheetah and asked him for an autograph.

"I don't sign autographs for free," Cheetah said.

"This for charity," Mitch said.

Cheetah said, "What charity is that?"

Mitch said, "The United Negro Sandwich Fund."

"Fuck you, man," Cheetah said, turning away.

Two holes decided it. We played one-under through the first five, me saving three pars, Cheetah missing two short birdie putts.

When we came to the "donut" hole, the 170-yard sixth, the par three, I clubfaced an 8-iron in there about three feet from the pin. Evidently Cheetah wanted to show me he could gorilla a sand wedge 170 yards—Tiger style. Which was how far he hit it, but unfortunately for him the shot flew into the unique pot bunker in the middle of the green and buried.

"Goddamn it, you fucking asshole!" Cheetah yelled at himself and slung the club over to his dad. Murmurs ran through the gallery around us on the tee.

Walking to the green, I looked at Mitch and whispered, "Thank you, George C. Thomas."

"Who that be?" Mitch asked.

"The architect who designed the course," I said.

"Man who put the bunker in the middle of this green?"

I nodded.

Mitch said, "Well, bless his goofy ass."

Cheetah took two to get out of the bunker, and by then he was so scalding hot and impatient he three-putted for a triple bogey six. When all that was over, I staggered in the birdie putt. It was a four-shot swing. Suddenly I wasn't two strokes back, I had a two-shot lead.

Now it was *my* tournament to win or lose. In that moment I'd have given $500 for a Marlboro, but I settled for a mouthful of Milk Duds.

We both parred the next three holes, which sent me to the back nine with the two-shot lead over Cheetah—and no one else was in contention. The leaderboards on the course told me that everybody else in the field had put it in reverse, including the media-hated lurkers.

The tenth at Riviera is one of the niftiest little par fours on the tour. It's only 311 yards, slight dogleg right, and your big hitters are tempted to try to drive it. But the small green sits on a crown, and if the drive misses the green, the ball is likely to disappear down a steep slope and pull a kikuyu blanket over its head. That basically eliminates the birdie possibility and often even eliminates the par.

Kikuyu grass is an African weed and gives you another reason not to go to Africa, although not as good a reason as your mambas.

Most of us never try to drive the tenth green. It's smarter to go with a two-iron off the tee, put yourself in position for about a hundred-yard pitch shot. Which is what I did perfectly with a slight fade.

"Hello, Golf," Mitch said.

Now I stood with Mitch and watched as Cheetah's dad handed him the three-wood, and said, "Time to turn up the volume, kid. We're due for a kick-ass back nine."

Suitably inspired, Cheetah stepped up and launched a satellite high and long, heading straight up over the trees toward the green. But the ball slowly started curving left—and went even more left.

"That's right, hook!" Cheetah hollered at the ball. "Now hook some more, you cocksucking, motherfucking piece of shit!"

He took an angry swing with the three-wood, but this time he was aiming at the ground. The clubhead took up a foot of turf. He kicked at the divot he'd dug, pitched the club over in the direction of his daddy, and stormed off down the fairway.

"Did he leave anything out?" Mitch said to a group of fans behind the ropes in back of the tee. Everybody laughed but Cheetah's daddy.

I cozied a sand wedge in there about ten feet from the pin for a birdie putt and delighted in waiting to see what Cheetah could do with his second shot. He'd driven it 330 on the carry, a little beyond pin high, but it had hooked thirty yards left and the ball was five inches deep in the kikuyu grass.

He opened the face on his sand wedge and took a Tiger Woods slash at it, but he didn't get a Tiger Woods result. He only moved it ten yards, but now he could at least see the ball. A lob shot from there put him on the green, but thirty feet away, and he three-putted for a double bogey six. When I drained my birdie putt, I took a four-shot lead with only eight holes to go.

Mitch said, "We don't need nothin' from here to the house but fairways and greens, my man. Let's do this thing."

Play conservatively, he meant. Don't do anything risky. Pars were good enough.

"Hit eleven, stay on twelve," I agreed.

Although I hadn't been straining to find Cheryl in the large gallery, I'd spotted her once on the front nine. She was strolling along apart from the crowd, trying to ignore a couple of college punks who were impressed with her bod. She was wearing large round sunglasses, snug khaki pants, and a tight pink knit top that did a swell job of displaying two of her major assets.

Cheryl finally made herself conspicuous to me on the eleventh tee. She worked her way up to the ropes, gave me a little thumbs-up sign. I wondered if she was thinking about the $615,000 first-place paycheck. I was reasonably certain that my two exes, Alleene and Terri, were thinking about the $615,000 first-place paycheck.

You could call that amount of money obscene, and you'd be right. I am more than grateful to the heroes who came before me to make it possible—Hogan, Nelson, and Snead . . . Palmer, Nicklaus, and Tiger. One by one, they kicked the tournament purses upstairs.

And I don't buy the argument that we deserve this kind of money because we can play golf better than Joe Jack Billy. Schoolteachers out there teach school better than Joe Jack Billy, but they still make crapola.

I honestly wasn't thinking about the money at Riviera. The W itself was more important to me in terms of pride.

It was ice cream all the way to the cabin. Cheetah made two more bogeys, just to prove how mad at himself he could get, and I parred the last eight holes in cruise control, and it was *Buenos noches,* coaches.

I closed with a light-running 68, three under for the round, and a winning total of 275.

Your faithful golf followers may have noticed that I wound up winning by four shots over somebody named Mark Elliott, a certified lurker that Cheetah let slip past him for second.

Cheetah somehow scared up the decency to congratulate me on the eighteenth green, backhanded as the compliment was.

Shaking my hand, he said, "If I were you, Bobby Joe, I wouldn't go to another dance without that putter."

Mitch replied for me. "We buyin' it a corsage."

13

CHERYL WAS ON MY ARM AS I WAS led into the press room by three tournament officials who were trying to hide their disappointment that I wasn't Cheetah Farmer.

The first person to greet me in there was a smiling Irv Klar. He offered me a high five, and I took it.

"What are you doing here?" I said.

"Hey, I came up today to root for my buddy," he grinned.

His buddy.

I quickly introduced Irv Klar to Cheryl and asked him to look after her while I went up to sit at the table where the microphone was and do my birdies and bogeys and try to give the Point Missers and Rally Killers something to write about.

Fort Worth's own Jim Tom Pinch, the New York sportswriter who'd coined lurkers, had also come up with Point Missers and Rally Killers. Some years back he'd explained to me that half the people in any press room—in any sport—were Point Missers and Rally Killers. A Point Misser could often be a Rally Killer, too, but there was a tiny difference.

The Point Misser was adept at asking naïve and pointless questions that had nothing to do with what happened in the sports event, and the answer wouldn't appear in anybody's story but the Point Misser's.

Meanwhile, the Rally Killer was adept at interrupting an athlete in the middle of revealing something fascinating about himself to ask a naïve, pointless, and completely off-the-subject question.

Like, for example, a golfer could be saying he stabbed his wife to death that morning with a butcher knife because she threw away his KKK hood, and the Rally Killer would interrupt him to ask if he planned to play at Doral next month.

I went through my round quickly. I said it was good to be back in the winner's circle—it had been a year and a half. I lied when somebody asked me about Cheetah Farmer's collapse. I said he got a lot of bad breaks today. I gave credit to Roy Mitchell, my caddy. I was in the process of talking about Mitch making me switch putters to the Armour and how it had made the difference in my game the last two rounds when a Point Misser interrupted me.

He wanted to know if I planned to play at Doral next month.

A studious writer was aware that I was single and had two ex-wives in my background, and brought it up. He asked which was easier, to play good golf, single or married?

I pointed out Cheryl Haney in the back of the room, said she was my fiancée, and said I'd been trying to talk her into becoming my third ex-wife but she was insisting I sign a pre-nup agreement first.

I waited for laughter. Nothing.

Minutes later, while I was talking about how much it pleased me to be from Fort Worth and win a tournament on a course where Ben Hogan had won three times, and Byron Nelson had won once—I thought the Fort Worth angle was interesting—a Rally Killer stood up, frantically waving his hand at me.

I stopped in midsentence, looked at him, and said, "Yes . . . ?"

He said, "What iron did you hit to the eighteenth?"

The Rally Killer was groaned at by his fellow journalists.

The rest of the interview was pretty much a dogfight between Smart Money and Rally Killers.

I was on my way out of the press room when Irv Klar asked me where we were going to celebrate tonight. He said Cheryl invited him to join us.

I said, "Do you own a pair of long pants?"

He said he came prepared, having had immense faith in me.

We were a party of four in the Polo Lounge that night—me, Cheryl, Mitch, and Irv Klar. Those three had never been in the Polo Lounge before and were excited about having a passel of celebrities to look at.

I gave "Pepe le Moko," the maitre d', a hundred-dollar bill to make sure he seated us in one of the booths on the left as you enter. Pepe le Moko was Charles Boyer's name in *Algiers*, I explained to Irv Klar. As for the booths on the left, it's a well-established fact that the booths on the right are Bulgaria, and all of the seating in the back is Albania. If you can't sit in one of the booths on the left in the Polo Lounge, you might as well go to a Denny's.

The maitre d' glanced at the hundred and gave us the big round booth in the left corner and a telephone and two platters of guacamole with chips.

I asked the maitre d' if he'd ever been to Algiers.

Nothing.

We all drank quite a number of adult beverages until it was time to order shrimp cocktails and cheeseburgers, then we drank adult beverages through the shrimp cocktails and cheeseburgers.

Irv Klar, my new young journalism friend, had to be told to shut up at least three times throughout the evening. Those were the occasions when he kept directing the conversation back to himself.

As I vaguely recall, he'd decided to make *Sports Illustrated* hire him right away, he'd write for them for five years, but by the time he was thirty he planned to be running a TV network or a movie studio.

I was yawning when Irv said to me, "I want to help you with your book. You'll need a wordsmith. That's me. My name will have to be on it, too. By Bobby Joe Grooves *with* Irving Klar. Like that. I'd never write without a credit, no way. I already have a great title, you ready? *Tees and Sympathy.* Huh?"

My yawn that time came with a whimper.

Mitch barely spoke all evening but he was relaxed, enjoyed himself, and was tickled by the glances he drew from passing waiters and other customers. His slick bald head glistened like Michael Jordan's, and he wore a light gray pinstriped suit with a blue handkerchief in the pocket, a dark blue button-down shirt with a lighter blue silk tie, and a pair of shades.

Pepe le Moko treated Mitch like he must be somebody famous, but he never could think of who.

14

GOING BACK HOME AS A TOUR-
nament winner meant granting some
local newspaper, TV, and radio inter-
views, but I didn't get to play the con-
quering hero too long. A big mistake
caught up with me.

The big mistake, I came to find out,
was the one I made at the Crosby. Which
was telling Nonnie Harrison what Cheryl
Haney's name was and where Cheryl
worked.

Cheryl was over at my place late one
afternoon about three days after we came
home from LA, and, as luck would have
it, while I was out running errands—
going to the cleaners, the drugstore,

picking up ribs and brisket from the Railhead for dinner—she'd received this phone call.

Guess what the first thing was Cheryl said to me when I walked back in the house. Never mind. I'll tell you what it was. She said:

"You fucked that woman in Pebble Beach!"

Under a surprising and immediate attack like that, I said what any man would say.

"What are you talking about?"

"I'm talking about Nonnie Harrison," she said, eyes blazing.

"Nonnie Harrison?" I said. "Yeah, Nonnie. She's married to that guy, J. Rodney. He was my amateur partner at Pebble Beach."

"I just spoke to her."

"You just talked to *Nonnie Harrison* on the phone?"

"Yes. The woman you fucked in Pebble Beach."

"Wait a minute," I said. "I get a phone call from a woman I barely know and that means I fucked her? Why'd she call here? I mean, how'd she even know the number? I'm unlisted. I sure didn't give it to her."

"She knew my name and where I worked. She called my office for your phone number, and my office gave it to her—as if that is of any goddamn importance in the light of things."

I said, "Cheryl, let's slow down a minute here. What exactly did Nonnie Harrison say, and what did she want?"

"She wanted to know what your travel schedule is over the next few months. She said to tell you she'd been thinking about you ever since the evening you two spent together. She said . . . I don't fucking believe this—she said to tell you it had been a long time since she'd been with a man as sensitive as you are."

"And you think that means I nailed her?"

Her look said what kind of a fool did I take her for?

Oh boy.

She said, "You know what almost makes it worse? Her fucking name is Nonnie! You fucked a *Nonnie*, for Christ sake!"

Six or eight fucks right off the bat, incidentally, was no NCAA record for Cheryl.

I momentarily wondered if it would have made any difference to Cheryl if Nonnie's name had been Mary Ellen. I also momentarily wondered whether it would be better to stonewall it or confess, beg for mercy.

That was decided for me in the next instant by Cheryl, who said, "Bobby Joe, if you don't tell me the truth right now, I am walking out of this door and you will never see me again. I mean it."

I said, "Why do you want to put me in a jackpot like that? If I say I didn't screw her, you'll call me a liar. If I say I did, you'll hate me."

"I won't hate you," she said. "I will know you are man enough to stand up and tell me the truth. I can't live with a liar, Bobby Joe."

I took a deep breath and said, "Okay, we . . . fooled around."

"You fucked her, you mean?"

"Well . . . it was more like she fucked me."

"I hate you!"

"See there?" I said.

"You rotten bastard!" she said. "How dare you? How *dare* you?"

All I could think about was, I knew I should have gone with popular theory. Like any sane man. Never confess, no matter what. Even if they have game films.

"You are double stupid," Cheryl said. "On top of not having any respect for me, you go off and fuck a bitch named *Nonnie*."

I thought about telling Cheryl that Nonnie had a sister named Neenie, but I wisely kept that to myself.

"It was an accident, is what it was," I said.

"It was an *accident*?" Cheryl said. "Your dick wandered off by itself and wound up between her legs?"

"It didn't *mean* anything," I said. "A big mistake on my part, yeah, but it was nothing. It was like, you know . . . I believe any understanding, clear-thinking person would consider it a sports event."

"Really?" Cheryl spoke with folded arms. "Maybe I'll go fuck a Dallas Cowboy . . . call it a sports event."

"Offense or defense?"

"Be funny. That'll fix it."

"Any normal guy in the same situation would have done the same thing, believe me."

"Wrong. Any miserable asshole with no character in the same situation would have done the same fucking thing. I thought I meant something to you."

"You do, babe."

"Don't call me babe."

"Look, I'm guilty. I did it. But it was a weird circumstance. It was like, you know, *strange*. It's never happened before in all the time we've been together, and it'll never happen again."

"Not till another Nonnie shows up."

"That's not true—and refresh my memory about something. We're not married, right?"

"Oh, that makes it okay?"

I said, "It makes it something less than a federal offense. It makes it less of a sin, a big deal, doesn't it?"

"You know what? It makes *you* less of a big deal, is what it fucking well does."

I said, "I'm sorry. I'm sick about it. I did a terrible thing to you. I wish I'd been stronger, had more willpower. Call me a weak shitass. Shoot me, stab me, slit my tires . . ."

"The only goddamn thing you're sorry about is you got fucking *caught!*"

"There is that," I said.

"Keep being funny. See what it gets you."

"How bad do you want me to feel, babe?"

"Don't call me babe!"

"What can I do about it now? That's all I want to know."

"You can catch a venereal disease."

"Now who's being funny?"

"Damn it, what a dumb shit you are. You've got a nifty lady who loves you, who cares for you, and you can't wait to fuck it up."

"I'm curious about something," I said. "What did you say to Nonnie when she asked you what my schedule was?"

"I told her it was none of her fucking business, and that my real name was Gambino—and if she ever put her cunt in your face again, she'd hear from my nephew Guido. That's about all."

I wanted to laugh at that, but held it in. Then I said, "There's one thing you ought to understand about Nonnie. She's a viper, man. She's the kind of woman where . . . if I hadn't done it with her, she'd have told you I *did*."

"My God," said Cheryl. "It was self-defense!"

15

CHERYL STAYED HOT THE WHOLE
two weeks I was home. We didn't see
much of each other, and when we did, I
was the recipient of what you call your
silent treatment. That was on the one
hand. Her wise mouth was on the other.
Not many civil responses to anything I
said. Punishment deal.

All in all, I was reminded from prior
experience with two wives that when a
woman gets as hot as Cheryl was, the
anger just has to run its course. Like my
daddy used to say, you might as well try
to fight a house fire with a garden hose.

Even flowers didn't do shit.

Another mistake I made was not staying out on the Tour, keep playing after I won at LA. You tend to play in streaks. I knew that. If my putter was on a roll, why didn't I let it keep rolling? I should have remembered the old gambler's motto. You need to make a bet on something every day—you might be walking around lucky and not know it.

But I felt like I stayed sharp hitting practice balls and playing a few friendly rounds out at Mira Vista while I was home, and I was feeling confident about my game when I went down to Doral.

To tell you the truth, I still don't know exactly how to tell anybody how to get to the Doral Country Club Resort & Spa in Miami, even though I've played in the tournament ten times.

I know it's way west of anywhere you'd want to be—downtown, the ocean, Key Biscayne, Coral Gables, South Beach, Coconut Grove, Miami Beach, Joe's Stone Crab, Bal Harbour, the airport.

The first two or three years I played in the Doral I actually thought it was named for a cigarette or a flower you put on a wreath. Of course I eventually found out the name came from humans. It came from Al Kaskel, who built the resort, and his wife, Doris. I guess Al Kaskel could have called it Aldor, but putting his wife's name first obviously made it sound better, and may have even prevented an argument at home.

There are five 18-hole courses at Doral, but the tournament's always played on the "Blue Monster," which was the first course built and the one designed to be a championship test.

When Al Kaskel had the idea for the resort forty years ago, a resort in the middle of nowhere, Dick Wilson was the trendiest architect around and was hired to do the course. Wilson had made his name designing Meadow Brook and Deepdale on Long Island, Laurel Valley in Pennsylvania, and several other Florida layouts, plus he was in the redo business. He'd carved out changes on such respected courses as Seminole, Colonial, and Inverness, although I can't imagine why anybody thought they needed it.

For my money, Wilson basically ruined Colonial at home by enlarging and flattening all the greens and cutting back trees. I've always wished I could have played Colonial when it was as tight and tricky as it was during Hogan's prime.

Doral's "Blue Monster" is flat and long, all eighteen holes rambling through and over and around a bunch of man-made lakes. Dick Wilson must have pushed his foot down six or eight times. Year in and year out, it's a 275 to 279 golf course, although Greg Norman caught it in a calm one year and stitched a 265 on it.

I went to Doral feeling okay about my game, less okay about my life. I stayed at the resort. It's not the most convenient place to stay if you want to go see exotic Miami, but as a wise man once said, that's what limos are for.

Buddy Stark and Jerry Grimes and I bagged the Tuesday night bridge game and hired a limo with an English-speaking driver—a rare thing in any city on the East Coast—and went off to fondle Miami's delights. There were free Buicks at our disposal, courtesy of the Tour, but we'd never have found our way back to Doral.

First stop was Joe's to get on the outside of some stone crabs. After that, all we did was pay rent on an outside table at the News Café in South Beach and sit there the rest of the night and watch it all go by.

And it did. A steady parade of fashion models, crack dealers, whore ladies, limpwrists holding hands, tugboat lesbos holding hands, bodybuilders, revolutionaries, Jennifer Lopez look-alikes, pickpockets, and now and again your Art and his lovely wife, Deco.

Due to a gesture on the part of Jerry Grimes, we were joined at our table by Brandi and Amber, two no-slack dirty legs in string bikini tops and cutoff jeans. The cutoff jeans were cut off right up to home plate. They passed for cute, but they'd have been cuter if it hadn't been for the tattoos on their upper arms and thighs and cheeks. The tattoos were of insects and flowers and, I think, guns. Buddy called them tootats.

He said to them, "I bet those tootats were a source of pleasure and pride for your mom and dad, huh?"

"My parents suck," Brandi said.

"Mine suck more," said Amber.

Jerry offered to buy them several beverages of their choice. Brandi, the taller one, said they were hungry. We watched them mop up cheeseburgers and fries while we drank some of that Cuban coffee that makes you want to run to Billings, Montana, and back.

Buddy Stark asked them what they were reading these days.

Amber said, "What do you mean?"

Jerry said, "We have a limo and we're staying at the Doral. They have lots of food at Doral."

Brandi said, "Cool."

I said, "Jerry?" He looked at me.

"I have a question," I said.

"What?" he said.

"How you gonna get back down that hill?"

I wasn't trying to sound like Paul Newman in *Hombre*, but the line is a keeper. Suitable for any number of occasions, and this was one.

Jerry got the drift and we politely blew them off.

After Brandi and Amber were gone, I said to Jerry, "I didn't think you'd want to wake up broke and dead tomorrow."

"With no towels either," Buddy Stark said.

AS SOON as the tournament started it looked like I couldn't wait to stagger, stumble, and falter. I never broke 70, even scared up a 75 in the third round, and my 290 total left me in a tie for 74th place, which only paid me a chiseling $5,700.

My putter kept working, but I couldn't get to the greens fast enough. I made the discovery that Doral has more bunkers around the greens than I remembered. I kept shooting at pins and kept missing. I saved a number of pars out of the bunkers, but pars were cheap. Kmart pars, Mitch said.

I was following through nicely on the sand shots, taking wide shallow divots like you're supposed to. Swinging through the shot and finishing high so my body was facing the target on the follow-through.

Mitch complimented me on my bunker play.

"We hit us some good photo ops," he said.

Knut Thorssun, cheater, enjoyed one of those weeks where God turned his head and allowed an asshole to win a golf tournament. Always makes you wonder what school God went to. Knut posted a 273 and took it by five shots over Ernie Els and Rickey Padgett.

Knut commuted to the tournament. He choppered over to Doral every day from his mansion in Palm Beach. One of his toys. A six-seat Eagle Bat Luxury Osprey, or whatever it's called. Air-conditioned, stereo, TV, Dell computer, snacks on board. Some guy flies it for him.

One day Knut brought the unruly little shits with him, Sven, 8, and Matti, 10, along with their nanny. The nanny, Renata, is 28, a blonde from Germany who has big tits and all the other moving parts. I'd often wondered what Knut's wife, Cynthia, thought of Renata.

Buddy Stark, who'd been there, certainly thought highly of Renata. He liked to say she was a very generous, fun-loving, good-natured person, given enough deodorant.

One thing the unruly little shits like to do at a tournament is get a putter and a ball from their daddy and hit line drives on the putting green. Telling them not to do this—they might injure someone—had never seemed to work. We've all learned to keep a sharp eye out and give them plenty of room.

The day they came to Doral, in a moment when Renata was having a warm chat with Buddy Stark, they stopped hitting line drives long enough to come over to where I was, on a remote corner of the putting green. Matti wanted to tell me a joke.

He said, "Has my dad told you the blonde's nursery rhyme?"

"The *blonde's* nursery rhyme?" I said. "What do you know about blondes?"

"Have you heard it?" Matti said.

"This is a joke your dad told you?"

"Have you?" he whined.

"No," I said, eager to get it over with, "I have not heard the blonde's nursery rhyme. What is it?"

"Hump me, dump me," he blurted out.

When they stopped giggling, I said, "Isn't that a little advanced for you guys?"

"Fuck, shit, piss!" Sven hollered, and they ran off to throw flying tackles on Renata.

Guess not, I thought.

THE HONDA tournament started out more than thirty years ago as Jackie Gleason's Inverrary Classic. It's always been played somewhere around Fort Lauderdale, which must be a city of 700 million people if you judge it by the traffic jams and condos you find there.

This time it was held at a new course called TPC at Egret Landing. It's one of those "stadium golf" designs the players are supposed to be proud of because the Tour builds them.

But Egret Landing is more of an embarrassment, is what it is. The architect was Barney Rivers, a club pro whose only qualification for the job was that he's married to our commissioner's sister. Barney is from Houston, so naturally he was more familiar with humidity than he was with how hard the wind blows on Florida property near the ocean. Nevertheless, Barney Rivers ripped off Pete Dye's TPC Stadium design and even tried to outdo it. The fairways are too narrow, the greens are too small, and waste areas are everywhere, gobbling up your tee shot on every hole. It's a carnival ride when the wind's strong.

The course has been called everything imaginable by our own people. The best description I've heard came from Buddy Stark. He called it "a surefire cure for constipation."

I should have stayed in my Fort Lauderdale motel that week, not even played. I could have had more fun hanging around the gift shop and counting the sales of denture grip. I shot 72–74 and missed the cut by a shot.

There's only one thing worse than missing the 36-hole cut, and that's missing it by one fucking shot. You blow one lousy six-footer somewhere, and it costs you a paycheck. All you can do the last two days is hit practice balls. You could leave town, go to the next stop, but you've already paid for the motel room so you might as well hang around and work on your game.

Buddy Stark and I agreed that the Honda Classic and the TPC at Egret Landing both got what they deserved. A lurker won the tournament. I honestly don't remember his name.

The highlight of my week may have been the message Cheryl left on my phone in the Lauderdale motel Saturday evening. I pushed the message button and heard her voice saying:

"It hasn't been easy to follow your progress. I was afraid you might have been ill or injured. I couldn't find your name in the paper. Then I realized I should have been looking for it under Other Scores or Failed to Qualify. Hope you're enjoying all the Nonnies in Florida."

Click.

This was good, I told myself. She was obviously thinking about me or she wouldn't have called.

16

WHEN YOU CONSIDER THAT ARNOLD Palmer owns the Bay Hill Club in Orlando, lives nearby, and presides over the Bay Hill Invitational, you'd think the golf course—out of respect for Arnold, if nothing else—wouldn't have let so many dogs win his tournament.

I can use the word dogs and get away with it because I'm one of the dogs. I won the Bay Hill four years ago. Rope-a-doped my old hook right into Victory Lane. Clipped Nick Price by two strokes.

The dogs have been plentiful around Bay Hill. If you look back at the past champions, you discover a lot more dogs than guys you find on Wheaties boxes or doing TV commercials.

A dog is a guy who may have won on the regular Tour, even more than once, but he's never won a major, your Masters, your U.S. Open, your British Open, or your PGA. Until he wins a major, he don't move up.

Dogs are a step above lurkers, but they're still dogs.

It's a mystery deal because Arnold and his partner, Ed Seay, completely remodeled Bay Hill after Arnold bought the property. They turned Dick Wilson's original design, which was weak, into a stiff championship test. The course is now almost 7,200 yards long, has a bundle of doglegs, and presents you with a lot of nervous shots to greens that are protected on one or two sides by water.

Buddy Stark's explanation for Bay Hill producing so many goofy winners over the years is that Walt Disney World is nearby—what else would you expect?

MY *LIVEWIRE* agent, Smokey Barwood, of Dotted Line, Inc., headquarters in New York City, New York State, came down to Orlando to see me over the weekend.

He wanted to "go over some projects" he could line up for me, see if any of them appealed to me in "the jing department."

I think he actually wanted to see if I'd been hit by a truck, seeing as how I'd missed my second cut in a row at Bay Hill. Shot me a couple of defensive linemen, 74 and 75, and went Dixie by four strokes.

There wasn't even any suspense to it. I turned the sixth hole into a commode and flushed it.

The sixth is a par five, 543 yards. It curves all the way around the big lake on the left. Clubface your tee ball out there near 300, you can go at it on your second, if you don't mind risking a shot into the water, which is on your left and behind the green. I'd put a drive out there pretty good, and Mitch estimated there was 254 left to the green, a little wind helping in case I wanted to go for it.

Tiger can get there with a two-iron, but I required a four-wood. As it turned out, I needed Tiger's swing. I pull-thinned the shot into the lake. Dredging up a triple bogey, it was the kind of undernourished shot that invites a comic to ask, "Does your husband play golf, too?"

But Mitch didn't say that. All he said was "Well, we got this one over in a hurry."

Smokey Barwood is a thin little guy in a three-piece suit and thick glasses. He wears his hair Wall Street–wethead style. He looks like one of those smarts on cable TV who tries to tell everybody how it is in politics and the financial world.

My agent thought he was doing me a favor by taking me to dinner in the "gourmet" restaurant at his hotel, which was dangerously close to that whole Disney World deal.

Nash, our waiter, brought me a little one-bite salad with a circle of lime green bath gel squirted around it. I wished for a camera, but drank my Junior and laughed at it instead.

The salad was followed by my entree, a little raw hen sitting on a bed of mashed sweet potatoes.

I said, "Nash, old buddy, take this sparrow back to the chef and ask him to cook it—and you can lose the sweet potatoes, too."

Nash said, "I'm afraid Gar won't serve it any other way."

"Gar?" I said. "Gar is the chef?"

"Yes. He's quite accomplished. He came to us from the Culinary Institute of Upper New York State."

Handing the plate to Nash, I said, "Tell Gar I'll pay a hundred dollars to watch the blood roll down his chin after he takes a bite of this."

Nash looked off, hand on his hip. When he gathered himself up, he said, "May I bring you something else, sir?"

"You can bring me a phone."

"A telephone?"

"Yeah, so I can call Domino's and get something to eat."

You can't miss a cut and go to a "gourmet" restaurant all in the same day without being testy. That's what I say.

I made do with Juniors, coffee, and bread while my livewire agent ate his raw pork medallions on a bed of mashed sweet potatoes and went over the business opportunities I could take or leave.

First he wanted to know if Irving Klar was real.

"Irving?" I said.

"He says Irving is his pen name. He called me. He's called me more than once, actually."

I said, "He's a young sportswriter who got hold of my pants leg in California and I can't shake him loose. He's harmless."

Smokey said, "Modesty is not his finest trait."

"You noticed that?"

"He says he's going to be the 'mechanic' on your book. I didn't know you were writing a book."

"I'm not," I said.

"It's not the worst idea to come across my desk lately. An inside look at the Tour . . . scrape the underbelly . . . not a tell-all, but a tell-*some* . . . it would have to be gritty."

"Irv Klar may be writing a book, but I'm not."

Smokey floated the latest business opportunities past me.

No, I didn't want to take a group of auto parts salesmen for a round of golf on Lake Buena Vista Country Club at Disney World. It wasn't worth twenty-five grand. I said I'd been to Disney World once—I'd rather spend a day with Knut Thorssun's kids.

No, I didn't want to do a freebie next week that would be good for my "image," a pro-celebrity tournament in Clearwater for the benefit of the Fellowship of Christian Athletes.

I said, "Half the guys I know who joined the Fellowship of Christian Athletes are no longer *in* the Fellowship of Christian Athletes. They made three bogeys in a row one day and said fuck this shit, I resign."

No, I didn't want to do a two-day outing with Japanese bankers in Rancho Santa Fe, California, on the Monday and Tuesday before the U.S. Open at Winged Foot in New York. It would leave me only one day of practice for the Open, and besides that, they were Japs.

No, I didn't want to play an exhibition in Mexico City. Mexico had tried to kill me twice. Mexico had scorpions bigger than squirrels, and they were territorial.

No, I didn't want to go to Düsseldorf in June to play in the German Open for expenses and a $25,000 appearance fee.

"Why in the world not?" Smokey asked.

"It's in Germany," I said.

I added that if I ever *did* enter a European Tour event, I'd take Curtis Strange's advice. Never win it. Always finish second. That way you get a big check and don't have to go back to defend.

I said yes to the *QE2*.

I was going to the British Open at St. Andrews anyhow. Sail over, fly home. I'd have a big cabin next to the captain's, I could take along the lady of my choice, or select one onboard. Smokey said it was five days, six nights on the ship after you sailed from New York. He swore it was usually smooth in the summer. Give one lesson to geezers on an outdoor deck, do a couple of Q-and-As, swoop fifty large, *Buenos noches*, coaches.

I didn't ask if I could have my own private lifeboat in case we did an iceberg thing.

Driving me back to the Bay Hill Club where I was staying, my agent brought up a touchy subject. The Ryder Cup.

17

THE RYDER CUP WAS A TOUCHY subject because in all my sixteen years out here, being a consistent money winner, nabbing the occasional W, staying exempt in the top 125, not molesting children and not dealing drugs in school yards, I was still 0-for-Ryder Cup.

The way I'm sure guys used to lust after Sophia Loren in the days when she gave true meaning to the low-cut peasant blouse—some say she won the first wet T-shirt contest—that was me lusting after a place on our Ryder Cup team.

We'd fielded eight U.S. teams since I'd been on the tour, and the only thing I'd been able to do was salute the guys who made it, root for them, and tell them how great they looked in their uniforms. Two years ago I was seventeenth on the final point list, seven spots out of it, but that wasn't really coming close. That was coming about as close as a skydiver trying to land in Fort Worth and hitting the ground in Austin.

I said to Smokey Barwood in the car, "My goal at the first of this year was to make the Ryder Cup team. That was it. That's what I told Mitch. That's what I told Buddy Stark, Jerry Grimes. . . . Cheryl . . . Alleene . . . Terri . . . all my wives."

"And that's what you told me," he said. "But that's what you told me the year before, too. Maybe the year before that."

"I'm a better player now," I said. "I'm peaking. This is the year. Look at the start I've got. Sixth in the Hope, fourth in the Crosby, W in LA."

"And two missed cuts in a row," he said. "What's that all about?"

"It's a game of slumps," I said.

"I've heard you say baseball is a game of slumps."

"Golf's a better example."

"When was Tiger's slump? I must have missed it."

"Any year now. It'll come with a bad marriage."

Smokey said he couldn't overstate the value of making the Ryder Cup team. It would double my outing fees, enhance my endorsement possibilities, dramatically increase my appearance money if I were to enter foreign events.

"I don't care about any of that," I said. "The Ryder Cup is our Olympics. It only comes around every two years. It's the only time we get to represent our country. I just want to be part of it one time. I want to put on the uniform, see USA on my bag, hear the anthem, and throw a side-body block on a European."

My agent asked me to walk him through it again, one more time, how you make the team.

It's all based on points, I said. A year and a half of top ten finishes. You get more points for this year, a Ryder Cup year, than last year, the year in between. And you get a lot more points for winning a major than you do for winning, say, your basic Colonial.

This year in regular tour events you get 150 points for a win, 90 for second, 80 for third, 70 for fourth, and so on down to 10 points for a 10th place finish. I got 150 points for winning L.A. Last year I would have gotten only 75. And I got 50 for my sixth in the Hope, and 65 for my tie for fourth in the Crosby.

"That's 265 points," Smokey said. Quick with numbers.

"I have more than that," I said. "You count last year, too. Last year I finished tenth twice, and eighth and sixth. That gives me fifty more."

"So you have 315. How many more do you need?"

"It depends."

"On what?"

"On what everybody else does," I explained. "Right now I'm in sixth place, but there are a lot of tournaments left. They count points through the PGA in August."

"It stops there? Why?"

"They need a month to get the uniforms ready. The shirts, slacks, sweaters, blazers. You're asking a man who's never made the team. What do I know? Ask an apparel salesman."

"You'll make it. When the going gets tough. . . ."

I said, "I'll have to do it on points. Larry Foster has two captain's choices, wild cards, but he'd never pick me."

"Why not?"

"No Ryder Cup experience."

"How did Larry Foster become the captain? He's on the Senior Tour."

"The usual way," I said. "Larry's a past PGA champion, but that alone doesn't do it. The officers of the PGA get together, talk it over, try to find a guy who's never called any of them a shithead. Larry's always been a diplomat. I think he's been campaigning for Ryder Cup captain a long time. Remembers names, writes thank-you notes, telephone freak, comes complete with fleshy blonde wife. But he'll be a good captain. He'll leave the team alone. He won't try to tell anybody where the v's oughta point."

Smokey said, "It would be nice if we could bring closure to this Ryder Cup spot . . . sooner than later."

"Closure," I said. "I'll look it up."

18

IT RAINED LIKE A BITCH THE DAY
before the Players Championship in Ponte
Vedra Beach, but if you knew anything
about Florida you knew the rain wasn't
going to delay the start of the tournament.

Rain doesn't bother Florida golf
courses. Florida rain goes straight down
through the grass and dirt and sits there.
Maybe some of it trickles on down to
China, I don't know. But mash your foot
down hard anywhere in Florida and
you've got an instant lagoon.

If I can pin down Ponte Vedra Beach
for you geographically, it's on the Atlantic
Ocean halfway between Jacksonville and
Geezerville, better known as St. Augus-

tine, which claims to be the oldest town in America. The Fountain of Youth is in St. Augustine. Big tourist attraction. This may also mean that St. Augustine has the oldest water faucet in America. I went there once and watched geezers buying bottles of Fountain of Youth water to take home and drink before they died.

Ponte Vedra, I think, may be Spanish for real estate development.

It is definitely the leader in the clubhouse for security gates. The security gates are in place to protect the homeowners from muny golfers and help pizza deliverymen find the right neighborhoods, which all look alike but have different names—Quail Joint, Smuggler's Grape, Gator Cove, North Ditch, etc. The security gates also provide a stern obstacle course if you try to drive anywhere in Ponte Vedra between the ocean and the intracoastal canal.

Halfway between the beach and the canal is where you find our PGA Tour headquarters and our TPC Stadium course with its famous seventeenth hole, the short par three with the island green. It's by far the best course that's ever been built entirely out of lumber.

Just kidding. I know Pete Dye, the architect, can take a joke. Pete did introduce railroad-tie bulkheads to American golf course design.

The best thing Pete did when he was routing the layout out of the forest and swamp, he let loose a herd of goats to get after the esses. The goats killed untold hundreds and chased hundreds more back to the Everglades where they belong. Which reminds me that it'll be a better world when the Everglades gets paved over. Let the fuckers bite into concrete, see how they like it.

Tour headquarters consists of these rustic-type buildings at the entrance where you turn to drive up to the golf course. In one of the buildings you'll find our new boss, Commissioner O. P. Giddings. Buddy Stark says the O. P. stands for Over Paid. In the other buildings you'll find our two thousand lawyers and accountants.

The Tour's been run by numerous commissioners through the years, dating back to Walter Hagen's day. Commissioners used to be known as tournament managers when such gentlemen as Bob Harlow and Fred Corcoran held the job, and they were frequently disposed to "pass the hat" to raise prize money. That, of course, was before we became a big business and felt the need to have our own CEO to make rich.

Two things did more than anything else to help us become a big business—Arnold Palmer and TV. They came along at the same time in the mid-'50s and it's been a zoom deal ever since.

Buddy Stark and I were talking about all this at dinner in the Sawgrass Marriott dining room the night before the Players. We were at a table by the windows, where we could watch the rain hammering down and see the lightning dance over the tops of the pines.

"Florida gives good storm," Buddy remarked.

We tried to name all the many departments the Tour now has. I got Business Affairs, Corporate Marketing, Business Development, Retail Licensing. Buddy got Agronomy, Television, Player Relations, Finance, Communications, Tour Operations. Somewhere in one of those buildings, he said, there was bound to be a Department of Lunch and Dinner Reservations.

We had no idea where O. P. Giddings came from. The Policy Board knew, but we couldn't name any of the players or captains of commerce currently on the board. They never told you any secrets anyhow.

We knew O. P. didn't play golf. We'd heard he used to work in "food products," and before that he jacked around in MTV, and Buddy said he'd heard the thing that locked up the commissioner's job for him—after Tim Finchem retired wealthy—was that he'd once been a disc jockey in Dallas.

Buddy said, "I don't much care where he came from as long as he keeps the train on the track. So far he seems to be doing it, mainly by staying out of sight."

PLAY GOOD, putt bad. Putt good, play bad.

That's every golfer's complaint. You can't have it all. God won't let you. So you go out to play a round and you either expect to play good, putt bad, or putt good, play bad. Usually you find out which way it'll go on the first two or three holes.

Like you stripe the tee ball down the fairway, cut an iron in there close to the flag, but blow the birdie putt. Right away you know it's a day when you're going to play good, putt bad.

This lets you pull the old Tommy Bolt act. When the birdie putt curls out of the cup, you look up at the sky and say, "Me again, huh? Why don't you come down here and play me *one time?*"

The great ball strikers in the past—Hogan, Snead, Nelson—they never played good, putted good. They played good but putted . . . just okay. It's the way it was in their day.

On the inconsistent greens they had to deal with, putting was always a problem. They had to read grain, shadows, splotches, even on bent, no matter how manicured the greens might look to the spectators.

That's why Hogan, more than anybody else, studied a course intently in practice rounds. He decided where he wanted to be on every green. He'd rather face a slick 30-footer on the right side, where he knew the speed, for example, than a 15-footer on the left, where the speed was guesswork.

Hogan played "target golf" before anybody knew to call it that.

We, meaning all of us today, don't have that worry. Most of the time we can stick it in there anywhere and we know the speed will be consistent, reliable, no matter where we are on the green.

All the advances in turf manufacturing and greenskeeping techniques have given us greens that putt true everywhere we go. We rarely see uneven greens. Lanny Wadkins said it best one time. He said, "The greens are so true now, we make six-footers the way we used to make two-footers."

Jack Nicklaus was the first golfer to play good, putt good. Aside from his awesome ability, Jack was a positive thinker. He's said, "When I was at my best, I never missed a putt in my mind."

Good golf tip, is all that is.

Now we have Tiger Woods. In case you haven't noticed, Tiger is the first golfer ever to play great, putt great. Which is why he laps the field about every fourth time out. It's why he's "Black Jesus," as some of the guys out here refer to him, behind his back, of course, envious of his talent, his wealth, his smile. Play great, putt great is why Tiger is up there on a level nobody ever knew existed. He can make the rest of us look like we're swinging hickory and hitting the feathery.

Tiger lapped the field at the Players Championship. He scorched Pete Dye's lumberyard with a 259 in a week when the nearest score to him was was the 280 that four guys tied with.

It was one of those "other world" performances he does so well. On the TPC Stadium course that most of us still think is pretty tough, and while most of us were glancing off the bulkheads, wandering around in the waste areas, and diving into the water around that frustrating little island green, Tiger steer-jobbed the fairways, threw darts at the flagsticks, and one-jacked the greens.

Tiger's total broke Greg Norman's tournament record of 264, and on top of that Tiger contended with an occasional wind, unlike the Shark in '94, when nothing was moving but the mosquitoes. What Tiger strapped on the Stadium course were rounds of 66, 61, 67, and 65. Uh-huh. Sixty-fucking-one in Friday's second round.

That's when Jerry Grimes said, "I don't know about you, Bobby Joe, but the sumbitch done bit my neck and sucked out all my blood."

Jerry was in second place at the time, but eight strokes back. He played extremely well and wound up in that four-way tie for second with Cheetah, Duval, and Mickelson. They only got beat by 21 shots.

I was only thrashed by 24 shots. I rolled into the garage at 283, tied with Buddy Stark and Justin Leonard for seventeenth. I was $90,000 better off, but no Ryder Cup points.

I DID get me a swing tip from Tiger, though. Somewhere down the line it might pay off.

We were hitting balls next to each other on the range after the third round. Guys with swings that aren't very picturesque, shall we say, don't like to practice near Tiger. I guess they're afraid he'll say something like "Can't you go to a doctor and have that removed?"

My swing's not a bad-looking golf swing, even when I get a result that doesn't exactly put me on the bluebonnet highway.

In an idle moment for Tiger, when he was taking a breather, fiddling with a grip on a club, I said to him, "I don't suppose you'd care to show me how to hit that knock-down two-iron of yours, would you?"

He took the two-iron out of his bag and addressed a practice ball.

"This the one you're talking about?" he said, and burned a low 220-yard draw down the range.

"That's close enough," I said.

He said, "I use this shot a lot when I have to keep the ball in play off the tee, coming down the stretch . . . or when it's windy."

"I've noticed," I said.

He addressed another ball. "I play it back in my stance, with my hands a little forward," he said. "And I sit a little lower in my setup. The key thing—for me, anyhow—is to bow my wrist at impact and abbreviate my follow-through."

He hit another shot, doing all that. Immortal.

"But you take a full backswing," I said.

Mr. Observant.

"Yeah, I do," he said, "You need quiet feet to do that."

"Quiet feet," I said. "I'll work on it."

I hadn't enjoyed many private talks with him. I had more questions.

"I read somewhere that you once ate fourteen tacos all at one time." I said. "Is that true?"

He said, "It was when I was in high school, before a match. This guy and I had a five-dollar bet on who could eat the most. He ate twelve. I won."

I said, "When I was in college a bunch of us were in a tavern one night and I watched this guy who was on the football team—a defensive tackle—eat six dozen hard-boiled eggs."

"Did he win the money?"

"There was no bet," I said. "He was just hungry."

Smiling, Tiger did a stretching exercise, holding a club, moving his shoulders back and forth as I came up with another question.

"You really make your own bed every morning?" I said. "At home *and* on the road? Even when you're staying in a—you know—Ritz Carlton, somewhere like that?"

"Yeah," he said. "It's a routine."

"Do you scrub baseboards, too?"

He laughed. Good guy. One of your nicer immortals.

19

THE GREATER GREENSBORO OPEN fell between the Players and the Masters, but it's never been one of my faves. It's as much of an outdoor cocktail party as it is a golf tournament. Your Carolina Bubbas tend to get themselves overserved. So it didn't take much thought for me to board the Pasadena-Sayonara Express and go home for a week to try to put a patch on my non-marriage to Cheryl Haney, my non-wife.

As soon as I got home, however, I found out there were other things that needed to be taken care of as well.

One thing involved George and Louise

Grooves's two-story condo. My folks suddenly felt the need for an elevator in their home.

"Stairs go first," my daddy said, feeling around on his left knee, where the arthritis was attacking him, and rubbing on his right hip, where an Oriental rot had set up shop.

"His legs are killing him," my mama said, "and I won't even bother to talk about my own pains."

I said, "Why don't you turn the living room into the master bedroom and forget about the upstairs?"

"Where would we entertain?" my daddy said. "You want us to play bridge on the bed when the McAllisters come over?"

I called an old high school buddy who was in the construction business and asked him to recommend an elevator guy. He recommended a "good old boy" named Glenn Tabor and I met Glenn Tabor over at the condo when my folks were out limping around the Hulen Mall.

"Aw, boy," he sighed as he looked the job over. Tough one.

I asked if it could be done, the elevator.

He said, "Aw, I can do it. Run it up that storage room and into that closet up there. Might cost you Colorado, Idaho, and Wyoming."

"That where you like to go?" I asked.

"Yep. Me and my gun. Hide out up there."

"Mad Dog Roy Earle," I said.

"Who?"

"Humphrey Bogart in *High Sierra*. With Ida Lupino."

Glenn Tabor squinted at me.

I faked a cough. "You fish up there, too?"

"Aw, yeah," he said. "Fish is everywhere. They send you postcards. But I just kiss 'em and throw 'em back."

"No problem on the money, whatever it is," I said. "Can my folks live here while the work's going on?"

"They can," he said. "It could get a might loud."

"They can't hear too good anyhow," I said. "Let's get it on."

He said, "It's on, Bubba."

I went to see my folks a day later and told them they were getting the elevator. My daddy asked if I wanted to see what his left knee looked like today. Pasadena, I said. He said try to visualize a skin-colored, oversize grapefruit, or a soccer ball. That was it.

I said I'd do that.

My mama said she suffered a migraine last night that would have blinded an elephant at the Forest Park Zoo. I said maybe the elevator would help. She said nothing can help a migraine—it was God's way of punishing women. I said men get migraines, too. Not as bad as the ones women get, she said. I said I'd forgotten that.

They thanked me for the elevator, gave me a cold meatloaf sandwich on Mrs. Baird's white bread, and said I was a good son.

THE OTHER thing involved my second ex-wife, Terri Adams. There was a message to call her at Red Taggert's law office. I called and when she answered the phone I said, "Hi. I just shot and killed two people in cold blood—how busy is Red?"

"Why'd you do it?" she giggled.

"No reason. They just pissed me off."

"We're pretty busy around here, but Mr. Taggert will be happy to talk to you about it if you have access to any money. How are you, Bobby Joe?"

"Back home, is all. What's up?"

"We are *so* busy. Ray Ron Moreland's trial started this week."

I said, "As you know, Terri, I travel a good bit. Who is Ray Ron Moreland?"

"Ohmygod, you don't know who Ray Ron Moreland is?"

"No idea."

"He's the guy who cut off his wife's head and buried it out behind their double-wide. But he didn't kill her. Red is sure he's innocent and he'll get Ray Ron off. Ray Ron is a very nice person. He sells containers that hold things."

"Like heads?"

"Bobby Joe! Yuk on you!"

"If Ray Ron didn't kill his wife, Terri, why'd he cut off her head?"

"It was a bad decision. I won't argue that point."

It was impossible not to laugh.

She said, "It's not funny, Bobby Joe. You have to understand Ray Ron's thought process. He and Paula Dean Adcock—that's his girlfriend—came home and found his wife murdered. She had been stabbed to death twenty-seven times. Ray Ron naturally thought if he called the police, they would immediately think he did it, or *they* did it."

"I can see where the cops might think that," I said.

"So he did the only thing that came to his mind," Terri said. "He cut off Myra Jean's head and tried to make it look like some kind of maniac came in and did it."

I said I didn't want to get all caught up in this, but I did wonder why Ray Ron was bringing his girlfriend home when his wife was there. Terri explained that the three of them lived together. I laughed. Terri said she was glad I found it was so hilarious. A good man's life was at stake here. Just because Ray Ron did something foolish, like cut off his wife's head, Terri didn't see why he ought to have to go to Huntsville and hit the slab like he'd actually murdered somebody.

"They used to ride Old Toasty in Huntsville," I said.

"Yes, they did," she said. "Now they catch the Big Needle."

"Kinder and gentler," I said. "Why'd you call me in the first place, Terri? You need a character witness for Ray Ron Moreland?"

She said she wanted to alert me to what I was going to find on her Mira Vista club bill. Which was the $2,500 she spent on a new set of golf clubs. Which she badly needed, seeing as how she was entered in the Ladies Club Championship next month.

I asked what her handicap was now.

"I'm a 23, but they won't let me have more than 18 in the tournament," she said. "We play one match a week. Alleene's entered, too. She's a six. What if we met in the finals? That'd be interesting from your standpoint. A wife-off."

"*When Worlds Collide*," I said.

"Huh . . . ?"

"Old science fiction movie . . . with Barbara Rush."

"You might have to referee," Terri said.

I said, "I might try to be out of town for that one. How was it possible for you to pay $2,500 for a set of clubs?"

"I went state of the art," she said. "Callaway Hawk Eyes all the way, except for the Tight Lies seven-wood. I got the Hawk Eye one, three, and five woods . . . two Cleveland wedges . . . and a Scotty Cameron putter."

"You didn't have to spend that kind of money, Terri. I could have gotten you all that for free."

"It was an urgent thing. I need to get in a lot of practice with the new clubs before the tournament starts. You bein' a golfer, I would think you of all people would understand that, Bobby Joe."

"You'd think," I said.

20

I USED WHAT LITTLE TIME I HAD
at home to lavish dinners, gifts, and apologies on Cheryl, my non-golfing non-wife.

I took Cheryl to two elegant restaurants, La Piazza and Del Frisco, bought
her two pieces of antique jewelry—a ring
and a pin—that I was assured any woman
would love, and begged forgiveness every
minute I wasn't eating, drinking, or
sleeping.

"I can't believe you'd pass up Greensboro with so many big names missing,"
she said during dinner at La Piazza down
on University Drive. She was having the
veal chop and I was having the sausage
and rigatoni with white cream sauce.

"You've always said you like those tournaments where more money spots are available."

"I've never liked trying to hit golf shots with empty beer cans dropping on cart-paths," I said, "even though Jerry Grimes calls it the Sound of Music."

Soften her up with humor first.

I said Greensboro was still known for the year—'78, I think—when they had this guy with a deep Southern accent announcing the players coming up to the eighteenth green the last day, and the guy uttered his memorable remark about Seve Ballesteros. Seve was about to win his first tournament in America.

I couldn't help laughing as I recalled the incident, now part of lore.

Even if the guy with the deep Southern accent had been sober, I said, I'm sure he couldn't have pronounced Ballesteros. So what he said to the crowd of Carolina Bubbas was:

"Okay, folks, let's give the little spick a big old hand."

"Charming," said Cheryl.

True story, I said.

The dinners were punctuated by long periods of silence. My apologies were deemed "too cynical." And the jewelry was judged to be too small. "I like big rocks," she announced.

However, it can be said that I did reduce myself from a "low-rent, weak-willed Nonnie-fucking disappointment" to the simple and more manageable "spineless asshole."

There was a moment at the last dinner, over steaks at Del Frisco downtown, when I pointed out to Cheryl that the *Fort Worth Light & Shopper* runs both Ann Landers and Dear Abby, and maybe I ought to write them a letter asking this question—if a man makes a terrible mistake and is genuinely ashamed of himself and knows he's badly hurt the woman he loves, should he be punished for it the rest of his life, even if he's willing to cut off his dick?

Cheryl said, "That would be no big sacrifice for you. You'd cut off your dick before you'd cut off your Armour putter. You can still have oral sex with your Nonnies."

"A man's got to make a living," I said. Still exploring humor, I added, "And oral sex don't count against you. A President of the United States taught me that."

She almost grinned, but fought it off.

"Why don't you come home with me tonight?" I said. "We'll discuss everything at greater length."

"No thank you."

"All right, we don't have to discuss anything," I said. "We can just watch a movie . . . or a war."

"What war?"

I said, "There's always a war on cable. Bunch of silly sumbitches who'd rather shoot each other over some religious bullshit than play golf or watch football. A-rabs and Skullcaps . . . thin Balkans and fat Balkans . . . Shirts and Skins."

"Shirts and Skins?"

"Yeah, you know. Irish deal."

"Jesus."

I said, "What does it prove, Cheryl? Staying mad for so long. It's a waste of time . . . or else you enjoy it."

"Screw you. Go home and sleep with your million-thirty."

"Hold it," I said. "You know how much money I've made this year?"

Call me amazed.

She said, "I don't know how much you've won. Somebody in the office mentioned it. They saw the money list in the paper."

"But you *remembered* the figure," I said. "A million-thirty. You're not even an ex-wife, but you know how much I've won? What's that supposed to tell me, you're just a fan?"

She said, "I might just as easily have said a million something else, whatever. So what?"

"But you got the number," I said. "I'm surprised you didn't say the exact amount—one million, thirty thousand, seven hundred. If there'd been forty-three cents on there, maybe you'd have got that, too."

"You're not turning this around on me, Bobby Joe," she said. "I'm the one who has a right to be angry. If you want to make things better between us, you're going to have to admit you're a sorry, weak-willed, spineless asshole to screw that bitch, and you're only sorry you got *caught*."

"Fine," I sighed. "I'm only sorry I got caught. I'm a weak-willed . . . spineless . . . what else was it?"

"Never mind."

IT DIDN'T help matters that I got caught again before I left for Augusta. Caught in a different situation. What happened was, Alleene Simmons called and wanted us to have lunch—there was something we needed to discuss in regard to the catering business.

I met her at Mi Cocinita, my favorite Tex-Mex joint. It's a small café in a converted garage tucked away on Bryan Street over by the grain elevators on the South Side. You've got to want to get there.

She showed up looking like a soccer mom, but better than any soccer mom I was acquainted with. She wore sneakers, tight purple leotards—those things women wear when they exercise—a short little khaki skirt on top of the tights, a baggy gray sweatshirt, and a white headband.

I said, "Alleene, you don't have to shed a single pound. It all looks perfect the way it is."

"Don't flatter me," she said. "I'll do a Patsy Cline. Fall to pieces."

We ordered the delicate cheese enchiladas and rice and beans with two church-lady tamales—the mild ones—on the side. She had a diet Coke in rebuttal to the lunch. I went with ice tea.

In the course of small talk I learned that Phil Murcer, her live-in and catering business helper, was history.

I said, "What happened? He got tired of playing Warden's Daughter and Escaped Convict?"

"Naturally that would be the first thing you'd think," she said.

She explained how Phil Murcer had wanted to be a partner, and how she couldn't afford another partner—she had me—and how his work at the catering business slowly fell off after he realized he couldn't become a partner. He'd pretend to be sick, stay in bed, want to be waited on, ask for chicken noodle soup, cough syrup, Advil. She realized she'd never been in love with him. All he ever had was a cute ass, and then he didn't have that, staying sick, so she told him to take a hike.

"I'm sorry," I said.

"Don't be," she said. "He was a lazy shit."

"Who's the new guy?"

"I don't have one. I have a dog. A Maltese. He's a year old, about this big, a little white guy. A River Crest lady gave him to me. She already has three. I named him Cary—for Cary Grant. He's gorgeous. He sleeps with me, right up against me. I'm insane about him."

"You keep showing off your legs in those tights, you'll have a new guy in no time," I said.

"I'm not really looking. I've hired a young girl to help with the business. Might hire somebody else. Listen, I have something for you." She dug into her shoulder bag, came out with an envelope, passed it over to me. "Your cut for the last seven months," she said. "I wish it could be more."

It was a check for $27,516.

I said, "Thanks, Alleene, but I don't need this right now if you can put it to better use."

"I know you don't," she said. "You've won a million thirty thousand this year."

I laughed. "You left out the seven hundred."

"What do you mean?" she said, then broke into a grin. "Oh, I get it. Female keeps up with male's money list."

"Cheryl told me how much I've won, too," I said. "Maybe I should call Terri, see if I can hit a trifecta."

"I've always kept up with your career, Bobby. You know that. It's not like we parted enemies. And don't get too excited about the money I gave you. I'm setting you up for something bigger."

"Hit me with it now," I said.

She said eagerly, "Okay. There's a piece of property I want. It's a place on Berry near the TCU bookstore. Stubby's Cafe. You may have eaten chicken and dumplings there. I have. It's for sale and exactly what I need. I don't want it for a restaurant—God, no. I want it for our catering headquarters. For Alleene's Delights. I can't keep working out of my home, Bobby. My kitchen's too small for the business we have now. I'm picking up garden clubs and charity organizations and more rich ladies."

It momentarily crossed my mind that I'd once been married to Fort Worth's Martha Stewart.

"How much are we talking about?" I asked.

"They're asking one twenty-five. It will take another fifty, maybe less, to fix it up. It needs an office for one thing."

"So you need one seventy-five?" I said.

I let it sit for a moment, acted like I was mulling it over, then said, "Well, that's no big blister."

"Great!" she yelped. "I'll tell you this, Bobby. It's going to be a very good long-term investment."

I said I'd talk to my agent, Smokey Barwood. He was also my investment guy. He'd tell me what my tax situation is . . . see if we wanted to borrow the money or handle it with whip-out.

"You're wonderful," Alleene said, taking my hand from across the table and smiling sweetly at me.

I moaned to her about how I'd been taken hostage in Pebble Beach, and how Cheryl had found out about it and was making me piss blood, and how the Pebble Beach scamp, Nonnie Harrison, wife of a rich guy, was occasionally leaving messages on my answering machine. I said I wasn't about to return any of her calls, give her any ideas about the future.

"Bunny boiler?" Alleene said.

"No, I don't think so," I said. "Just a fun-lover. But trouble."

Alleene was still holding my hand and smiling sweetly at me when I heard the familiar voice behind me.

"That's cute," the voice said. "How romantic."

I looked around to find Cheryl with two of her real estate friends, Bonnie Lasater and Jolene Frederick.

Bonnie, in her forties, the oldest of the group, usually wears so many bracelets and necklaces I'm surprised I didn't hear the clanking sounds when she came in the front door.

Jolene, a cute blonde thirty-something, is given to having *Sex and the City* parties, I hear. She invites a bunch of her chick friends over to drink wine and make fun of guys' dicks.

Jolene is also known for the engaging messages on the T-shirts she wears. The one today read:

TREAT MEN LIKE SLUTS.

"Hey," I said pleasantly to Cheryl and them, releasing Alleene's hand. "You want to join us? Our business meeting is over."

Glaring at me, Cheryl said, "Oh, really? The business meeting's over? No, I believe I'd rather try this one—go fuck yourself."

With that, Cheryl split for the door, saying to Bonnie and Jolene, "Let's go someplace where I don't have to look at an asshole."

"I'm tight with that," Jolene said.

Bonnie said, "We can probably get in the Paris Coffee Shop by now."

And they were gone.

Alleene smiled at me sympathetically, took my hand again.

I sighed and said, "Good send-off to Augusta, huh?"

21

PEOPLE ARE ALWAYS ASKING ME
what I like best about the Masters, which
they only know from color TV. Like
whether it's the beauty of the Augusta
National itself, or the challenge of Amen
Corner, or the ghost of Bobby Jones, or
the excitement of it being the first major
of the year. Of course it's all those things
together, is what it is, and most folks
could figure that out if they weren't
dumber than Knut Thorssun. So what I
usually tell people is that my favorite
things are the sandwiches, pimento
cheese or egg salad, they sell on the golf
course.

I'm only half-joking. Those sandwiches

are what you call scrumptious, and I've been eating them the whole ten years I've earned my way into the tournament. Another thing is, I hear they've always been good—they haven't changed in fifty years.

Tell me that Clifford Roberts, who used to run the tournament in a no-back-talk style, wanted those sandwiches made the way he liked them. On white bread with no lettuce. They say he'd eat more than anybody during Masters Week.

Clifford Roberts is a familiar name around golf. He was Bobby Jones's good friend and the tournament chairman from the beginning in 1934 until a few years back when he hauled off and killed himself. Roberts had become so incurably ill—the Big C and Big M were jacking around inside him—he decided it was time to go play the Big 18.

One evening at the club he went outdoors and took himself there with a pistol, which he rightly figured was the fastest route.

One thing your modern-day golf architects find time to do at the Masters is salute a pine tree or an azalea bush in memory of Dr. Alister Mackenzie. I mentioned Mackenzie earlier when I was talking about Cypress Point. It was Mackenzie's design of Cypress that caused Bobby Jones to hire him to do the Augusta National, Jones working with him.

I've often wondered why Mackenzie is so revered. Cypress Point was a no-brainer—here's the land, there's Carmel Bay. And if Mackenzie was so smart, how come Augusta's incomparable back nine was the front nine originally? The course played that way in the first Masters in 1934. Funny deal. If it had played that way one more year, Gene Sarazen wouldn't have had the fifteenth to double-eagle. Then what?

Here's a string of the greatest seven holes in all of golf—the tenth through the sixteenth, which includes Amen Corner and offers a total of five water holes—but Mackenzie saw them as a start rather than a finish.

Another thing. In Mackenzie's book, *Golf Architecture*, he lists the rules for designing the ideal golf course, and one of the rules says,

"There should be no hill climbing." So what does he do at Augusta National? The first, eighth, ninth, and eighteenth holes are all uphill.

A wiseguy might even suggest that if Dr. Alister Mackenzie was so smart, how come he didn't know how to spell Alistair?

A *BIG* moment for me that week was running into my agent, Smokey Barwood, and Irv Klar, the sportswriter, on the golf course.

It was Wednesday morning. Mitch was complaining about the fit of his official caddy coveralls, white with my name in green on the back. The coveralls were too large. "I reckon they don't have no alterations department around here, do they?" he said. I was playing my last practice round with Buddy Stark. I found Smokey and Irv—they were together—waiting for me on the seventh tee.

Smokey was eating a pimento cheese sandwich and Irv was eating an egg salad sandwich, but I wasn't scoring.

They'd only been able to acquire practice-round tickets, which had cost Smokey a painful amount of whip-out from a scalper working out of the flea market across the street from Magnolia Drive, the club's main entrance. The flea market grows bigger every year. It offers rip-off Masters souvenirs and fake Tiger Woods autographs on phony Augusta National flags and other items. Smokey and Irv's tickets were good for Wednesday only. Smokey's agency, Dotted Line, Inc., didn't have the stroke that IMG does. All week IMG scatters its agents around the course like dogwood, and puts more of its agents on the veranda than the veranda has tables and umbrellas and members in their green jackets. Irv wasn't able to acquire a press credential, even though he'd applied on the letterhead of his LA County newspaper, the *Daily Planet* or whatever it was.

"According to them, I'm shit," Irv said. "Don't step in me."

I said, "But it won't be a problem next year, will it? You'll be with *Sports Illustrated*, won't you?"

"Fuckin' A," he said.

They walked along outside the ropes as I played the last three holes of the front nine, which was all I intended to play on Wednesday.

I glanced at them and saw Irv Klar gawking at the soaring pines and steep hills. I imagined he was thinking what everybody else thinks the first time they see the course. Like how big it is. Bigger than any course you've ever seen. And how steep the hills are. You can't appreciate it when you're watching TV. You have to see it in person to understand that there's not a level lie on the whole course.

They walked with me up to the ropes and security guards surrounding the clubhouse veranda, which was as far as they could go. Hundreds of people stand outside these ropes every day, staring at the privileged folk who can enter and lounge about—contestants, contestants' wives, working press, club members, longtime clubhouse credential holders. People stand outside the ropes and watch the privileged folk eat, drink, chat, mill around.

Staring at the clubhouse, Irving said, "What's upstairs where that balcony is?"

"Grill room and bar," I said. "Place to eat breakfast and lunch and drink—and the past champions' locker room."

"What's over there on the left?"

"Players' locker room, where I'm headed."

"What's on the right?"

"The Trophy Room. Basically a dining room."

"All these people inside the ropes legitimate?"

"They obviously have the proper credentials. If they don't, they get apprehended and sent to live in Newark, New Jersey."

Irv said, "They ought to put up a sign on that big tree in there."

"What kind of sign?" I asked.

"One that says 'You're Scum and We're Not.' "

Smokey Barwood said he had what he called good news. "Bobby Joe. I think we have a publisher for your book," he said. "Sleeping Giant Press. It's a small house in New York, but on the way up."

"I'm not writing a book," I said.

"I'm writing it," Irv said. "You talk, I type."

Smokey said, "Five figures now, but six-figure advance if you win a major."

I said, "If I ever win a major, I'll be smart enough to type my own book. Tell me winning a major makes you smarter than Stanford."

We were interrupted by a middle-aged woman in shorts, golf shoes, and a floppy hat. She accused me of being a golfer. I confessed. She asked me to autograph two pairings sheets for her. I gladly did. She wondered if I would go in the locker room and ask Knut Thorssun to autograph a pairing sheet for her. I said I was in a business meeting right now—and Knut Thorssun wouldn't do it anyhow.

"He won't do it?" she said.

"No ma'am," I said. "Knut only autographs for money."

"How much?"

"The last I heard, he was up to seven hundred and fifty dollars . . . well on his way to a thousand."

"Well, *spit up* on him!" she said.

"I couldn't put it better myself," I said as she walked away.

Smokey continued. "The editor at Sleeping Giant is a bright young man. Lars-Flynn Bostick. He recently took up the game. I would describe him as very keen and quite earnest."

"Keen and earnest," I said.

Smokey handed me some folded pages of paper, white, 8x10, typewritten. "Just go over them when you have time. We'll talk about it on the phone next week."

Irv added, "It's the opening chapter of your book. Just a first draft. But I think I captured your voice pretty well."

"I'm not writing a book," I said.

"Maybe you are," said Irv.

I stuck the pages in my hip pocket.

Smokey said, "I rather like what Irving's done. I have another job for him in the meantime. He's going to do a golf instructional with Salu Kinda. It should do well in the Far East."

"Salu Kinda is a client?" I said, surprised to hear it.

"As of two weeks ago," Smokey said. "He was unhappy with All-Star Sports in Dallas. Something about their arithmetic. Knut recommended him to IMG, but IMG wouldn't take him on, so he called me."

I looked at Irv. "What do you know about golf instruction? You don't even play the game."

Irv said, "Hey, man, I'm a pro. You're a golf pro, I'm a journalism pro. I've got a copy of *Harvey Penick's Little Red Book*. No sweat."

22

MY FIRST THOUGHT WAS, IRV
Klar has to be hung by his thumbs. Here's
why:

Tees and Sympathy
By Bobby Joe Grooves
with Irving Klar

Ah yew bet, I'm jes' a ol' boy from
Texas who likes to golf his ball for a
livin' on the PGA Tour. Yep, that's
where you can find me—in a covey
of birdies or in a nest of your female
pubics.

Yeah, I like the ladies. I want to
set that straight real quick. Too

many people think golfers are limpos because we dress fancy instead of like roofers and dry-wallers.

Whur at ol' boy gonna geedat? That's a question they used to ask about me before I was even old enough to jack off or go shit in a lake. But when I picked up my first set of golf utensils I knew I wanted to be some kind of Ben Hogan or Bobby Jones, only not as short or dead.

Speaking of pubics . . .

I didn't read the rest, and it was a good thing Irv left town that night because after I read that embarrassing shit I would have tracked him down and put an overlapping grip on his throat.

His uninvited book effort upset me so much, I couldn't sleep good the whole week of the Masters. There's no question that what he wrote was the main reason I didn't score better.

True enough, I tied for eleventh place, but I never broke 70 in any round, I never came close to climbing on the leaderboard, what we call the high rent district, and I came away with no Ryder Cup points. Xerox.

Sure, I'm happy with the $125,000 I swooped, and there was no telling how much the amount might have made my ex-wives whoop.

But all I did in Augusta was moan and stew and fret. I showed Irv's first page to Buddy Stark in the locker room one day, and after trying fight off a grin the only thing he said was:

"Utensils?"

I showed the first page to Mitch on the practice range after I'd struggled to my first-round 74.

"What lake you shit in?" he said. "I know you shit on Amen Corner today."

I did butcher the twelveth and thirteenth The wind held up my seven-iron to the twelveth and it landed in Rae's Creek. El Splasho.

I went to the drop area and just as fast as I could I chunked the sand wedge into the front bunker. I was lucky to get away with a double. And I followed up that comedy act with a three-jack at the thirteenth after I reached the green in two. Perfect.

I chunked four wedge shots the first three rounds. Mitch finally figured out what I was doing. You have to make solid contact with the ball on your pitch shots, which I'd more or less forgotten.

I wasn't letting my wrists cock on the takeaway. What you want to do on your pitches is play the ball in the middle of your stance and put your weight a little forward and keep your hands slightly ahead of the ball, which prevents any urge you may have to scoop it.

You want to hit the ball, then the turf, and let the loft of the club get you up in the air. No big thing to do—unless you've got *Tees and Sympathy* on your mind.

While I was scraping it around eight shots out of first and three shots out of Ryder Cup points, Ernie Els caught a hot putter and let it drag him to that two-stroke win over Tiger. Tiger accepted the loss graciously. Broad smile and pat on the back for Ernie.

It's easier to be a gracious loser when you're Tiger Woods. Man walking around with a six-pack of majors in each hand.

IT'S POSSIBLE to eat dinner free all week in Augusta if you want to take advantage of the mess of invitations you receive.

Everybody entertains, including some of the top players, who rent private homes for the week instead of staying in hotels and motels like most of the field, including me.

A lot of the parties are quite lavish. Ice sculpture involved.

The USGA has a party, the PGA of America has a party, the Golf Writers Association has a party, television has a party, golf magazines have parties, golf equipment people have parties, golf apparel people have parties, European tourist boards and golf societies have parties, and rich guys you'd rather have a head wound than be bored by rent the biggest houses and have parties.

The parties are all catered. You can find every adult beverage and dine on all the country ham, redeye gravy, fried chicken, sliced steak, cheese grits, black-eyed peas, and biscuits you can force down your neck. Same spread everywhere. Maybe some shrimp thrown in.

I stayed at the Magnolia Inn as usual. It's not far from the course, but over in an older part of town near Augusta College, which was a Confederate arsenal during the Civil War.

The inn is on Walton Way, a main boulevard, and from the looks of some of the huge old pre–Scarlett O'Hara mansions that still line the boulevard, not to mention others that are even bigger on the side streets, you might guess that the neighborhood was once a good place for Confederate generals to retire to.

I kept to my room most of the week, but I did venture out socially one evening, Saturday night. I went with Buddy Stark over to Knut Thorssun's party at the huge old pre–Scarlett O'Hara mansion he'd rented for the week.

It wasn't far from the Magnolia Inn. I drove there with Buddy but figured I could crawl home if I had to, after I'd eaten, or after some corporate all-star had bored a hole in me, telling me all about his own golf game, or after Matti and Sven, the unruly little shits, had terrorized me long enough.

The mansion was tall, wide, and white with columns and enormous trees and grounds and statues and fountains and flowerbeds, but it wasn't any larger than the mansions across the street from it or on both sides.

Juvenile Delinquent, one of the valet parkers, took Buddy's car and we went inside.

Nobody was in the living room but two housekeepers. They were down on their hands and knees with cleanser and brushes, trying to clean up the puddles of black ink that Matti and Sven had poured on the white carpet.

We moved into the library, where a workman was trying to scrape splotches of red paint off a white door.

"Kids do that?" I asked.

The workman said, "If they was mine, they'd be drowned by now."

I was reminded that for obvious reasons Knut has to rent a different private mansion every year for Masters Week.

The buffet spread was in the large kitchen, and a few people I'd never seen before in my whole life were picking around at the food. They wore bright colors.

Sitting in a chair over in a corner of the kitchen with her own bottle of white wine and smoking cigarettes was Knut's wife, Cynthia. She waved a hello at us. Her pretty face was slightly flushed, the look of a woman who'd already gotten half-boxed.

"Food's there, guys," she said. "Bars are outside. Please introduce yourself to anyone you don't know."

"I don't want to know anybody," I said.

"I don't blame you," Cynthia said.

"Where are the boys?" I asked. "I noticed coming in they've been having their idea of fun."

"Aren't they wonderful?" Cynthia said. "They could be outside right now puncturing tires, who knows? Yesterday morning I caught them upstairs in the master bedroom breaking open the wall safe and trying to steal the owner's jewelry. Incredible. I'm a good person. I really am. But I've given birth to two children and they're both throwaways."

She sipped her wine, dragged on a cigarette.

I said, "I don't understand why Knut doesn't do something about those kids."

"I know one reason," Cynthia said. "He's too busy fucking Renata."

"Him too?" Buddy Stark said.

Cynthia laughed. "Or maybe it's Celia this week," she said. "Could be Linda . . . possibly Melissa . . ."

I dodged that subject and said, "It sounds to me like old Matti and Sven are ripe for a military academy."

"I'm working on it," she said. "Knut keeps saying they're just boys, they'll grow out of it, but he's never the fuck around—what does he know?"

"Where *is* the host?" Buddy wanted to know.

Cynthia said, "I'd say he's either outside sucking up to a rich asshole or on his cellphone talking to one of his bimbos."

I didn't want to embarrass Cynthia by asking her about the story now circulating around the tour. Ask if it was true. That she caught Knut daytime screwing a chick on the deck of their 120-foot boat when it was docked at their Palm Beach home. During the Doral, the story went. Cynthia had taken five other golf wives home for lunch, the ladies wanted to see the new boat. Cynthia went down to the dock first to make sure the rooms were clean, got halfway down the dock, and bingo—there was Knut getting it on in the bright sunshine with Miss I. M. Port.

You didn't have to wonder how a tale like that could be circulating around the Tour. Cynthia had shared it with another golf wife, and that was like telling NBC, CBS, ABC, CNN, and Fox News.

"Well," I muttered as Cynthia poured herself more wine, "I guess we'll go grab a beer."

Buddy said, "Is the money worth it, Cynthia?"

"You bet your ass it is," she said. "But I won't be around much longer. I'm gonna be outta here. . . . So Buddy . . . when I'm a wealthy divorcée and the kids are in lockup, you gonna give me a call?"

"James Taylor," Buddy smiled.

Cynthia said, "I've got a friend?"

Buddy said, "Winter, spring, summer, or fall."

When we were outside having a beer at one of the bars, and were finished looking around at the brightly colored conversation groups, I said to Buddy, "You're not really gonna take a shot at Cynthia, are you?"

Could be his retirement run, he said. Cynthia still had her looks and she was going to be richer than bent greens after she took Knut to the cleaners. Be a win-win deal.

I said, "Tell me a rich wife is hard-earned money."

Buddy said, "Dollar a word, they say. But it can't be any harder than playing golf."

We never paid our respects to Knut. He looked too busy to interrupt, standing by himself in a corner of the lawn, a drink in his hand, talking on his cellphone.

CERTAIN SPORTSWRITERS LIKE to complain that the Tour between majors is a trip to Downtown Glaze City. I can see how it can be—unless you're winning so much money you're telling jokes to total strangers.

You get a taste of the big time at the Masters—the enormous crowds, the swarms of press—but you don't get another taste until the U.S. Open two months later. After that, you go back to Triple A for a while. Then comes the British Open in July—huge—then it's back to the minors again until the PGA in August. Less huge, but big.

Everything in between, the sportswriters contend, is some kind of MCI-Compaq-FedEx-MasterCard-Verizon-NEC-Kemper-Buick Classic. I've thought it myself. Wake me when the sponsors in their blazers stop thanking all the volunteers, and the lady courtesy car drivers in their designer outfits have stopped going down on Knut Thorssun.

But don't get me wrong. I admire to win any kind of tournament, even if the trophy looks like a glass basketball and you can't find the results in the sports section of the paper till you look on Page 9-C.

Not that I'd taken any victory laps lately. I'd played in five tournaments since the Masters and all I'd done was get myself Windexed, Ajaxed, and Cloroxed.

The Heritage came right after Augusta, and even though I have a hard time finding Harbour Town's fairways, the way they're hidden among the pines and magnolias and Spanish moss and railroad-tie bulkheads, it's still a course I like and respect.

Harbour Town took famous the minute it opened in 1969. When Pete Dye turned a South Carolina low-country swamp on Hilton Head into a fantastic, new-old-looking layout, it was the start of modern golf course design. That's a definite. Ask any course designer today, or read a suitcase-size book called *The Architects of Golf*—if you can lift it.

Length and cow pastures were out, charm and accuracy were in. All of a sudden Pete Dye's bulkheaded bunkers and bulkheaded ponds and natural waste areas were in vogue.

Since Harbour Town, there's no telling how many swamps have been transformed into golf courses along the eastern seaboard, from Myrtle Beach, South Carolina, to Ocean Reef, Florida, real estate developers running around like wild dogs. Hilton Head Island not only invented swampfiend golf, it invented The Gated Community.

This time at Harbour Town in the MCI Classic, or what I still call the Heritage Classic, I stepped on my dick at the seventeenth and eighteenth holes all four rounds. The par-three seventeenth is one tough hole—190-yard shot over water and sand—and I missed the green every trip. The eighteenth, the long par four that plays to the lighthouse, was into the wind every day, and I skillfully managed to put my drive in Calibogue Sound twice, then put my second shot in Calibogue Sound twice. Pull-hook deal. My mistakes added up to 281 and left me in a six-way tie for twenty-seventh.

Big payday. Banked $21,000. Or $21,466.66, as my ladies back in Fort Worth might have counted it.

I left Hilton Head again without knowing what MCI stands for. All I know about MCI is, I get these phone calls when I'm home. Sometimes it's a recording that says, "Listen closely for an important announcement from MCI," and sometimes it's an actual human voice that says, "Hey, Bobby Joe Grooves! How you doing today? A good friend of yours gave me your number. They know you'll be interested in a terrific offer from MCI."

Whichever voice it is—recorded or live—my response before I slam down the phone is the same one I give to any other telephone hustle. It tends to run along the lines of "Hey, pal. Bite my ass, don't ever call me again—and go get a real job."

I WENT back to the Houston Open for the first time in five years and remembered why I stopped going. It's not played in Houston.

It's played about thirty miles north of Houston at Woodlands Country Club, a course carved out of a forest of oaks and pines by Bruce Devlin and Robert von Hagge.

It used to be accused of being in Houston, but whoever said this might as well have said it about Mars and Jupiter, too. Today it's officially said to be located in Woodlands, Texas—the golf course begat a town—and now it's more like a hundred miles from Houston in traffic.

In the Houston Open's earlier years, long before my time, it was played on classy courses like River Oaks, Brae Burn, Memorial Park, and Champions. I only know those layouts from the days when I'd go down there to play in an amateur tournament and get waltzed out of town by some guy who called himself Bayou Slim. A guy who wore a hard hat, smoked Camels, carried his clubs in a little white canvas bag, and could solid play for his own money.

The Houston Open I'd most liked to have seen was the first one in 1946 at River Oaks. It marked the last time Byron Nelson, Ben Hogan, and Sam Snead finished 1–2–3 in a tournament. They occasionally did that. And two of them often finished 1–2. This was back in the days when they were the Biggest Big Three that ever dominated the game.

My dad would say that I played in the Houston Open at Woodlands like a man standing in line to give up. I fired a string of 74s and tied three lurkers for sixty-eighth at 296 while another lurker I'd never heard of won it with a 279.

Mitch said we could take heart in the fact that the total unknown only dusted us by seventeen shots. Funny old Mitch.

I NORMALLY only go to New Orleans to rediscover acid indigestion in the French Quarter. Now I stand before you to announce that if I ever go back again, that'll be the only reason. It won't be to play golf.

I hadn't been back to the New Orleans Open since it moved from Lakewood to English Turn Country Club, a course Jack Nicklaus plopped down in the Mississippi Delta. That was about ten or twelve years ago. But Buddy Stark talked me into entering, saying the course was perfectly suited to my game.

It looked like Buddy was right after the first round. I shot a five-under 67 and was only one back of Julius Claudius, who put up a 66. But then came the near-fatal heart attack in the second round, when I walked onto the fourth green.

There the sumbitch was, curled up comfortably on the back left edge of the green, a goddamn rattle ess—and no dwarf either.

I was paired with Jerry Grimes and Rickey Padgett.

Jerry said, "That deal right there ain't no rub of the green."

"I bet he's four-foot long," Rickey said. "I'll call a rules guy on my cell. Tell him to bring security."

I said to Mitch, "You ever see a man run like a spotted-ass ape? You're getting ready to. I'm outta here."

Mitch said, "We talkin' about WD? We close to leadin' this Mother Goose, man. They'll chase him off. Ain't nothin' to it."

I said, "Ain't nothin' to it? You crazy? You know how many nephews and cousins and aunts and uncles that sumbitch has around here? We chase him off, he's gonna tell every one of 'em about me. He knows I'm here. I saw him looking at me."

"You the crazy one," Mitch said. "Think about we can win this thing. We playin' good."

"Fuck this thing," I said.

"We can scoop us some Ryder Cup points. Think about that."

"Fuck the Ryder Cup."

"Fuck the Ryder Cup, too? We fuckin' everybody."

"It's not worth dying for," I said.

The rules guy arrived about a minute later, and as soon as he stepped out of his golf cart, I slid into it and burned rubber. Withdrew wins Indy.

Later on I started thinking about what I'd done and couldn't resist calling Cheryl. I thought she'd find it amusing. I reached her at the real estate office.

"Your phobia is *not* funny," she said. "You could have won the tournament. First prize is $615,000!"

"Dadgumit, I forgot about that," I said. "I should have sat down and tried to reason with the cocksucker!"

I called Alleene next. I was certain she'd think it was amusing, being more familiar with something in my past.

Alleene had closed the deal to buy the place on Berry for Alleene's Delights, but she was still working out of her kitchen in the house on Hilltop. I caught her in a pile of herb-crusted salmon.

I told her what had happened.

"That's the fastest exit you've made out of anywhere since college," she said.

We relived the incident on the phone.

My second year at TCU I made this drastic mistake of signing up for Biology 101. I needed to take a science course and everybody told me biology was easier than chemistry or geology. The first day I nonchalantly walked into the classroom and took a seat. But as I casually glanced around the room I noticed three or four students and the professor, Dr. Pinhead, which should have been his name, looking on the floor for something, peeking under desks, tables, chairs.

"What are y'all looking for?" I asked a fellow student.

"Three of the snakes got out of the jar," he said.

"Jesus fucking Christ!" I yelled and leaped up and raced out of the room in two long-jumps. Dropped the course in that instant.

Alleene said, "It's my vivid recollection that you spent the rest of the day and night creeping brews in the Hi Hat Lounge."

"As we said in those days," I laughed. "True. It was the nearest joint."

THE NEXT tournament was the Byron Nelson Classic in Dallas. I could have commuted from home every day, but I dropped an intellectual thought on it and decided not to penalize my golf game like that. Better to stay at the swank Four Seasons Hotel, right there in Las Colinas, where the two courses are, the ones they use for the Nelson, the TPC course and Cottonwood Valley.

So my first order of business back home was to smooth-talk, beg, and bribe Cheryl into staying with me at the Four Seasons. If something important came up at the real estate office, I said, she could always dash back to Fort Worth, but meanwhile she could lounge around the hotel, take it easy, or, while I was playing golf she could visit the North Park Mall and hit on Neiman's and all the other fancy Dallas stores that women like to slap around with their plastic.

I was counting on my secret weapon to be the fact that Cheryl found it hard to turn down luxury. I was right. She agreed to come over on Thursday, the first day of the Nelson, and planned to stay through the weekend, provided our room was equipped with two beds and I promised not to make any sudden moves. She was still into punishment.

It would have been a good plan if it hadn't been for the two golf courses. Both the TPC at Las Colinas and Cottonwood Valley are spread out on a sorry piece of ground—windy and treeless—and they're a mixture of designs by Robert Trent Jones Jr. and Jay Moorish, who've done their best work in other cities on other prairies.

It's birdie heaven around there, is what it is, and they come cheap. If you can't shoot 61 or 62 every round, you might as well not enter.

A good example is what I did. I shot a 68 on Thursday and another 68 on Friday, I'm four under par, but I miss the cut. Uh-huh. Seventy-four guys shot better than 136.

I was plenty hot and packing in our room at the hotel when Cheryl came back from slapping around Neiman's.

I told her what I'd done.

"We could still stay the weekend," she suggested. "It's an awfully nice place."

"And do what?" I snarled. "Gallery some lurker in the Nelson? Some shitass who shoots sixty-fucking-two? Maybe we can follow him the last two rounds when he shoots 63, 63! Never misses a fucking putt. Maybe we can ask him for his autograph on a cap! Maybe we can get a snapshot of the two of us standing next to him holding the trophy."

"Anything else?" she said.

"Yeah. I love Byron Nelson but piss on Dallas."

"Well, I certainly enjoyed my stay," she said, starting to throw her own things in a bag. "The maid service was swell. The bathroom was spacious. The minibar came in handy. I enjoyed the morning paper. We really must do this again sometime."

I said, "Cheryl, you've got to understand something. When you miss the cut out here, you just want to *get down the fucking road*. I'll find a way to make it up to you."

"You seem to be piling up a lot of things to make up for, don't you?"

I said, "You enjoyed saying that. I could tell by the look."

Slinging more things into her bag, she said, "You want to leave? Well, haul ass!"

We were out of there pretty quick after that.

24

THE COLONIAL NATIONAL INVI-
tational Tournament, which is now called
the MasterCard Colonial, was first made
famous by Ben Hogan, who won it a lot—
like five times in the early days—and
then it was made famous by tits and ass.

No tournament on our tour offers a
skin festival like Colonial Country Club
does for one week in May every year. It's
where I met Cheryl Haney, after all. But
she was your honest shapely adorable.
No dirty leg, she. Dirty legs never make
it to their thirties anyhow. Some go
chunko, some wind up in the joint, some
marry U-Haul Charlie.

The Colonial became a skin festival in

the late '60s, the members remind you. In the middle of the drug craze and The Pill and make-love-not-war and all the other enlightenment of the time.

Now at Colonial every year it's like some showbiz producer goes out and rounds up every no-slack dirty leg and cut-slack dirty leg in the territory, pitches in a ton of steel bellies of your collegiate persuasion—and announces that what we're going to have here is not just a golf tournament, folks. What we're going to have here is a convention of hip-hugger, choke-crotch hot pants and skimpy, heavy-load haltertops—we're going to Downtown Skin City. And what this does is bring out the grown man's battle cry of "Good god-a-mighty, tell my wife I'm out on the course with Crenshaw, but get my ass to the margarita tent."

Out on the Tour the Colonial has earned some nicknames. That's because it's a known fact that more than one guy out here has dumped his present wife and met his new one in the gallery, the clubhouse, or the margarita tent.

Buddy Stark calls it "the Tammy Wynette Classic." Go to Colonial and get yourself a d-i-v-o-r-c-e. But for my money it's Jerry Grimes who's been the most inspired by the skin festival. Jerry's lately taken to calling it "the Masterbate Colonial."

Colonial draws some of the biggest crowds of the year, and not just because of the skin. Once a year it gives thousands of people a chance to hang around a fancy private club.

The course, too, is an attraction. It's a winding, shady, riverbottom layout smack in a beautiful old residential neighborhood only five minutes from the TCU campus—as the sorority Porsches and fraternity Range Rovers fly.

The course is not as tough and narrow as the original design of John Bredemus and Perry Maxwell, back when it held the U.S. Open in '41, or even as it was during Hogan's '50s, but it's still a challenging par 70, even without much rough and with wide fairways and larger greens.

A big reason it's popular with the contestants is it treats them better than most tournaments from the standpoint of food, facilities, transportation, lodging, marshaling, and overall friendliness. Everybody is made to feel important, even your lurkers.

I grew up watching the Colonial as a little kid, when players like Billy Casper and Gene Littler were winning it, and then as a teen rat later on when Lee Trevino and Tom Weiskopf were winning it.

I didn't always have a ticket, but there were ways around that. One way was to dangle a string out of the pocket on my shirt, and walk fast.

Back when I was a teen rat I never dreamed I'd someday become a Colonial member with full access to a great course, not to overlook the Wednesday night fried chicken buffet and the Navy bean soup and cornbread on Saturdays.

I'd played the course hundreds of times over the years, therefore my pals on the Tour always expected me to have a home court advantage when the tournament rolled around. I should, I agreed, but I never seem to be a threat. Try too hard, maybe, in front of the home crowd.

This time I was something less than a threat, finishing tied for twenty-first at 282. Won $42,000 but no Ryder Cup points. Did that while the Great White Swede, Knut the Nuke, cheated his way to another victory.

It was windy all week, the wind coming from every which way, but Knut shot three rounds below 70 and put up a 276 that was good enough to nudge Cheetah Farmer and Fred Couples by two strokes.

Everybody knew he cheated if they bothered to read that Friday's *Light & Shopper* after his opening round 68.

Knut went to his interview in the press room and bragged about how his caddy's compass had told him where the wind was coming from on several key shots. One of the Colonial officials in the press room said, "Excuse me, Knut? Your caddy has a compass?"

Knut proudly said, "Yes, my caddy is Ernie Shockley, and he is very helpful to me."

The retarded jerk didn't know it was against the rules to use a compass, but he's a Swede, right? *Har, har,* bang fist on table.

This was all reported in the paper.

A Colonial official, Doc Matherson, quickly consulted the rule book to make sure his memory was correct. And right there in front of everybody he informed Knut that Rule 14–3 specifically prohibits the use of a compass to assist a player in determining wind direction—and the penalty for the violation is disqualification.

"I'm sorry, Knut, but you're DQ," Doc Matherson said.

A giant hush fell over the room, according to the paper, but Knut scrambled out of it, thinking quicker than I knew he was capable.

The paper quoted Knut saying "Uh, well . . . you see . . . the situation is . . . we only used the compass in practice rounds."

Like shit, is what I thought about *that*.

Doc Matherson bitterly opposed the decision, but the other officials took Knut's word for it—no DQ—and he went on to win the whole Mother Goose, stuffing $720,000 in his bulge.

Buddy Stark said we should be in awe of what Knut did, considering how many times he got laid during the Colonial. Buddy said to be seriously pussy-whipped and still win a tournament was some accomplishment, boy, even if Knut lied like an A-rab.

In a way, Knut couldn't help himself. Fort Worth has these well-known, good-looking "husband helpers" around town—fortyish-type businesswomen—who like to sport-fuck rich married men, rich divorcés, rich widowers, and any celebrity who turns up and makes himself available.

They all took a swipe at Knut, one by one. He was their pick this year.

Although I'd never been one of their draft choices, and I'd never known their real names, I did know them by sight and by the names certain gentlemen among the Colonial membership have given them. There was "Crime-Spree Kitty," "Get 'Em Up Gloria," "Racehorse Rita," "Do Me Twice Dottie," "Tasty Pie Tina," and "Earth Mother Lillian."

Such ladies exist in other cities, of course, but it's a widely held opinion on the Tour that Fort Worth offers the best-looking, best-natured, and fun-lovingest of them all.

Something else besides the tournament to make the city proud.

25

THE TEMPTATION AROUND MY
house was to blame my poor play in the
Colonial on the epidemic of wives in my
gallery. They were all out there at one
time or another, the Great Triumvirate.
In another time and place they were
known as Vardon, Taylor, and Braid. At
Colonial they were Cheryl, Alleene, and
Terri.

I was on the putting green before I
teed off in the first round when Terri
beckoned to me. A little wave and smile.

I walked over to the ropes to say hello.
She was with Cliff Doggett, the great
American and wonderful human being
she lived with. He didn't look any

different than the first time I'd seen him, when he'd reminded me of Brad Pitt in *True Romance*. Sleepy-eyed guy, three-day stubble on his face, soft voice, messed-up brown hair.

"Hey man," Cliff said. We shook hands. "I sure like knowin' a celebrity . . . even though Terri says you're just people."

"That's me," I said. "One of the people flock."

"Good-looking shirt," Cliff said.

I glanced down at myself. It was just a yellow Sahara with a stand-up collar. Went with my khaki slacks and solid white shoes.

Terri was quick to tell me Cliff was working now. He was cooking three nights a week at The Old Neighborhood Grill. I knew the restaurant. A home-cooking joint over on Park Place.

"Cooking's a new gig for me," Cliff said, "but I'm all over it."

Walking toward us came a couple—a gizzard-lip, stuck-for-an-answer-looking guy in a checkered sport coat, and a pale, lumpy bimbo in a short black skirt, pink satin blouse, and black high heels.

I recognized the couple from a photo in the *Light & Shopper*. It was Ray Ron Moreland and his girlfriend, Paula Dean Adcock. The same Ray Ron Moreland who'd murdered his wife and chopped off her head, but had beaten the rap thanks to Red Taggert.

The verdict was outrageous. I agreed with the local columnist who wrote that Red Taggert had outfoxed the DA again. Red had been shrewd enough to arrange for a jury of twelve men who were obviously unhappy at home with their own wives.

Terri greeted Ray Ron and Paula Dean with "Hi, there. I see you picked up the badges Red left for you at will call. Good."

I would liked to have said, "Hey, it's Walter Neff and Phyllis Dietrichson," but I was reasonably sure Ray Ron and Paula Dean wouldn't recognize those names from *Double Indemnity*, even if they'd ever seen it. Also, I wasn't crazy. Fuck with a head-chopper? What I did do, I dropped a couple of Titleists on the putting green and pretended to work on my stroke.

"We was in the clubhouse for a while," Paula Dean said. "We just come from there. Everybody was real nice. Ray Ron signed a bunch of autographs."

"I did," Ray Ron nodded. "I sure did."

Terri pointed Ray Ron and Paula Dean toward the margarita tent, saying she and Cliff would join them in there later—after they watched a few holes of golf.

Ray Ron said, "Who's Cliff?"

Terri gestured at Cliff, who seemed to be studying something in the distant treetops.

Ray Ron said to Cliff, "Yo, man."

"Huh?" said Cliff. "Oh . . . yeah . . . for sure."

When the wife murderer and his fiancée had strolled away, I said to Terri, "High heels at a golf tournament? He killed the wrong woman."

Terri let that sail on by and said, "I thought we'd follow you awhile, till it's time for Cheetah and Couples and Knut to go."

I said I was honored.

Terri mentioned that if she and Alleene both won their matches at Mira Vista this weekend they'd meet in the finals of the Ladies Club Championship next week. "You may have to skip Hartford," she said. "How could you resist watching two of your exes clash on the links?"

"Tempting," I said.

AFTER MY second round Friday, Alleene caught me on my way to the clubhouse. She was dressed for golf, like she might be going out to hit balls later. White shorts to mid-thigh, blue knit shirt, white visor, white shoes. Hard not to notice the perfect tan on her perfect legs. She said she'd watched me play sixteen, seventeen, and eighteen and was impressed with how casually I three-jacked two of the greens from twenty feet.

"I was impressed, too," Mitch said.

I introduced Roy Mitchell to Alleene Simmons. I couldn't believe the two of them had never met.

"This the first one?" Mitch asked me, nodding at Alleene.

"First or second, I never can remember," I said.

"Is he always that funny, Mitch?" Alleene said.

Mitch said, "He tried to imitate a golfer today. Didn't work out."

Alleene asked if I wanted to come see the catering joint on Berry that I'd financed. She was now moved in. I said why not—I didn't need to practice to keep playing this good. I showered and met her there.

Alleene's Delights got my full approval. Good sign, plenty of space, lots of stoves and pots and pans. A big walk-in freezer. Nice office. Desk, chair, cabinets, file drawers, window to look out on Berry Street traffic and a Walgreens.

Two young people were working for her in the kitchen, a black kid and a Mexican girl. Their names were William and Mary.

"William and Mary?" I said, grinning at Alleene.

"I know." She returned the grin.

"Wonder what the odds were on that?"

"Good," she said.

"Probably not as good as they'd be on Oral and Roberts."

"William and Mary are good workers," she said.

This guy Terri lived with, I told her, was cooking at The Old Neighborhood Grill these days. She might want to keep him in mind for a job someday. I described Cliff to her. She said she made it a practice never to hire burnouts—or do anything else with them.

She said, "If Terri and I are in the finals of the Ladies Club next week, will you come out and watch? I'd love to have you there. I really would. You're still my favorite guy, you know?"

I told her I'd have to miss the Hartford Open—they'd changed the dates again, to satisfy the new title sponsor. Imodium.

"This is more important," she said.

"You should know that Terri has a new set of clubs. Hawk Eyes."

"What she *has* is eighteen strokes. I'll be giving her twelve. I'll have to play my butt off to beat her."

"You seriously want me there, Alleene?"

"I do, yes," she said. "Unless it'll upset Cheryl. How's it going in the love department?"

"Rough sledding," I said. "But . . . although I'm no good at being noble . . . it doesn't take much to know that the problems of two little people don't amount to a hill of beans in this crazy world."

"Thanks for reminding me of that, Rick."

I promised her I'd think about skipping Hartford if her match with Terri took place. I said it might add a new dimension to the excitement of women's golf.

CHERYL CAME out for a while on Saturday with her pals Jolene Frederick and Bonnie Lasater. They followed my group through the first six holes. I was in a pairing with Nick Price and Fuzzy Zoeller, two of the last remaining smokers on the tour. It took me back to a happy time.

Nick and Fuzzy weren't scoring any better than I was, which was why we were paired together. Their names attracted a small gallery, although I doubt if they attracted more attention than Jolene's snug white T-shirt with the purple lettering on the front. The message said:

Applaud These

I had a moment with the ladies while our group was forced to wait on the fifth tee—somebody had sliced into the Trinity River up ahead. As we stood there I said to Jolene, "I can't help but admire your T-shirt."

She said, "Most of the comments have been favorable."

"I imagine," I said.

Cheryl said the new bumper sticker on Jolene's Audi A-4 was better than any message on her T-shirts. I learned that the bumper sticker proudly read "I Date Your Husband."

I asked the ladies if I could take them to dinner tonight.

Jolene said, "Thanks, but I have a home to wreck."

"I have a bridge game," Bonnie Lasater said.

"I play bridge," I commented.

Bonnie said, "Oh? Are you a Jacoby Transfer person, or do you bid the Stone Diamond?"

"I just play bridge," I shrugged.

I may have noted the sneer of a bridge Nazi as Bonnie walked away with Jolene, letting Cheryl and I have a moment together.

Cheryl permitted me to take her out for some barbecue that evening. The Railhead was too crowded, so we went to Angelo's and ate ribs and drank beer and continued our discussion of my tragic character flaws.

26

MY TWO EX-WIVES WON THEIR
semifinal matches at Mira Vista to set up
their championship confrontation, but
the other news around Bellaire Drive
South was what the mail brought me—a
manila envelope containing Irv Klar's latest stab at literature.

A personal note was included. He
apologized for taking so long with this
version, but the scum-level newspaper he
worked for had been keeping him busy
covering "high school crap." He'd also
spent some time preparing his resume to
send off to *Sports Illustrated*, the *New
York Times, Washington Post*, and *LA
Times*—everything in between sucked—

and he'd lost two weeks when his mom and dad made him come up to San Jose and help take inventory at their discount jewelry store.

He hoped I liked what he'd done. Smokey Barwood liked it. But he was sure I'd have some suggestions—hey, it was going to be my book, wasn't it?

I tried to read what he'd sent, purely out of curiosity, but stopped halfway through the first page to kick a chair. Small wonder.

Tees and Sympathy
By Bobby Joe Grooves with Irving Klar

Hidy, podnoos. I'm just a yodelin' country boy from down on the farm in Texas, but I never milked no cows, seein' as how I was busy learnin' how to whap that ol' golf ball around, which I do pretty good these days on the PGA Tour.

Although I've won some tournaments and I have a bank account a lot of women would like to go down on, I don't need a Greyhound bus to tell me I'm not any Ben Hogan.

I'm just your average money winner out here who scores his share of pussy along the way, and it don't matter none to me if they're spitters or a swallowers.

I picked up my first golf utensil when . . .

My immediate thought this time was, I wish I was my old lunatic high school basketball coach, Baldy Toler, and Irv Klar played for me. Irv would get fifty licks from my paddle on his gym-shorts ass, do a hundred push-ups on his fingertips, and run laps till his chest exploded.

27

THE TRUTH IS, I'D NEVER SEEN
Alleene or Terri play golf.

But I was given ample opportunity the
following week on a bright warm Sunday
when I was skipping the Hartford Open
in order to attend the Ex-Wives Classic at
Mira Vista.

I suppose it was Alleene who talked
me into staying around for the match. To
be honest about it, I guess I was rooting
for Alleene to win. Alleene wasn't living
with a guy who'd even failed hippie, or
working for a loophole criminal lawyer.

And Alleene was taller.

My ex-wives both over-rehearsed for
about an hour and a half, hitting balls at
opposite ends of the practice range.

For the occasion Alleene wore a dark red shirt, a short white skirt—six inches above the knee, my eye measured—and white visor. Terri wore navy blue shorts, light blue shirt, black visor. They both wore white shoes and those little anklet socks that men look precious wearing when they play golf in shorts.

I stood off in the background behind the ladies, studying each of their swings for about ten minutes before I retired to the locker room and drank coffee and waited for the bell to ring.

On the range Alleene looked like the better player by far, which was why she was a six and Terri was an eighteen.

I was pleasantly surprised at how good a swing Alleene had. I liked the slope of her right shoulder and the way she was centered behind the ball when she set up. Her left-hand grip was a bit weak in my opinion, but when she came through the ball she compensated for it in the way her body uncoiled. I wouldn't want Cora Beth Kenny or Perkie Haskins to hear me say it, but I thought Alleene had perfected a man's golf swing for herself.

Terri had a long, slow three-piece swing, the kind that often gets cussed by somebody playing behind her. A lot of good things had to happen between the takeaway, the pause, and the follow-through for Terri to bring off a good drive, or a decent shot with any club in the bag. I assumed she must be a pretty good chipper and putter or she'd need 28 instead of 18.

I was up-front with Cheryl Haney, telling her where I was going to be that day. This was to prevent Cheryl from finding out about it later and accusing me of going out there in the hope of enjoying an Olde Lang Syne fuck with the winner, spineless asshole that I was.

Cheryl had intended to go with me for the bizarre fun of it all, but business kept her away. Her boss, Donald Hooper, had assigned her to play hostess at an all-day "open house," which, I'd learned from Cheryl, was something a real estate firm did when it hoped to unload a joke of a mansion that would only make sense to buy if a Ferris wheel and roller coaster could be connected to it.

The piece of property that day was a big "modern Victorian" deal in a flush neighborhood that could be called either "out there around Shady Oaks Country Club" or "down there in New Westover Hills."

It had two wraparound porches, one up and one down, where you could stand and look at nothing, Cheryl said. It sat in a hole and didn't even provide a view of the Shady Oaks golf course. You entered into the game room, of all things, and then you had to go through the dining room before you found the living room, and then you had to go through the kitchen to reach the master bedroom, and it wasn't even near Canterbury Drive where Ben and Valerie Hogan had lived.

Cheryl said, "I'm going to have to stand around the house the whole afternoon and watch people laugh at the fucking place and eat all the Krispy Kreme donuts."

Alleene and Terri were scheduled to play at one o'clock. The pro shop let me have a golf cart to follow their match. I rolled down to the first tee on No. 1, a downhill par four. Got there before they did and sat there in my cart, chewing gum and wishing I still smoked.

The ladies came along shortly in their own carts, their golf bags strapped on the back. They stepped out and walked over to me, drivers in their hands. If they'd expected a gallery, it was just me.

Well, it was me most of the time. There was a phantom club member in a straw hat with a big black dog riding around in the golf cart with him. The man turned up every three or four holes during the match and looked like he was explaining what was going on to the dog. I swear the dog would nod and look as if he understood everything.

Now on the first tee, Terri said, "I'm glad you came out, Bobby Joe."

I said, "What's riding on this? Like . . . what does the winner get?"

Alleene said, "Oh, there's a trophy, and I think there's a $200 certificate for merchandise in the pro shop."

"And you get your picture hung on the clubhouse wall," Terri said.

I said, "I know you're both nervous. You've been hitting balls all morning. Don't worry about your drive on this hole. Just take a normal, easy swing. Your tee shot here is only one shot out of all the strokes you're gonna take today. Just one. I've played some of my best rounds after I've bogeyed the first hole."

Alleene said, "Great, Bobby. You're telling us we're going to bogey the first hole. Thanks. We needed that."

"No," I said, "I'm telling you not to get discouraged if you *do*."

"Why in the world did we ask him to come here?" Alleene said to Terri with a laugh.

"Big mistake," Terri said.

"Good luck," I said. "Y'all play good."

And I drove off, heading down to the first green.

28

THE RULINGS I WAS FORCED TO make had a dire effect on the Mira Vista Ladies Club Championship. Fortunately, they weren't judgment calls, the kind a zebra comes up with in a football game that breaks your heart and makes your wallet look like Arnold Schwarzenegger stepped on it. They were decisions that came right out of the Rules of Golf.

The first one occurred immediately, on the green at No. 1. Alleene hit a good tee shot to the edge of the bluff and played a respectable mid-iron down to the green. She was on in two. Terri drove well enough but thinned her second and was way short. She barely reached the front edge of the green with her pitch. She was on in three, but she was getting a stroke a hole, so if they both two-putted, they would halve the hole, Alleene with a four, Terri with a five.

When Alleene couldn't find a coin or a ball marker in her pocket she casually marked her ball with her car keys. She dropped the keys behind the ball. I'd left my cart and walked over to attend the flag.

Terri instantly said, "You can't do that, Alleene!"

"I can't do what?" Alleene said.

"You can't mark your ball with your car keys."

"I don't have a coin," Alleene said, "and I forgot to grab some ball markers in the shop."

"That's a penalty stroke," Terri said. "You lay three."

"Oh, for God's sake," Alleene said impatiently. "Did you hear that, Bobby Joe?"

"Terri may be right," I said.

Alleene said, "Are you *kidding* me? A penalty for *what?*"

"I'm not sure," I said. "I know our Tour rules say you can't mark your ball with anything but a coin or a 'similar object,' I think it's called. If you do, it's a one-stroke penalty."

"See there?" Terri said to Alleene.

Alleene said to both of us, "Since when are we playing PGA Tour rules? It's just a goddamn country club tournament!"

I said, "That's true. You're probably playing USGA rules—and I'm not positive those rules are the same as ours. Anybody have a rule book?"

"I do," Terri said. She went over to her golf bag, pulled out a rule book, came back, and handed it to me. She said, "The reason I know it's a penalty is because Mrs. R. K. Fowler called it on me in our quarterfinal match. I couldn't find a coin in my pocket and marked my ball with my cellphone and she called it on me. I learned a lesson real good."

It took me a few minutes to find the rule and longer to make sure I understood the language. I learned that the USGA would indeed allow you to mark your ball with car keys, a hotel room key, the toe of your putter, or several other things. However, the rule went on to say that the object had to be placed precisely behind the ball before the ball was lifted. If not—and I read this out loud—"the player cannot be considered to have marked the position of the ball with sufficient accuracy and shall incur a penalty of one stroke."

Terri said to Alleene, "You just plunked your car keys down somewhere near your ball. I watched you do it, and I don't call that marking your ball with *sufficient accuracy*. You lay three."

Alleene turned to me. "Are you going to let her hold me to this crap?"

"The rule book's on her side," I said. "You can take it to court, but she'll win."

Alleene angrily two-putted the hole. Then Terri two-putted the hole, Alleene refusing to give her a six-inch tap-in.

Walking off the green, Alleene said to Terri, "So you made a net four with your phony handicap and I made a five with my penalty stroke, is that it? You're one-up?"

"Yes, I am," Terri said.

Alleene slammed her putter down in her bag on the cart, saying, "Boy, is that some kind of chickenshit deal or *what*?"

ALLEENE PLAYED extremely well, only two over par through the tenth hole, but Terri was still one-up. Getting a stroke a hole, it only took bogeys for Terri to tie Alleene's pars, and when Terri made a couple of doubles, those were the holes where Alleene bogeyed, so she gained Xerox.

The next incident that required a ruling came at the eleventh, the outstanding hole on the course in my book. A par five.

Mira Vista is a par 71 course and it was designed by Jay Moorish and Tom Weiskopf back when they were partners. The eleventh was their signature hole. The drive takes you to the brink of a creek. The hole then doglegs sharply to the right and you have an option. The fairway is split by trees and a gully. You can play up the left side or up the right side of the trees and gully. Both are slender openings. That leaves you with a difficult pitch to a slightly raised green that's guarded by bunkers. Great hole.

The ladies skillfully avoided all the trouble—the trees and gully— and reached the green in what was regulation for them, Alleene on in three, Terri on in four.

They were a good distance from the cup, which was back right. Alleene's ball was on the front left of the green, about fifty feet away. Terri's ball was on the front right, a little closer, maybe forty-five feet away.

I was tending the pin when, to my complete surprise, they both putted at the same time.

I was still tending the pin when the balls started to break inward and roll toward each other.

This can't happen, I thought. Couldn't happen but it did. About eight feet short of the cup the balls collided with each other, one going this way a few feet off line, the other going that way a few feet off line.

Alleene yelled at Terri, "What in the name of Christ were you doing? I was away!"

"I thought *I* was," Terri said. Then she looked at me, and said, "What do we do, Bobby Joe?"

I said I'd need the rule book again.

It took a while but I found the answer under Rule 16. Terri, who was closest to the hole, incurred a two-stroke penalty for putting out of turn. After three-putting the green, she ended up with a nine. There was no penalty for Alleene in the collision. She was permitted to replace her ball and putt again. She three-putted for a bogey six but won the hole.

"We're all even," Alleene said to Terri as they left the green.

Terri frowned and muttered something under her breath. Something from the Scriptures, I gathered.

THE MATCH was still square going to the sixteenth, and that's where the last ruling came into play.

The sixteenth is a short par four that runs through a tunnel of trees and ravines. If your tee ball can thread the needle, it's only a drive and a flip, even for the short hitter or the good lady player. A crooked tee shot and you could be looking at a double bogey or worse—something they haven't found a name for yet.

Alleene steer-jobbed her drive down the fairway—no nerve ends showing—and then played a little run-up shot onto the green, giving herself a birdie putt of fifteen feet. Terri skied her drive but it found the fairway. She topped her second but it went straight and left her short of the green by about fifty yards. Next she bladed her pitch, but the ball ran straight again and rolled up on the green, leaving her about twenty feet from the flag.

I knew what Alleene must have been thinking as she watched Terri do all that. Three bad shots but the lucky bitch will probably halve the hole anyhow—she has a stroke.

They marked their balls and began circling the green slowly, kneeling, squinting, reading their putts from every angle. Female Greg Normans.

It was Terri's turn to putt first, but I noticed her looking around on the ground for something in the vicinity of where she'd marked her ball.

"Terri, are you going to putt *today?*" Alleene asked.

"I can't find it," Terri said.

I walked over to Terri. So did Alleene.

"You can't find your ball marker?" I said.

"I don't believe this," Alleene said.

"It was right here," Terri said. "It's gone. It's just gone, that's all."

"Look on the bottom of your shoes," I said. "Maybe you stepped on it by accident."

"I wouldn't do that," Terri said.

"Can we look?" I said.

Terri raised up her right foot—and there it was, a penny. Somehow stuck to the sole of her golf shoe.

"This has to be a violation of *something,*" Alleene said.

"Why?" Terri asked, putting the penny back on the green, the spot where she thought it belonged.

"*Why?*" said Alleene. "Because it *does*, that's why. Right, Bobby?" Another rule-book deal.

Five minutes later I found the answer. Terri's ball marker had been moved *after* she had "completed the marking process." When this happens, says the USGA, even if it's accidental, you suffer a one-stroke penalty.

The penalty cost Terri the hole. She was now one-down to Alleene with two holes to play, and Alleene knew she had her. Time for a little lip.

As Alleene addressed her ball on the seventeenth tee, waggling her driver, she said to Terri, "How do you like your rule book now, honey?"

And with that, Alleene solid-nailed a solid drive. Center-cut job.

I was kind of proud of Terri for not dying easy. She dug out bogeys on the last two holes, forcing Alleene to make pars to hold her one-up lead and capture the coveted championship.

They shook hands politely on the eighteenth green.

"You're a lot better golfer than I am," Terri said to Alleene. "You deserved to win."

"I know," Alleene said with a straight face. Then laughed.

I gave both my ex-wives a hug and said, "You adorables played a hell of a match. I saw a lot of good golf shots today."

Alleene said, "It's a good thing you were here to interpret the rules, Bobby. If we'd been by ourselves, we'd still be somewhere out on the course scratching each other's eyes out."

Alleene, the winner, insisted on buying the drinks in the clubhouse.

I had too many, according to Cheryl Haney later.

29

AS IT RELATED TO MY MEDIOCRE career and stagnant personal life, I asked Buddy Stark, "What the fuck am I doing?"

This was the first week in June and I was down in Austin playing in a two-day charity event as a favor to Buddy. We were having breakfast at Barton Creek Country Club.

"I haven't done anything but stick my pick in the ground for two months," I said. "I've slid three places in the Ryder Cup standings. I'm hanging by a thread in ninth place with a whole pile of Steve Pates snipping at my heels."

"What?" said Buddy. "You don't like a challenge?"

"All I need is one more top five finish to nail down a spot," I said. "I've got time. Three more majors . . . and as many tour stops as I can squeeze into my busy social life, what with all these charity events."

"This one is special," Buddy said. "It benefits the local Hispanic community."

Repeating a line I'd heard from Willie Nelson the previous night at the tournament party, I said, "Yeah, well . . . remember what Jesus said to the Mexicans—y'all don't do anything till I come back."

Buddy said, "Who's already locked up a spot, besides Tiger, Phil, Davis, and Duval? Cheetah, I guess."

"Right. Cheetah . . . and Rickey Padgett . . . Justin . . . Hal Sutton."

"It's already a hell of a team."

"We'll need it," I said. "Europe's looking sturdy. Knut the Nuke, Sergio, Colin, Jesper, Ollie, Westwood, Clarke . . ."

"Rommel . . . Goebbels . . . Himmler . . ." Buddy said.

I said all I could do from here on was drop a little "hello, golf" on the case. If I made it, I'd be the proudest guy in a USA logo. But . . . if for some reason it didn't work out . . . I'd just have to flop down on my sofa and say, 'Mother of Mercy, is this the end of Rico?' "

One distraction I hoped I'd gotten out of the way, I said to Buddy, was the book thing. I admitted I'd secretly been intrigued with the idea at first, if it sounded like me and if it was a real book—not one of those instruction deals with dots and arrows crawling all over the photographs.

Buddy said, "My 20 Ways to Make You Sneaky Long, Even After You've Had a Big Lunch."

"Something like that," I said. "I called Smokey. I told him to put the book idea on indefinite hold. Irv Klar wasn't working out. Maybe I hadn't mastered Ronald Colman yet, but why let the world in it? Smokey called Irv, and Irv called me. Irv said he was just trying to write something people would read. I said what people—the devoted fans of Minnie Pearl? He said he was only trying to give it a 'hook.' I said hook this. That's pretty much the way we left it."

Buddy said, "Maybe Emily could write the book for you. My scholar's not too busy. She's not fucking anybody right now but me and some guy named Dostoyevsky."

ONE NIGHT after I got back to Fort Worth my folks invited me over to have dinner, ride the elevator, and hear about their aches and pains. My mom knew I couldn't refuse if she promised to cook hamburger steak with brown gravy and onions, pinto beans, and mashed potatoes.

In the department of aches and pains, my dad revealed that he now had "one of everything" and "two of some things."

He couldn't see out of his left eye or hear out of his right ear. Both of his hips hurt so bad most of the time they ought to be donated to the Museum of Natural History after he was gone.

His left knee still popped on a regular basis and took it upon itself to swell up and go back down for no reason, and there was no telling what that muscle on the right side of his neck was up to.

He was also suffering cramps in his calves in the middle of the night. They were so painful, it was all he could do to roll out of bed and walk around to make them go away.

"Old Pavarotti don't holler *that* loud," he said.

And it wasn't helping George Grooves that all of the local pro teams were letting him down. He'd spent years being faithful to the Texas Rangers, Dallas Cowboys, and Dallas Mavericks, but now look what they were doing to him. They were throwing off, losing games to gimps, and they didn't care because they were too rich. It was a better world once.

He said we used to have athletes on the planet who took pride in winning for the sake of winning, but those heroes were gone now, replaced by sissies who ought to change their names to "Dow Jones" and "Salary Cap" and "Stay Hurt."

He said, "Bobby Joe, I guarantee you, if I was one of them rich team owners, I'd fire every overpaid joker who pulled a hamstring or a groin or a quadriceps in any way other than in a violent collision on the field."

I assured him a great many Americans felt the same way.

I PRACTICED for two hours at Mira Vista the next day and afterward, like I was the Manchurian Candidate and somebody suddenly showed me the queen of diamonds, I hopped in my car and drove straight to Alleene's Delights.

I might have been fooling myself but I didn't fool Alleene.

When I found her in her office doing paperwork, she looked up and said, "Let me guess. Cheryl still hasn't come around, you're lonely, and you have this idea that I'm lonely too, right?"

"You are very quick," I said.

"Poor cupcake," she grinned. "Come on, I'll take you to lunch."

In separate cars we drove out to Cousins on McCart for barbecue. My choice because the odds were a thousand to one we wouldn't see Cheryl Haney out there—and didn't.

We ate chopped beef sandwiches and cole slaw and lingered over coffee for an hour, Alleene saying that if we both still smoked we could turn it into an all-afternoon, student days, cigarettes-and-coffee session.

I said I'd heard college kids didn't do that anymore—sit around in daytime and smoke and drink coffee and talk about stuff, either their woes or the world's. What they *did* do now, I'd heard, was study five days a week and reserve the weekends for getting shitfaced and fucking people who didn't have last names.

I asked Alleene if a motel was out of the question this afternoon.

She patted my hand and said it was too bad she hadn't liked golf when we were married, but we didn't need to complicate our lives now.

"Well, shit," I said.

She insisted she liked her life nowadays. She loved her work, loved playing golf, loved her dog, Cary Grant, and she'd begun to like living alone. Cheryl must be a dynamite babe, she said, or I wouldn't have been fooling around with her for two years. Surely I could repair the damage with Cheryl eventually.

I said I was looking at another dynamite babe right now.

Alleene said thanks, but she was working so hard these days she wasn't feeling much like a warden's daughter.

I said I'd be the judge of that.

Outside, before going to our cars, we gave each other a wet kiss, and I said, "We'll always have herb-crusted salmon."

30

MOVIES AND BOOKS AND TV ARE always telling you how a man will do strange things when he believes he's in love, but sometimes even real life proves it. Take the deal I made with Cheryl Haney.

She agreed to take a vacation and go with me to New York for two whole weeks—for the Buick Classic at Westchester Country Club the week before the U.S. Open, and for the Open itself at Winged Foot—but only if we could stay at the Plaza Hotel in Manhattan.

That way we could go to some Broadway shows and eat at some of the "chic" restaurants in the city that she'd marked in a guidebook, the kind where it was a good guess on my part that a plate of pasta would cost more than a person could spend on clothes in a year.

"This will make it fun for me, too," Cheryl said. "I'll be in the city with things to do while you're playing golf every day. I won't be stuck in a hotel up in Westchester County . . . in some dirty, polluted little town where the rivers catch on fire and there's nobody to talk to but Tony and Connie in the local diner."

I went for it. I didn't even bother to mention what a hardship it was going to be on me to have to make the round trip from New York City up to Westchester County every day to play golf—one hour each way without a traffic jackpot or getting lost.

I made it as easy on myself as possible. I hired a limo and driver for the whole two weeks. Found me a cordial Russian in the yellow pages who owned his own company and worked for half the fee of any other company. He was a nice-looking young guy named Dimitri.

Dimitri had only been in the country two years, but he spoke English better than most people in Louisiana.

He greeted me every morning outside the Plaza at dawn with a poppy-seed bagel and cream cheese, an apricot Danish, coffee, and the newspapers.

On the way to the courses each day we'd stop at the Rye Hilton and pick up Mitch and my golf clubs. Some days Dimitri would watch golf and try to understand it. Other days he'd drive back to the city, take Cheryl wherever she wanted to go to shop or sightsee, and return for me. He even insisted on driving us in the evenings when we went to dinner and the theater. At the end of the two weeks Dimitri's bill was only $7,000, but I forced him to take $10,000 and considered it the best money I'd ever spent. It would have been twice that much if I'd gone with a brand name.

I wouldn't have seen much of Manhattan in the daytime if two practice rounds hadn't been rained out at Westchester Country Club. The limo whipped me back into the city and Cheryl made me go see some stuff I'd never have gone to see on my own.

Modern art, for instance. I got dragged to this museum and this gallery to look at paintings of blue, yellow, and red crisscross stripes, and white on white, and maroon bubble on green bubble, and men and women with big orange bodies and little pink heads, and the other way around, and men and women where the artist either intentionally or accidentally left off the arms and legs.

That was about all the culture I could handle without putting on a beret and growing a beard.

Cheryl led me to two department stores that were supposed to be well known for one thing or another. In Bloomingdale's I was privileged to observe dozens of skinny saleswomen with black shoe polish hair and arrogant expressions who wouldn't let you buy anything if you put a knife in their ribs. This was opposed to Bergdorf Goodman, right near our hotel, where I found helpful salespeople who were eager to sell you a box of mints for only $65 or an antique silver tea service for only $150,000.

On one of the days, Cheryl wanted to "experience" Central Park and made me walk through the park from the Plaza up to what they call the Boat Pond. The park was pretty and had more trees and shrubs and large rock formations and elevations of land than I would ever have guessed. I saw some areas that would make good golf holes.

When we arrived at the snack bar at the Boat Pond we were invited to a birthday party for a dog.

The birthday girl was a small two-tone poodle named Brenda. Balloons on strings were tied to a large iron table, gift-wrapped packages of toys and food were being opened for Brenda by humans gathered around the table, and the humans had brought all of Brenda's friends and neighbors to the party. We were given human cookies and introduced to Emma, Raymond, Webster, Feeney, Collins, Sue—yeah, a dog named Sue—Shelton, Beauregard, and Barbara Jane. All friendly and well behaved. Everything from a Canadian sheepdog to a Yorkshire terrier.

The Dog People. Best New Yorkers I met.

Our nightlife consisted of going to the chic restaurants on Cheryl's

list and going to the theater. Every day when I came home from golfing my ball in Westchester County, I'd barely have time to shower
and shave and dress up for my evening out. "Hurry" was my middle
name.

The chic restaurants were all noisy and crowded. As best I recall,
their names were Millie Vanilla, Metro Luther, Mario Andretti, and
Tookie Dondo. Wherever we dined, our waiters turned out to be rude
and slow. I assumed they were taking it out on us because they'd
never seen us before. For dinner I usually ordered a veal doohickey,
hold the pot plant and bath gel. It was a New York experience.

So was the theater.

We went to the hit drama first. It was about a black woman slowly
strangling a family of white Southerners to death with a Confederate
flag. Why the hit comedy was a hit, we'd never know. We only know
we spent two hours listening to a group of fags and lesbians brutally
ridicule every straight, hardworking, law-abiding, God-fearing Christian in the United States of America.

Both shows received wild standing ovations as we sprinted out.

We also went to two hit musicals. The first one was great. The
songs had tunes I recognized and the dancers danced their asses off,
particularly a girl in a yellow dress. In the other hit musical, none of
the songs had tunes and the dancers only danced with their arms.

Leaving the theater after that tuneless award-winner, Cheryl made
me laugh till I coughed when she said, "I didn't hear a lot of 'Yankee
Doodle Dandy' in there, did you?"

We went back to our hotel after the theater that evening and had a
couple of drinks in the Oak Bar.

This was the night Cheryl began to act a little affectionate in small
ways, and there in the bar she said, "I'm sorry this trip is so expensive.
I know it's costing you a bunch."

"Aw," I said, "you can't put a price tag on culture."

"Thank you for not saying what you really think," she said.

"What might that be?" I asked.

Grinning, she said, "That this is turning out to be the most expensive piece of ass you've ever had."

On the heels of that remark, I may have set a Plaza Hotel speed record for a man signing a bar check and hauling a lady up to his room.

It had been a while since I'd helped Cheryl slip out of her duds.

Definitely worth the money.

31

SOMETIMES YOU DON'T KNOW dick. Maybe I was just in a mood to play well in the Buick Classic. That's what I did anyhow. I shot 70, 66, 70, and 73 for 279. Some other year that would have put me near the top. This time it merely earned me a tie with five Corey Pavins for eighteenth and a check for $38,000. Not to complain about the amount. It helped pay for some of the chic dinners and culture I soaked up on Manhattan Island.

Mitch took credit for what he called my "improved play." He said it was directly related to his suggestion that I shorten my preround practice routine. I was beating too many balls on the range, staying out there for an hour or longer, and this might have been making me grow tired on the closing holes.

He said the day of the first round, "We shorten it to twenty-five minutes. We just hit some pitches, some irons, a few woods, some sand shots to see what the sand is like. We in our rhythm. Then all we do is putt awhile and go."

Maybe the new routine helped. I'd stick with it awhile and see.

I said to Mitch, "I guess the trick will be not to get to the course too early—unless I bring along a book to read."

Some of our better players don't like the Westchester tournament or the golf course, and they faze it for those reasons, but I like the tournament and the course for all the reasons they don't.

I like it because Westchester C.C. is one of the oldest courses on the Tour. It was designed back in 1922 by Walter Travis, who was sixty years old at the time and by then was known in golf circles as "the Grand Old Man."

Travis was a native of Australia who didn't move to the United States until he was in his twenties. He didn't even take up golf until he was thirty-five, but once he did, he won the U.S. Amateur three times and the British Amateur once. He was forty years old before he started designing courses.

Westchester's course has since been doctored by four or five designers over the years, but it still retains the old-fashioned look of Walter Travis's day with its blind shots, sharp doglegs, and sporty length—only 6,700 yards—the layout winding through trees and small hills.

Travis designed a lot of other antiques that are fun to play. One treasure is Garden City Golf Club on Long Island—if you can manage to beg your way on. Another is Ekwanok in Manchester, Vermont, which looks like the place where trees were invented. Still another is Cape Arundel up in Kennebunkport, Maine, where one of the hazards during summer months might be a Secret Service detail. And people should know that it was Travis who brought golf to Sea Island,

Georgia, when he finished the first two courses there shortly before he died in 1927.

I even like the Westchester clubhouse although guys on the tour laugh at it. It's eight stories high, bigger than a stack of Wal-Marts, and still reeks of the Roaring Twenties when it was originally known as the Westchester-Biltmore Hotel.

Pals on the Tour complain about the crowds at Westchester, saying they're too loud and too dumb about golf. It's a regular-guy crowd. Working stiffs. Cabdrivers, bookies, plumbers, horse players. But I say it's part of the charm. There's no other stop on the Tour where we can hear guys in the gallery holler: "Yo, Adrian, there's Freddy Couples, show him your tits!" . . . "Yo, Shark, the three-putt, forget about it!" . . . "You talkin' to me?"

Wouldn't surprise me someday to hear a natty guy in the crowd say, "If anybody turns yellow and squeals, my rod's gonna speak its piece."

Probably not. Golf would bore "Little Caesar."

THERE'S THIS about Westchester County: You never know what town you're in. Cross a road and you think you're in Rye but you're in Harrison. Or turn a corner and you think you're in Scarsdale but you're in Mamaroneck.

But I knew I was in Mamaroneck, New York, the week of the U.S. Open because that's where Winged Foot is.

Somebody once called Winged Foot the "Yankee Stadium" of golf. I think it deserves the compliment. For my money, Winged Foot combines golf course, clubhouse, scenery, and history like no other club.

The clubhouse alone lets you know you've arrived at someplace big-time and intimidating. It's built out of rugged brownish, grayish stone, has the world's greatest outdoor veranda under a candy-striped awning that overlooks the finishing holes. In general it looks as if two stately English mansions have been shoved together. It's huge, old, multigabled, formidable-looking, important-looking, haunted-looking. To me, that's what a U.S. Open clubhouse is supposed to look like, including haunted.

A Hall of Fame of Golf has worked in and around Winged Foot's pro shop. Craig Wood and Claude Harmon, a couple of Masters champions, are among the head pros of the past, along with a successful Tour player, Tom Nieporte, and Harmon's lineup of assistants over the years included Jackie Burke, Dave Marr, Mike Souchak, Al Mengert, Shelly Mayfield, Rod Funseth, and Otto Greiner. And all that says nothing about the fact that Tommy Armour was a longtime Winged Foot member.

Both 18-hole courses at Winged Foot, the West and the East, were designed in the early 1920s by A. W. Tillinghast, or "Tillie the Terror" as he was known—my pick over Donald Ross and Alister Mackenzie as the best of your "Golden Age" architects.

Tillinghast, who enjoyed his fame, his cocktails, and hanging out with Broadway celebs, wrote the pilot film on protecting greens with bunkers when he did those layouts at Winged Foot. He carved both courses out of the trees and foothills and craggy boulders of an area only thirty-five miles north of Manhattan, and labeled both of them his masterpieces.

Tillie believed greenside bunkers should be blended into the landscape and they should be irregularly designed—large, small, steep, steeper, shallow, curving—and punishing. The shot to a well-guarded green, he insisted, should be the stiffest test on the golf course.

It was a sheer accident that Winged Foot West became more famous than Winged Foot East in the first place. When the USGA awarded Winged Foot its first U.S. Open, the one in 1929, it named the East Course as the site. East is a little shorter, a little sportier. But three holes on East didn't recover quickly enough from a heavy rainstorm a few weeks before that Open was scheduled, so the championship was moved to the West Course. Then Bobby Jones sank that putt on the seventy-second hole in the '29 Open—"the greatest putt in the history of golf"—and went on to win that Open, and this made the West course so revered, the East's rep has suffered unfairly.

Since then, every men's major at Winged Foot has been played on the West—the U.S. Amateur in '40 where Dick Chapman, a club member, local knowledged all opponents, the Open in '59 where Billy Casper never missed a putt, the '74 Open where Hale Irwin became a magician with his four-wood, the '84 Open where Fuzzy Zoeller waved the white towel at Greg Norman, the '97 PGA where a rainbow greeted Julius Claudius on the final green, and this past Open where Knut Thorssun benefited from one of the dumbest rulings ever made by a U.S. Golf Association airball, meaning rules official.

I'll get around to that in a minute, but first I've got to get this off my basic chest: we're mainly a zebra-free sport. What I mean is, we don't generally have to put up with blind, stumble-bum, inconsistent zebras calling pass interference, or holding, or illegal block, or walking, or no foul when it's clearly a mugging, or any of the other phony shit that's threatening to kill my interest in football and basketball.

For example, I don't have to worry that after I sink a thirty-foot putt for a birdie, I may look around and find a yellow flag on the ground. Like some idiot ruled I took too much time, maybe, and I have to putt the ball again, but this time from thirty-five feet, after a five-foot penalty.

Golf does have rules, of course, and we do have officials—our own zebras—to interpret them. But in almost every instance, a ruling that might go against you, deny you relief, or penalize you a stroke happens during play, and you have an opportunity to overcome it before the round is over.

And yet the three biggest zebra deals in golf history occurred after the tournaments were over. Each one had a killer effect on the final result, and one of the cases even added to the lore of Winged Foot.

All of the rulings seem to me to have been pretty close to nit-picking bullshit, but of course I'm an anti-zebra kind of guy.

Love my horror stories about zebras.

The 1940 U.S. Open at Canterbury in Cleveland was where Porky Oliver got shafted. This was the championship eventually won by Lawson Little in a playoff over Gene Sarazen. But Oliver, who started the last round three strokes out of the lead, caught both men with a final round 71 and posted the same 287 total they did. In fact, he finished ahead of them and looked for a while like he might be the winner. But Porky didn't even make the playoff, thanks to a ruling.

It came to the attention of the USGA that the pairing of Oliver, Ky Laffoon, and Claude Harmon, along with the pairing of Johnny Bulla, Dutch Harrison, and Leland Gibson, had started the last round five minutes ahead of their scheduled tee times.

The reason they started earlier was because they thought they saw some bad weather approaching and wanted to get out on the course before the storm hit. Bad answer, the USGA said. And against the rules to boot. All six were disqualified. Oliver broke down in tears when he was informed that he not only hadn't tied for the biggest championship in golf, he was DQ'd.

Lawson Little and Gene Sarazen both pleaded with the USGA to let Porky's score stand and join them in the 18-hole playoff, but the bluecoats and armbands played bluecoat and armband. Not on their lives.

Then there was the sad case of Jackie Pung in the 1957 U.S. Women's Open on Winged Foot East. Yeah, East. The course that was supposed to have hosted Bobby Jones and them in '29.

Jackie Pung blazed home late in the final round of that Open with a 72 to overtake Betsy Rawls, the leader, and beat Betsy by a stroke with a total of 298 to 299. But in Jackie's excitement she made the mistake of not studying her scorecard closely enough before she signed it and turned it in. Her playing companion and marker, Betty Jameson, had accidentally put down a 5 instead of a 6 for Pung at the fourth hole, and Jackie didn't catch it. The total score was accurate on her card, the same 72 she'd shot, but the bluecoats and armbands deemed the little oversight on Jackie's part to be such a serious violation of the rules they disqualified her—and Betsy Rawls became the champion.

Although the USGA got soundly beat up in the national press over the incident—it wasn't like Pung had tried to cheat or anything—their zebras argued that they were given no choice under the rules, which clearly state to this day, "The competitor is solely responsible for the correctness of the score recorded for each hole and the penalty for error is disqualification."

Finally, there was poor old Roberto de Vicenzo in the '68 Masters. He blew that sole responsibility thing after he eagled the first hole of the last round for a deuce, holing out an eight-iron, and went on to shoot a 65 to tie Bob Goalby for the green jacket. Except *his* playing companion and marker, Tommy Aaron, accidentally wrote down a par 4 instead of the birdie 3 that Roberto had made at Augusta's seventeenth hole, and Roberto didn't notice the mistake before he signed the card. Well, lo and behold, his card added up to a 66 instead of the 65 he'd actually shot.

If it had been a U.S. Open, de Vicenzo would have been DQ'd in the grand style of Jackie Pung, but at the Masters the zebras wear green coats instead of blue, they can do what they please, and their zebras fumbled around and eventually came up with a "local rule" that let Roberto off with a one-stroke penalty.

It cost de Vicenzo a tie for the Masters and a chance to enter a playoff with Bob Goalby, but he was allowed to keep the $15,000 second-place money, the runner-up's silver medal, and the pair of crystal goblets for making that eagle deuce.

Not the only example of a golf zebra showing his generosity, however. How 'bout that deal the rules dunce let Knut get away with at the U.S. Open?

32

IT'S A TRADITION AT THE U.S.
Open for most of the contestants to
complain about the setup of the course—
the high rough, tight fairways, unfair
bunkers, and severe greens, too slick for
the undulations. Doesn't matter where
they play the Open from one year to the
next, whether it's Winged Foot, Oakland
Hills, Southern Hills, or some new club,
it's a cinch the layout is going to be
cussed at, bitched about, and called
everything but a white man's golf course.

Seems like every year the players forget that Open courses are supposed to be
tough, make you think, force you to play
more strategically than you do on most of
the pushover Tour courses we see.

All it takes is for a "name" player to storm through the locker room and criticize the course in a cloud of fucks. Immediately dozens of guys adopt the same opinion without even thinking about it.

They think a Cheetah Farmer or a Knut Thorssun is supposed to be intelligent because he's won some tournaments. But that's a big misconception about our sport. Cheetah Farmer can't think past his headlines, and Knut can't think past his zipper.

The press doesn't get it. The Irv Klars have never gotten it. They keep asking Tiger Woods how to solve world hunger and the problems in the Middle East because he wins golf tournaments, just like they used to ask Arnold Palmer and Jack Nicklaus what they'd do about Vietnam.

The practice rounds at Winged Foot were barely under way when Cheetah started cussing the layout and saying Ray Charles must have been the architect—old line—and they ought to put a circus tent over all eighteen holes, or better yet, just plow them up and start over. Other antiques.

And Knut. He's about as original as a Swedish meatball. He'd heard the line somewhere else, to be sure, so I was disappointed to hear guys laugh in the locker room when he said, "It is goofy golf. What it is they need to do here, they need to put a windmill on every hole."

Har-har. Bang fist on table.

My good pals Buddy Stark and Jerry Grimes even joined the list of complainers. Their games weren't sharp when they arrived, and then when we made some wagers in our two practice rounds together, and I put some hurt on their money clips, they launched into whining.

Jerry had no trouble finding nearly all of Winged Foot's greenside bunkers. While he was in the process of wearing out his sand wedge, he said, "This ain't no National Open, it's fuckin' Desert Storm."

The problem for Buddy was on the lightning-fast greens. There were no tap-ins. Even a one-foot putt could break two inches. Buddy wasn't holing anything in practice and he blamed it on Winged Foot's severe undulations, the way the greens were shaved down, and in some cases on the "asinine golf-hating maniac sicko" who set the pins.

He said, "USGA assholes want you to try to make a putt on top of Yul Brynner's head."

It was mandatory in Winged Foot practice rounds to spend a little extra time on the eighteenth green trying to duplicate "the Bobby Jones putt."

This was the twelve-foot putt for par and a 79 that Jones sank on the seventy-second hole in '29. It saved him a tie for the U.S. Open with Al Espinosa, a journeyman touring pro. Jones drowned Espinosa in the playoff.

A couple of renowned writers and Jones watchers, Grantland Rice and O. B. Keeler, have contended in books that it was "golf's greatest putt." The reason is because it rescued Jones from the most desperate situation he'd ever been in. Jones needed the putt not only to tie Espinosa but to keep from shooting 80 for the first time in an Open, and to avoid his worst collapse ever in a major. He'd blown a four-stroke lead with only four holes to go by bunkering his way to a triple bogey at the fifteenth and three-putting the sixteenth for a bogey. The watchers claim that if Jones hadn't dunked that putt at Winged Foot, the humility and embarrassment of his collapse would have made it impossible for him to win the Grand Slam a year later.

Old photos have told me exactly where the cup was set on the day of Jones's putt. It was middle-right. Jones had pulled his second shot into the left rough and his pitch stopped on the left side of the green twelve feet short of the cup. Jones faced a slightly downhill putt that broke left to right.

I was happy that somebody in the USGA was lugging around enough sense of history to have the cup positioned near "the Jones spot" all during the practice rounds.

Buddy and Jerry and I took dead aim at it both days of practice. Three tries apiece, closest to the hole for a hundred. Nobody came close to making the putt, but I won the money each day.

"Well, fuck the USGA," Jerry Grimes said, missing the putt one more time. "Fuck the USGA . . . fuck Winged Foot . . . and fuck that crippled sumbitch in the wheelchair."

"That would be Bobby Jones, or Franklin D. Roosevelt?" Buddy Stark inquired.

"Don't make a shit," Jerry said.

"Last I heard, they were both dead," I said.

"Not as dead as my golf game," said Jerry.

BITCH ABOUT the course all you want, you can't help but be pumped about the fact that you're playing in the U.S. of Open. I say you can't. Not unless you're a mummy who recently busted out of a pyramid and took up golf in time to qualify for the Open.

The atmosphere alone gets me excited. Flags flying over the clubhouse and big scoreboards, hordes of golf-wise crowds on hand, press swarming around like at no other tournament, football-type grandstands rising up in prime locations, TV towers here and there, and scads of hospitality tents off somewhere in the distance forming their own neighborhood, a one-week village.

I'll tell you one thing. I'm about half-proud of the way my ass played in the Winged Foot Open.

While I elect to give most of the credit to my sudden artistry with the lob wedge, Mitch said my stellar effort more likely had something to do with the fact that I was getting laid again.

Not having a lob wedge in your bag when you're playing a U.S. Open course, or any course with heavy rough, deep bunkers, and fast greens, would be like a rock star going on a concert stage without drugs.

The lob wedge has more loft and less bounce than your normal wedge, and I needed it often at Winged Foot out of the high rough and bunkers around the greens, to get the ball up quick and land it soft. The thing you have to guard against with the lob wedge is scooping the ball. Or chunking it. You can do this by keeping your left wrist flat and firm through impact and letting the club do the work. "Hit against your left side," as Mitch, the old swing guru, said.

I came out of the gate with a germfree 69, one under par, my best opening round ever in the Open. Naturally it didn't lead. By the end of the day it wasn't even close. There was the 66 by Knut followed by the four 67s by Rickey Padgett and the lurkers, and the five 68s by Tiger and Cheetah and the other lurkers. There was a grand final majestic total of twelve 69s in all, and I was in a tie for eleventh place.

Here I thought I'd played a good round in a major, but I read in the morning paper where there hadn't been any wind and the pin placements had been "inviting," so it turned out I hadn't done shit.

But my second straight germfree 69 on Friday was considered only one shot shy of magnificent. A stiff breeze whipped in and out, the pins were hidden, and some of the 67s, 68s, and 69s went so far Dixie they even missed the cut.

This greatly pleased the USGA and Winged Foot's members. They'd been shocked and the same thing as pissed off by the flood of low scores shot on Thursday.

Knut's 134 total kept him in the lead, but my 138 hoisted me into a tie for fourth and sent me to the interview area in the press tent. Which was where—and I don't even remember how it came up—I let drop the news that I was staying at the Plaza Hotel, commuting to the Open, and investigating some of Manhattan's pleasures in the evenings.

Slow news day, evidently. I was greeted in Dimitri's limo on Saturday morning with a headline on the back page of the *New York Post* that screamed:

BROADWAY BOBBY JOE!

And a big black headline on the back page of the *Daily News* that hollered:

GIVE HIS REGARDS TO WINGED FOOT!

It was even mentioned down deep in the *New York Times* story that a touring professional named Robert Joseph Grooves of Fort Worth, Texas, was curiously doing a "backward commute" to the Open championship.

I saved the newspapers for my mother's scrapbooks. I might also confess that I didn't mind the instant new nickname "Broadway" that Buddy and Jerry and Mitch each hung on me and were never going to let me forget. "Spin" had never done it for me anyhow.

All kinds of unexpected things happened in Saturday's third round.

Your serious golf fans might say that the most unexpected thing of all was that my satchel didn't fly open, meaning Robert Joseph Grooves didn't go brain-dead and shoot straight up.

It was a tough round. Start late in the day and you find your share of spike marks on the greens, the fans are a little more restless, and you have more time to think about stuff, like should you become more aggressive or play more conservatively to protect where you are. That kind of mental shit.

What I did was, I ignored my brain and turned myself over to my golf clubs. I played one shot at a time and managed to steer-job my way into enough fairways and save enough pars with my trusty lob wedge and putter to escape with a dig-deep 72, two over par. My 210 total at 54 holes was good enough after all the smoke cleared to leave me in a tie for fifth.

Knut Thorssun, Cheetah Farmer, Tiger Woods, Rickey Padgett, and Vance Clinter, a lurker, all squabbled over the lead most of the day Saturday. When everything unraveled, Cheetah led at 206. Tiger and Rickey were at 207. The lurker was at 209. And Knut, embarrassed and steaming, was tied with me.

There was a good reason for Knut to be hot—he blew to a five-over 75. In his press interview he blamed a stomach ailment for his poor play on the back nine, but the real reasons came out later, I learned, as he stomped around in the privacy of the contestants' locker room.

I was listening to Knut along with his IMG agent, Killer Tom McBride, the only agent with enough stroke to be in there. McBride sipped a Perrier and I drank a beer while we watched Knut slam things around and holler about the "she-bitches" who'd caused him all the problems on the course.

It turned out that one of Knut's traveling bimbos, Tanya something, had passed a note to him at the tenth tee. The note informed Knut that she deserved more out of their relationship. Like a bigger condo for herself in West Palm and a job in his organization for her father—otherwise Knut might be reading about himself—and her—in the *National Enquirer.*

"This is a crazy woman she-bitch!" Knut yelled. "She is wanting to be blackmailing me. Me! The Nukester! Tommy, you must be taking care of this she-bitch for me."

Killer Tom McBride said, "Tanya is a terribly fine-looking woman."

"Yes," said Knut, "but does this give her the right to turn into a she-bitch and try to ruin me?"

"I'll speak to Tanya," the agent said. "I'm sure we can work out a solution . . . something that won't be financially irresponsible on our part. She's a terribly fine-looking woman."

The other she-bitch was Knut's wife, Cynthia. She was at home in Palm Beach and called him long-distance on his cellphone while he was standing in the fifteenth fairway waiting to hit his second shot. She wanted to tell him the latest thing his sons—Sven and Matti, the unruly little shits—had done. Sven and Matti were going around knocking on doors all over the neighborhood and asking the people who lived there for money, and threatening to set their houses on fire if the people didn't give them any money. Knut had said to Cynthia, You're calling to tell me this while I'm playing in the Open? Can't you handle this yourself? Cynthia told him she had given up trying to handle the rotten little pricks, and she was personally taking great pleasure in springing this news on him while he was in the middle of a U.S. Open fairway. Knut had asked where the hell Renata was, and why wasn't Renata in charge of things? And Cynthia had said that Renata had taken the weekend off to go to Key Biscayne and fuck tennis pros and Miami Dolphins.

"I am surrounded by she-bitches," Knut said. "You cannot ask a man to play his best golf when he is surrounded by she-bitches."

I asked Knut if he'd thought about a divorce.

He said, "We have discussed it, but Cynthia says she will only agree to a divorce if I take the boys. What would I do with them?"

"No problem," I said. "Divorce Cynthia, marry Renata. Renata can take care of the kids—when she's not off fucking—and when she is, she can hire a babysitter."

Knut turned to Killer Tom McBride with a look that seemed to ask what the agent thought about my suggestion.

"Expensive," the agent said, "but it's got legs."

33

SAY THE NAME OF S. G. (SHUG) Hardisty to any of your knowledgeable golf fans today and there's a good chance they'll know who you're talking about. The man's name has gone down in infamy, or deeper. Shug is the USGA dolt who gave Knut that favorable ruling at Winged Foot.

Only six of us had a reasonable chance to win the Open in the last round. Six of us within four shots of one another. Everybody else was eating dust.

The last day pairings and start times:

1:47—Bobby Joe Grooves & Knut Thorssun.

1:56—Tiger Woods & Vance Clinter.
2:05—Cheetah Farmer & Rickey Padgett.

The first guy to go to Downtown Tap City was the lurker, Vance Clinter. Being paired with Tiger didn't help him—they had most of the gallery. Clinter doubled the first hole, doubled the second, bogeyed the third, tried to become invisible, and soared on to an 82, crawling back into his lurker's cave.

Tiger was the next to go, much to the surprise of everyone. The greens ate him up. He three-putted six times before he reached the tenth, the great par three. There, he five-putted for the triple bogey six. This was a shocking thing. Outrageous. Tiger not only reads greens better than anybody ever, his putts hug the ground like nobody else's, and they start looking for the cup the second they come off the face of the putter. He played pretty well from there to the clubhouse to finish with his unbelievable 79.

A grizzled historian like me could have told Tiger not to be embarrassed by the round. He was in good company. Ben Hogan had once skidded to a 79 on the last day of the Masters when he'd been the 54-hole leader, and Sam Snead had once slipped to an 81 when in the same position in a U.S. Open.

It was a sadistic layout in the last round, as Open courses usually are. The fairways look about two feet wide, the rough looks like you can lose your shoes in it, and the greens putt like a marble floor. You can find yourself in nerve-wracking situations where you feel like you want to vomit before you take the club back.

Early on it was easy to tell that the course was going to whip up on all of us. Rash of bogeys on the leaderboards. No red numbers. We were all over par after twelve holes, some more than others. It was a fistfight to save a par. I remember thinking that one or two over, a 281 or 282 total, might be good enough to take it.

Cheetah was losing it off the tee, Rickey was losing it with his irons, Knut was losing it in the bunkers, and I was losing it in my mind.

For one thing, you have to think you're *supposed* to win the U.S. Open—that you *deserve* to win—in order to win it. And I've never been mean enough, or dumb enough, let's say, to think that way. I've always been convinced that the only way I'd ever win a major would be if all the other contenders fainted or got assassinated.

History, of course, has told us that the Open and the other majors have produced some extremely unlikely winners over the years—total unknowns in some cases—but they were just lucky sumbitches is all I can say about it.

I have to be honest and admit that I wasn't even *trying* to win the Open. I was just trying to get to the house without getting hurt and grab me enough Ryder Cup points to nail down a spot on our team.

You could say that might be the reason why I didn't win the Open. Or you could give me and Mitch and my lob wedge credit for digging out those pars over the last four holes—each one a long, tough Mother Goose—and shooting that gut-wrenching 74 that brought me in at 284 and nabbed fourth place for me.

The round enabled me to swoop 140 beautiful Ryder Cup points— almost as many as I'd receive for winning a regular Tour event—and collect a young $217,000.

I honestly didn't give any thought to the prize money until Mitch, the wily old accountant, said, "Broadway, my man, we done stepped in a pile of smackeroons."

AS IT often is, the Open was decided on the last three holes.

Cheetah Farmer felt the heat and bogeyed two of the holes when he three-putted sixteen and eighteen. Cheetah and his arrogant, crew-cut daddy blamed spike marks for the disappointing 76 that gave Cheetah a total of 282.

Rickey Padgett felt the same heat and doubled the seventeenth and only managed to steal a bogey five at eighteen by no-braining a forty-foot putt into the cup. He'd sliced his drive, pulled his second shot, chopped a pitch, and flubbed another pitch. Rickey's 76 put him in at 283.

Cheetah and Rickey did all those things while knowing that 281 had become the score to beat. Knut Thorssun's 281.

But what they didn't know—and I did—was that a USGA rules official, the one and only S. G. (Shug) Hardisty, had more than likely won the Open for Knut back on the sixteenth hole.

That's where Hardisty, who owns a meat market in real life back in his hometown of Toledo, gave Knut the free drop out of the rough from behind the TV camera forklift. And out of what I guarantee you was a horrible lie that had double bogey written all over it.

Knut was one over, working on a 71, hoping to get to the cabin at 281, but he wasn't leading at the time. Cheetah and Rickey were behind us and had yet to encounter their difficulties on the closing holes.

Knut had pulled his second at the sixteenth far to the left of the green and into the rough behind the forklift. His ball was buried a foot deep in the thick grass. You could barely see it.

For the history books I'm happy to relate the conversation that took place between the three of us—Knut, myself, and the USGA dunce. It went like this:

Knut: "I believe I am entitled to relief."

Myself: "From what?"

Knut: "The machine there. It is an immovable obstruction."

Dunce: "I'm not sure what it is. Big old thing, though."

Knut: "It is an immovable obstruction. It is blocking my shot. The rules clearly state that a player is allowed a free drop from an immovable obstruction. I have seen this situation before."

Myself: "I'm sure you'd be real happy to get a drop out of *this* lie. That's a forklift, for Christ sake. For a TV camera. It's not an 'immovable obstruction.' It's got wheels on it! The network can move it. You have to play the ball where it is, *Nukester*."

Dunce: "I don't know. It looks immovable. Big old thing."

Myself: "You think it grew here, Shug? Tom Brokaw planted it—NBC's idea of a fucking tree?"

Dunce: "It looks to me like it would be a lot of trouble to move. I'm going to call it an immovable obstruction . . . allow relief."

Knut: "I should drop over here, do you agree?"

Dunce: "Yes, that will be fine."

Myself: "I don't fucking believe this shit."

Knut was permitted to lift his ball out of the deep rough, move around the forklift, and take a free drop on a nice firm patch of ground. From there he was able to pitch onto the green and save his par. Thanks to S. G. (Shug) Hardisty's ruling, he'd turned a six or seven into a four.

This inspired Knut to par the last two holes and win the Open sitting in the clubhouse.

THIEF STEALS U.S. OPEN!

That would have been my headline, but America's newspapers were more generous.

34

THE OPEN CHAMPION AND I CEL-
ebrated in different ways that Sunday night. Tell me Knut went back to
his Westchester hotel and comparative-
shopped the blowjobs of two light hooks
he met in a hospitality tent. I, on the
other hand, overjoyed that I'd made the
Ryder Cup team, went back to Manhattan Island to seek out food.

Real food. As in something to eat.
In other words, nothing from Cheryl's
lineup of chic restaurants, the fern joints
where I'd have to say to my waiter, Raoul
or Humberto, "Anybody want to explain
to me why it's taking so long to osso two
buccos?"

Dimitri, my driver, said he knew just the place. He took us to P. J. Clarke's, an old saloon and hamburger establishment on Third Avenue. First, however, we went to the Plaza Hotel, where I cleaned up and collected Cheryl. She hadn't gone to the last round of the Open because I'd assured her I wasn't going to win it.

She went to the ballet instead. A matinee at Lincoln Center. She couldn't remember the name of the ballet, but she said there were a lot of good hang-timers and butterflies hopping around on the stage. In the first act, all the hang-timers chased a butterfly, or maybe she was a swan. In the second act, all the butterflies or swans chased a hang-timer—and it was flat-out impressive that the hang-timer could leap so high, considering his bulge was larger than a volleyball.

Cheryl had returned to our hotel room in time to turn on the TV and watch the finish of the Open. She'd heard one of the announcers mention that I'd cinched the Ryder Cup team. She was happy for me and agreed that I deserved to have whatever I wanted for dinner.

I called Smokey Barwood, my agent, who lived in the city, and invited him to join us. My agent hadn't gone to the Open either. Another client was demanding all his time.

Smokey came to the back room at P. J. Clarke's and allowed that he was "this close" to arranging a new sneaker contract for the client. The client was Mucus Benson, the all-pro linebacker. This was the same Mucus Benson who had been acquitted two months ago of murdering his girlfriend, LaToya Boyette, the Olympic hurdler, with an axe.

"Well, who wouldn't want to give *him* a sneaker deal?" Cheryl said.

In a festive mood, I opened with three Juniors and got on the outside of a bowl of beef barley soup and two bacon cheeseburgers and a plate of home fries and closed with two more Juniors.

Our waiter went a long way toward making my night when he proudly revealed that the front bar, which looked out on Third Avenue, was where they'd filmed some scenes in *The Lost Weekend*—the old movie with Ray Milland. That movie had made the saloon famous in the first place.

"Jane Wyman," I said.

"Where?" the waiter said, looking around.

"She was in the movie with Ray Milland," I said.

"Oh," he said.

I picked up my glass of Junior and looked at Smokey.

"This shrinks my liver, sure, and it pickles my kidneys," I said. "But look what it does to my mind. It makes it soar. That's not Third Avenue out there, it's the Nile. Yeah, the Nile—and here comes Cleopatra on her barge."

"What are you talking about?" Smokey said.

Cheryl said, "It's just a wild guess, but I think he's doing Ray Milland in *The Lost Weekend.*"

"I can't remember all of it," I said.

Smokey said, "Well, I did Mucus Benson in *my* lost weekend."

I asked Smokey how our mutual friend Irv Klar was coming along on the Salu Kinda instruction book, which the golf world was eagerly looking forward to, no doubt.

"He's finished it," Smokey said. "He's done quite a nice job. I don't believe you can actually detect how much he borrowed from Harvey Penick, Ben Hogan, and Tommy Armour."

"What's the title?"

Smokey said, "Salu wants to call it *The Little Yellow Book*, but the publisher likes *For All Who Love the Game*. It's unsettled as yet."

I said, "Isn't that one of Harvey Penick's titles, *For All Who Love the Game*. I'm sure it is."

"You can't copyright a title," Smokey said.

"Really?" I said. "Hell, if that's the case, I'd just call it *Ben Hogan's Five Lessons: The Modern Fundamentals of Golf*, by Salu Kinda with Irving Klar."

Cheryl said, "Yeah, if that's the case, I'd think about *A Fish Called Wanda* . . . *The Great Gatsby* . . . *Gunga Din*. . . ."

"*Gunga Din*," I said. "Now, there's a truly great movie. 'Kill . . . kill . . . kill for the love of killing!' "

"What . . . ?" Smokey said.

"The goofy old guy in *Gunga Din*," I said. "The cult leader. That's what he yells. He said it first—before Jack Nicklaus."

I was the only one who laughed at that.

If it was all the same, my agent said, he would like to discuss my schedule. Ryder Cup participation was obviously going to change some of my plans.

I'd already thought about it in the limo coming back to the city, I said. Memphis would be the only tournament I could play between now and the British Open because of the QE2 deal.

Smokey was surprised that Cheryl wasn't going on the voyage with me, or to the British Open. She had already taken her two-week vacation from Donald Hooper Realty for this New York trip, she pointed out, and she had no intention of quitting her job—she liked it—and there were other reasons.

"I saw *Titanic*," she said, "and I've been to a British Open."

I'd tried to tell Cheryl that there are three British Opens. The one they play in Scotland, the one they play in England. And the one they play at St. Andrews, which is the best one.

But Cheryl had too many memories from our "wonderful" trip last year to Royal Lytham & St. Annes. Buddy Stark had come up with the bright idea for us to handle the British Open the way the high rollers do. Rent a house. We picked one out from the brochure the R&A real estate people provide every year. A "large and charming red brick cottage within walking distance of Royal Lytham & St. Annes" is what was advertised. A house with three bedrooms and two baths and "atmospheric grounds and gardens." The pictures looked good. And it was only $12,000 for the week. As British Open rentals go, the price was something of a bargain.

Buddy took Emily, the Austin scholar, and I took Cheryl. We flew nonstop from DFW to Manchester, England, which is only an hour or so from Lytham, where a travel agent had arranged for a car and driver to meet us. They didn't. That was the start of it.

We managed to rent a car, and Buddy drove on the wrong side of the road for the first two hours while we tried to find the house we'd rented. Cheryl finally insisted on taking the wheel after Buddy had painted the left side of our Saab green from the shrubbery he'd hugged—and had almost killed us on four different occasions at the roundabouts.

The cussing grew louder after we found our house. It not only wasn't within walking distance of the golf course, it wasn't within walking distance of a town, a grocery, or anything in sight, but we were able to enjoy the aroma from the atmospheric grounds of the cow pasture directly behind it.

A nice note from the owner, a Mrs. Dubbins, apologized for the fact that there was only one bathroom. She had intended to add on a second bath before we arrived but had run out of funds. She did not apologize, however, for the fact that there would only be enough hot water for one person to bathe each day. "Bummer," said Emily, the scholar.

Since we could never solve all the mysteries of the house in one week, like how to work the stove, the central heating, or find all the hiding places where Mrs. Dubbins stored her dishes and towels and what-have-you, we ate every meal out, risking collisions on the roads. We dined either in the small town of St. Annes or in quaint Blackpool, an old promenade–music hall–pleasure pier–roller coaster city where working-class Brits go to find family entertainment and sunbathe in the dark gray mist and icy winds conveniently provided by the Irish Sea.

We laughed about all that in P. J. Clarke's and reasoned that the lodging and death-defying trips in the car to the course and going out to eat may have had something to do with the fact that Buddy and I played lousy last year at Lytham—I tied for 62nd and he tied for 68th—and why Cheryl Haney was more than happy to stay home this time.

"See one place without enough hot water, you've seen them all," she said. "That's my travel tip for the day."

35

I WAS SITTING AT THE LOBBY
bar in the Peabody my first night in
Memphis in my brown cashmere sport
coat and khakis. I was fondling a Junior,
looking at the ducks in the fountain. I'd
watched the ducks march in and tried to
remember if there didn't used to be more
of them. I think I counted seven. I was
having thoughts about Memphis, a city I
liked, while I was waiting for Buddy Stark
and his "mystery guest."

Earlier in the day I'd gotten my Memphis fix out of the way. I'd done Graceland once, years ago, and once was too
many. You can't really do Graceland unless you've got curlers in your hair. But I

did the handy downtown trolley, the beautified riverfront, scrubbed-up Beale Street down and back, all the reminders of the blues guys W. C. Handy and B. B. King, and the big statue of Elvis on the corner. I'd wound up having a pulled pork sandwich at the Rendezvous, which is only a nine-iron from the Peabody.

You can't accuse "Mimfuss pull" of being even close to what a Texan normally thinks of as barbecue, but I take the position that there's no bad barbecue, even the chopped skin they brag about in North Carolina.

I'd been playing in the FedEx St. Jude Classic every year since I'd been on the Tour, and I'd always stayed at the Peabody. I like to know where I am and why it's there. Otherwise, all you ever see is a motel and a golf course. I don't call this stopping to "smell the flowers," as Walter Hagen said, but I do call it fighting boredom.

Most guys out here don't do it. They're motel rats, and not just because they're cheap. Their interest doesn't stretch beyond their own golf games is what it is, although some of them like to fish. They've never seen downtown Memphis.

For that matter, they come to the Colonial every year and never scout out Fort Worth, or even care to know what it's all about—they only know Ben Hogan was our Elvis.

One thing I thought about when I was in Memphis was something only another stat junkie might be aware of. It was in Memphis at the old original Colonial Country Club in 1960 that Ben Hogan did a last-hurrah thing. Hogan, who was forty-eight years then, tied for the Memphis Open that year with Tommy Bolt and Gene Littler. They played off at eighteen holes and Tommy Bolt won with a 68 over Ben's 69 and Littler's 71. But it was the last time that Ben Hogan—Hawk, Bantam, Wee Icemon—would finish in first place after the regulation seventy-two holes in any tournament. Landmark deal.

I may have been thinking more about Hogan than the ducks when Buddy Stark tapped me on the shoulder at the lobby bar in the Peabody.

"Come on over, we have a table," he said.

I went over and joined Buddy and his "mystery guest," who was none other than Mrs. Knut Thorssun, the former Cynthia Keeling.

My reaction: "You want me to say *Gott in Himmel*, leapin' lizards, or roast my Mother Goose?"

In a tight pair of designer jeans and low-cut green top and frizzy new hairstyle, she didn't look like any married lady, mother of two.

"You're not really that surprised, are you?" she said.

"Probably not," I said. "Buddy told me he was bringing a 'mystery guest.' I was hoping it would be you and not Renata."

"I'll take that as a compliment," Cynthia said.

"You should," I said. "You look great, Cynthia."

"Thanks again."

"I'm in love," Buddy said.

"I believe you," I said. "Who wouldn't be in love with this lady?"

"*We* . . . are in love," Cynthia said firmly.

I sat down and looked around for a waitress, and turned back to the two of them. "This love deal," I said. "This is something that's been going on awhile, behind my very back I take it?"

"We've always been attracted to each other," Cynthia said. "We've been good friends since I used to come out on the Tour, since Buddy was married to the exquisite Laura. We've shared a lot of feelings . . . laughter . . . problems . . . traded a lot of knowing glances."

"You slippery dude," I said to Buddy.

He shrugged.

Cynthia had been in Austin with Buddy, looking around for a castle to buy in Barton Creek. It was where she and Buddy planned to live after they were married. Which would be after her divorce from Knut, and after the settlement that was going to peel off Knut's skin. She had already filed—the day after he won the Open.

I said, "Cynthia, is it smart for you to be out in public with Buddy if you're in the middle of a divorce and a skin-peeling? Where *is* Knut, as we speak? I know he's not here."

"Munich," she said. "He's getting a million-five appearance fee to play in the German Open."

"*Gott in Himmel*," I said.

Cynthia wasn't sopping up the white wine like the last time I'd seen her, which was at Augusta. She was nursing along half a glass. She was still smoking, though, and I enjoyed being near it.

"You haven't heard the other good news," Buddy said.

The other good news involved Knut and Cynthia's boys, the unruly little shits as they were known far and wide.

Cynthia grew excited and a trifle animated as she talked about what she'd worked out for her sons. They were presently under house arrest in Palm Beach—Renata and two Miami Dolphins in charge. But within the month Sven and Matti would be put in chains and driven to a remote part of Virginia and enrolled in a military academy, the Jeb Stuart Institute for Young Men.

"The school is 150 years old and no one has ever escaped," she said. "The concrete walls are thirty feet high. The nearest town is twenty-five miles away, one of those Somethingburgs. They can have visitors one day a year. They wear uniforms. They drill. They study. They get their little asses beat regularly. They can't write letters or receive mail. They can't make phone calls or receive phone calls. Every two months they're allowed to go to town under armed guard for about an hour, to buy toothpaste and stuff."

Buddy said, "Tell him what they get to do for fun."

"Clean toilets," Cynthia said, smiling with satisfaction.

I asked how long Sven and Matti would be in the academy.

"Till they finish high school with honors," she said.

"Wow," I said. "That's a long time."

"Yes!" Cynthia said, her eyes sparkling. "Isn't it wonderful? The world will be safe for eight, nine . . . ten years."

I wondered if she'd inquired into what the future usually held for graduates of the Jeb Stuart Institute for Young Men.

She said, "They keep up with that. The vast majority go on to college, obtain their degrees, and become good citizens. Some pursue careers in the military, of course. And they freely admit that they sometimes *do* turn out a small number of homosexuals. That's what I'm rooting for."

"You are?" I said.

"You bet," Cynthia said. "The little fuckers won't reproduce. That's a blessing for society—and nobody will ever call me grandma."

I sipped my cocktail and said, "Well, Wilmer . . . Sven . . . Matti . . . I'm sorry to lose you as sons. But you can always get another son. There's only one Maltese Falcon."

The lovebirds were kissing. They didn't hear Sydney Greenstreet.

THE MEMPHIS tournament has been played on three different courses. It started on old Colonial, the Bill Langford course built back during the First World War, the course where Cary Middlecoff honed his game. Then it moved to new Colonial, the course Joe Finger did in the early '70s. Now it's played on one of our TPC things, Southwind, which Ron Pritchard designed in the '80s with Fuzzy Zoeller and Hubert Green looking over his shoulder as consultants.

Even though Southwind has a dozen water holes and small greens, guys tend to kick it around, which means it's normally not my kind of course. In the past I've shot even par for two rounds and missed the cut by six strokes. There's a fun deal for you.

But making the Ryder Cup team juiced up my confidence and this apparently put some "nonchalant" in my game, Mitch observed, and I spent the week watching my wedges nestle. I have no other explanation for why I got hung up on those 67s and shot me the 268 that tied me for fourth and garnered me a tidy $170,000.

I might have won the whole fandango if I hadn't played the ninth hole like Alleene or Terri. It's a 450-yard par four with water along the left of the fairway and guarding the green on the left. Twice I tried to see if my ball would float. The first two rounds I went double-double at the ninth just as straight as an Indian goes to shit.

But I was happy for Buddy Stark, grabbing himself a W like that, his first victory of the year. Looked like he came out doped with a 64. But he stayed in his funk and added 68, 67, and 66 for 265. It brought him home two ahead of Zinger and Sutton and swooped him a young $630,000.

"What the fuck got into you?" I said to him, giving him a warm handshake in the locker room.

He grinned, "Just showing off, I guess—for you know who."

Cynthia had used good sense in not going near Southwind all week. She watched it on TV. If a single caddy or Tour wife or player had seen her it would have been all over ESPN that evening.

Buddy did tell Jerry Grimes about the Cynthia deal, promising to kick Jerry's ass from Memphis to Cloyd Highway if he blabbed it around. Jerry took an oath and joined us for dinner.

Buddy, Cynthia, Jerry, and I celebrated that night at the Rendezvous. Buddy and Cynthia did a job on two bottles of white wine amid their cuddling. Jerry stuck with beer. I stuck with Junior.

We only hit the high spots of Buddy's triumphant Sunday round—he knew better than to take us eighteen holes. We all got around to agreeing that Knut Thorssun was a universal buttwipe, perhaps the all-time. Eventually we ordered as much barbecue as the waiter could carry.

It was the old food critic Jerry Grimes, after cramming another bite of "Mimfuss pull" in his mouth, sauce trickling down his chin, who looked up at us and said, "It's not very good . . . but idn't it good?"

36

AS SHIPS GO, THE *QE2* CAN LEAD my armada anytime.

I boarded that dude in New York on July 7, a week after Memphis and ten days before the start of the British Open. I confess I spent the first two days counting all the bars and restaurants on board—the thing is bigger than most Texas towns that have high school football teams. After that, I spent the rest of the "crossing," as we call it, wishing Cheryl had come with me.

It's a romantic deal, being on a luxury liner, especially if you have a suite like I did. Big bed, big bathroom, TV, phone, and glass doors instead of portholes.

Doors that opened onto my private outdoor veranda. I devoted some time to standing on my outdoor veranda, cocktail in hand, wondering how debonair I looked—and thinking about a line from a movie that seemed to fit: "What is it about being on a boat that makes everyone behave like a film star?" Amazingly, I couldn't remember what movie it came from, or who said it, for two days. Finally I remembered it didn't come from a movie at all, it came from a TV series, *Brideshead Revisited*. Which most of my friends would have bet the Under on me watching back when it ran, but I recall liking it. The parts I understood.

There were things to do on the ship other than look debonair during the six nights and five days it took to get from New York to Southampton. There's twenty-four-hour room service, a casino, shopping mall, bookstore, library, theater, concerts, lectures, dancing lessons, swimming pool, jogging path, and a driving net on an outside deck where I hit balls for a while every day, keeping loose. But mostly you dine and drink.

I do heartily recommend that everybody take a voyage someday, but only in the summer, when it's smooth. If you go any other time, according to my waitress at my regular table in the Britannia Restaurant on Upper Deck, you might find yourself trying to grab your salad plate as it goes floating through the air.

From my very own suite I could pick up the phone and call Cheryl—for only fifteen dollars a minute. I called her every day. But the first time, Jolene Frederick answered at Donald Hooper Realty.

"Hi, Bobby Joe," Jolene said. "Last night we were trying to think of all the names for the grail. Help me out here."

"The what?"

"The Holy Grail," she said. "You know. The juicy."

"Is Cheryl there?"

"Yeah, but help me out. We thought of beaver . . . wool . . . gash . . . donut . . . taco . . . c-word, of course . . . snatch . . . boat . . . box . . . clump . . . slice."

"*Slice?*"

"You don't listen to rap much, do you?"

"I assassinate rap. Put Cheryl on, please, this is costing fifteen bucks a minute."

"In a second. What do they say on the Tour?"

"I don't know, Jolene. I've heard caddies call it fringe . . . face . . . froghair . . . first cut."

She squealed, "Face! I love it! 'Gimme some *face*, baby.' Hold on. Here's Cheryl."

I asked Cheryl if Jolene ever sold any property. Lowering her voice, she said yes, occasionally, but not if it interfered with a chance for her to break up a home. Cheryl asked how was it out there in the Atlantic. I said she should be here—she'd enjoy sitting in a deck chair, watching fat Greek guys and long-tall Brits splash around in the pool in their little briefs.

Closest thing to royalty on board, I said, were the assorted pairs of snooty mothers and bored-looking daughters. Made only in America. Cheryl said if I tossed a move on any of the daughters I could stay in Scotland. I said the mothers were the threat. They'd had work done. But they weren't likely to be attracted to me—I didn't bring a tux and didn't know how to hold a brandy glass.

None of the other phone calls to Cheryl were that interesting, although some cost more than $200.

Three other so-called "celebrities" on board paid their freight by giving a talk and answering questions in this huge lounge. The most popular was the English lady mystery writer I'd never heard of. She filled the room and, unless I misunderstood, basically said that no other mystery writer, man or woman, knew shit.

I didn't bother to hear the former butler at Buckingham Palace, who I heard made a big hit by talking about how much the Queen liked her gin. I also took a pass on the German soccer star.

I drew the smallest crowd, maybe three dozen people. They found nothing to laugh at, and I cut it short after reading the disappointment on all their faces. Their looks said, How come I wasn't Arnold Palmer?

The penetrating questions they asked me were:

Do I know Tiger Woods?

What is Tiger Woods like?

How tall is Tiger Woods?

Part of the deal called for me to hit balls into the driving net outside after my talk. I was also expected to give some swing tips if the crowd asked for any. The crowd consisted of seven geezers in plaid wool caps with bills. James Cagney caps.

I went through the bag, hitting two or three balls with each club. The geezers didn't say anything, except one of them asked when it would be his turn. Each one hit some balls. I didn't cure any of their tops or shanks.

Smokey Barwood earned his agent's keep—or I should say avoided the loss of a limb—with the arrangements he'd made for me when I arrived in Southampton on July 12. We docked soon after breakfast.

I was met by a pleasant and helpful East Indian fellow with a limo who drove me the two and a half hours to London Gatwick airport and saw to it that I boarded the right shuttle, the one to Edinburgh. And an hour and a half later I was in the Edinburgh terminal, where I was met by a pleasant and helpful Scottish fellow with a limo who drove me the two hours it took to reach the Old Course Hotel in St. Andrews.

As I told Smokey later, by way of thanking him, if I'd had to work all that out on my own, I'd probably still be in Budapest.

37

THE OLD COURSE HOTEL IN ST. Andrews looks completely out of place. It's a big modern structure that stands a little apart from the ancient gray city, a city with spires sticking up and every building looking like a church or a ruin. But the hotel is convenient because it sits right by the seventeenth fairway—the Road Hole—and from all I've heard in discussions on the subject, it has the only up-to-date bathrooms in town.

It's primarily reserved for contestants and officials when the British Open comes along every five years. There are other okay places to stay, like Rusack's and Scores, a couple of relic-type hotels right there in town that are even closer to the R&A clubhouse, but if Americans want to feel like they've never left home, the Old Course Hotel is their joint.

Which, from my personal point of view, was what was wrong with it during my wonderful stay.

A full complement of American fans had managed to have enough stroke to reserve rooms there, too, and just after I passed muster with the registration people I saw one American of particular interest across the lobby—Nonnie Harrison.

And she saw *me*, and started toward me, looking pleased, border-line excited as I interpreted the look. I don't mind admitting I was stricken with terror.

"Oh, shit, oh, dear" is close to what I said to myself.

I had a few seconds to recover from the kind of shiver I hadn't known since I was a kid in a movie and saw Dracula for the first time, although it behooves me to admit that she looked pretty damn good for a lady who plays out of the Rich-Wife-Good-Little-Shopper Division.

As she was coming toward me I was standing there reading the note Mitch had left for me at the front desk saying he'd arrived, had a room in a B&B in town, and would meet me in the morning around nine—he'd arranged a practice round tee time for 11:30.

If I'd been quick, I would have said to the Scottish guy with my clubs and luggage on the roll cart, "Of all the eight-centuries-old linkslands in all the cities in all the world, she has to walk into mine."

But I was travel-weary. So all I could think of to say to Mrs. J. Rodney Harrison was "Hi, Nonnie. What in the world are you doing here?"

She insisted on giving me a hug and kissing me on the mouth, after which, with her tongue back in her own mouth, she said, "Rodney wanted to see a British Open, and I wanted to shop in London for a few days on the way, so here we are."

I slipped the guy with my stuff ten pounds, close to twenty dollars, to wheel the things up to my room as I chatted with Nonnie. He didn't act like I'd overtipped him at all, which gave the place something else in common with America.

I asked if Neenie, her sister, was with them. Making small talk.

Nonnie said, "No, Neenie's working in a boutique in Highlands this summer. She's staying in our cottage. Neenie's not looking for Mr. Right. She gets bored to intense sleep with any relationship that lasts more than a month. Her latest, she tells me, is a man named Casey something from Jacksonville, Florida. He's renting a cabin for two weeks in Cashiers. This is Neenie's summer to screw tourists."

I asked if Rodney was off playing golf someplace today, knowing that's what most Americans do when they come to British Opens—play more rounds of golf at various courses than the contestants do in the British Open. There's a golf course of some kind about every two miles in Scotland in one direction or another.

Yep, she reported. Rodney had gone off with three assholes from Atlanta to play North Berwick, wherever that was.

"Ah, my favorite course in Scotland," I said. "But it's two hours from here. You have to go around Edinburgh."

"They have a chopper."

I said, "It's probably my favorite *area* in Scotland. I mean, you play North Berwick West, North Berwick East . . . Dunbar, which Old Tom Morris designed . . . Gullane, which Willie Park designed . . . Gullane has three courses, actually, but Gullane No. 3 is the best. How do you like St. Andrews, Nonnie? Great atmosphere, huh? This is the birthplace of golf, in case nobody's told you."

"It looks like the birthplace of *death* to me," she said. "You'd think it might have occurred to them to plant a tree somewhere."

Chuckling, I said, "I know what you mean. The first time Sam Snead came to St. Andrews, he said, 'It looks like there used to be a golf course here at one time.' You have to play it to appreciate the subtleties."

She said, "Can we lose the golf encyclopedia? I want to *see* you this week. I'll work something out."

"I'm, uh . . . not sure that'll be possible, Nonnie."

"I haven't forgotten Pebble Beach," she said, "and I don't think you have . . . even though you didn't return any of my calls. By the way! Who was that dirt-bike bitch in Fort Worth who told me to get lost on the phone?"

I informed her that the "dirt-bike bitch" had a name. It was Cheryl Haney. And she was a whole lot of babe, and the woman I was in love with.

"Oh, *please*," Nonnie said.

"I'm not kidding," I said.

"She's in Texas, isn't she?"

"Yes."

"And we're here, right?"

"Yes."

"So?"

I tried to look ill. "Nonnie, seriously . . ."

"You can at least have dinner with us," she said. "Rodney will make reservations upstairs. Maybe I'll work something out for us, maybe I won't. We won't sweat it. You look tired, Bobby Joe Grooves. Go cuddle up with your fucking morality and get some rest. I'm off to buy cashmere."

She gave me a subtle feel-up as she pecked me on the cheek and was gone. I watched her leave, wishing like hell I'd skipped the British Open.

IT KEPT me up half the night, tired as I was, thinking about how I'd give Nonnie the slip all week. I could throw off, tank the deal, miss the cut, and be off the reservation by Friday night. But I'd still have four days to worry about. Okay, I could claim an injury and WD right away. Concoct a death in the family? Choke on a toenail I'd find in a pork pie or a sausage roll? Fake mad cow disease?

I shared such thoughts with Mitch the next day on the course while

I was reacquainting myself with all of the historic hazards at St. Andrews—the Swilcan Burn, Hell Bunker, the Principal's Nose, the Beardies, the Elysian Fields, Miss Grainger's Bosoms, the Valley of Sin.

Going way back, a handful of architects had tinkered with St. Andrews. The likes of Allan Robertson, Old Tom Morris, James Braid, Alister Mackenzie. But the Old Course—squeezed on one side by the town and lashed on the other by the winds from the sea, with its yawning double greens and hidden moguls and massive patches of purple flowers, your basic heather—was still the gem that Nature had designed.

Mitch was naturally concerned that with Nonnie on my mind I wouldn't play well in the world's oldest major. It dates back to 1860 and the Brits still call it "the Open Championship," like nobody else has one.

"Kind of funny, though, when you think about it," Mitch said. "Man tryin' to run away from a lunch wagon."

Lunch wagon. I'd file that away for Jolene.

"Nonnie Harrison is big trouble," I said. "The serious kind. Trouble in Downtown Cheryl Haney City."

"Hate them kind," he said. "Can't just trick fuck and let it go. Must be a white thing."

I said I hadn't thought of it that way.

"We have to de-flect, is what we have to do," he said.

"Deflect?" I said.

Mitch said, "Yeah, we spin her off . . . keep you out of the purple flowers this week."

"Spin her off on what?"

"You not usin' your head."

"It's not the first time."

"Think Knut," he said.

"Knut?"

Mitch said, "Spin her off on Knut. He a lunch wagon man. Hell, he been to lunch wagon *graduate* school. You can bust me if Nonnie don't go for a big old handsome white bread like Knut."

"I drop Knut on her and I skate?"

"Now you quick."

"Could work," I said, giving Mitch a low five. "I'll do this thing."

I DODGED Nonnie for two days by being on the golf course or in areas where she couldn't gain admittance. Like in the R&A clubhouse or out on the practice range. But I didn't escape her messages. One message said J. Rodney would be playing golf at Gleneagles all day Tuesday, and what were my plans? Another message said J. Rodney would be playing golf at Elie all day Wednesday and what were my plans? And another said dinner was on for Wednesday night in the hotel's upstairs dining room, no excuses.

I responded to the dinner message, telling her to count me in and have Rod make it a table for four—I was bringing a "mystery guest."

By then I'd recruited Knut for dinner. I'd finally caught up with him that Wednesday morning and he favored me with a chat on the putting green behind the big grandstand to the right of the No. 1 tee.

I was covered up in friendship and innocence—I needed his ass.

"The she-bitch!" he said. "Do you know what this woman has done, Bobby Joe? It is to be unbelievable! Cynthia, the she-bitch, is asking for a divorce. From me! The Nukester! This is a crazy woman, I tell you not."

"Gee," I said, "I had no idea Cynthia was unhappy."

"She is not unhappy," Knut said. "How could she be unhappy? She is married to *me*. I have given her everything—houses, cars, swimming pools, my name. Without me she would still be flying for Delta Airlines and stealing cups and saucers!"

"You've been a generous guy," I said. "Not every American wife drives a Mercedes *and* a Lexus SUV. That alone . . ."

"What it is, she is crazy," Knut continued. "Things have been put in her head by other she-bitches. This is what I believe to be true. Now she is wanting much of my money. I am told this is the way of she-bitches."

Knut said Cynthia was asking for $30 million for herself and a $20 million fund set aside for the two boys, Sven and Matti, a fund they couldn't touch until they were out of college.

He said, "Cynthia thinks she is hitting me where I hurt, and I am acting so as to be injured and complaining bitterly, but the joke is to be on the she-bitch. I will give her this amount and be done with her because what she does not know is, I am worth four times that much! *Har-har.*"

Unable to avoid humor, but keenly aware that most humor takes a detour around Knut, I said, "By God, that'll show her. Strap a little thirty million on her, see how she likes it."

I could only imagine how much Buddy Stark would like it.

The remark missed the Nukester like an air ball. Seconds later he was telling me about this great school his sons were going to enter. The she-bitch had found the school in Virginia, but he'd approved of the idea. With his busy schedule he couldn't very well take care of the boys himself, and Renata didn't want the full-time responsibility. The private school was a good solution, even if it was the she-bitch who thought of it. Sven and Matti were going to be getting the best education possible and receive some much-needed discipline at the Jeb Stuart Institute.

"For Young Men," I said.

"For who?"

"It's the Jeb Stuart Institute for Young Men."

"You have heard of this place?"

"Yes, I have," I said. "It's highly respected. You're a lucky father to have your sons enrolled at Jeb Stuart. They will learn many things and may become future generals in the army—maybe even for the United States."

Another air ball.

I carefully studied the crowd around the putting green and was happy not to observe any bimbette who might be traveling with Knut. With "Captain Wood." Another nickname Jerry Grimes had recently given him. If Knut had a honey with him, she'd be faithfully in the gallery at all times. He liked having them there. He'd once had *two* in Palm Springs—cut-slack Stacy walking on the left side of the fairway and no-slack Lori walking on the other. Dueling dirty legs.

"I take it you're alone this week," I said.

"Yes, this is unfortunately true," he said. "I have been looking, but I must tell you, Bobby Joe. I have never pulled a lot of pussy out of Scotland."

"Well, Knut," I grinned. "This is your lucky day."

38

J. RODNEY HARRISON WAS THE
proudest man in the rooftop restaurant of
the Old Course Hotel. Knut Thorssun
was at his table.

Rodney was so proud, I was mildly concerned that he might go down on Knut
before Nonnie could get around to it. For
a while that evening, the all-time jock-
sniffing record was in serious jeopardy.

Nonnie and Rodney were already at
the table when Knut and I came in. I
wangled a seat for Knut next to Nonnie. I
watched her size him up as I made introductions. She scanned his blond mane,
broad shoulders in a solid blue golf shirt
and snug white slacks, the slight bulge in
evidence.

She did the scan as Rodney was pumping Knut's hand and saying, "Goddamn, Knut Thorssun! I'll be goddamn. . . . I'll tell you what, stud . . . Knut the Brute. . . . Here he is, right here, sports fans. The United States Open golf champion! . . . Thor-more-nuclear! Shithouse mouse, I've got him tonight!"

Nonnie acted unimpressed with Knut and tremendously bored with golf chatter as the evening progressed, all of us having the grilled fillet of Dover sole. She smoked and drank as Rodney made Knut take him through many of the greatest rounds Knut ever played.

When Knut cleared his throat and leaned his elbows forward on the table for the third time, it was an ears-up for me. I dropped my napkin on the floor and leaned down to pick it up. This was in order to sneak a peek at what might be going on under the table.

As I suspected—and hoped—Nonnie's nonsmoking hand was free to be on Knut's thigh, dangerously close to the bulge. Also, the toe of her shoe was slowly moving up and down Knut's calf.

My major thought was that Roy Mitchell deserved a bonus. We'd spun off Nonnie and now I'd have a clear head to take on the purple flowers and devilish moguls and other challenges of the Old Course.

I raised back up in time to hear Rodney say, "Goddamn, Knut, good buddy, anything you want or need when you come to Atlanta, you got it. Stay with us in Buckhead, too, by God! You can have your own wing of the house. Hell, if it ain't already big enough, I'll build on."

Nonnie said, "I'm sure he would prefer a hotel, Rod."

"What is this Buckhead you are saying?" Knut asked.

Rodney said, "Aw, it's just a little old pissant neighborhood where Bobby Jones and Coca-Cola used to live."

Nonnie faked a yawn, said for some reason she was tired tonight. Then Knut yawned, said the same thing. They both stood up. Rodney said he had some more drinking to do. I told Rodney I'd stay with him—he could tell me all about playing Elie today and Gleneagles yesterday.

That's right. Threw myself on the fire. But it was a small price to pay, all things considered.

I NEVER saw Nonnie again the rest of the week. You'd think her charms wouldn't have bothered a gash man like Knut, but I was sure she'd caused him to miss the cut at St. Andrews. She spurred him out of the chute, I'd wager, and rode him till he bucked himself into that pair of 81s.

I know one thing. Having Nonnie off my case had more than a little to do with me playing good enough to finish tenth and waltz out of town with a parcel of pounds that translated into $122,000. I was never a serious enough contender to be invited to the press tent, but I did grant some one-on-one interviews about the Ryder Cup coming up in September at Muirfield Village, the Jack Nicklaus course in Columbus, Ohio.

I took care not to talk big, knowing I was certainly the weakest link in the USA's chain.

ST. ANDREWS needs wind to protect itself from low scores, and this time we got us a dose off the old Firth of Forth. Every round it was spinnakers-up going out on the front and a Trailer Park, Kansas, tornado coming home.

The wind turned the Road Hole into a par six. Made the little pot bunker on the left of the green look bigger than West Texas. Made the in-bounds road on the right look wider than a DFW runway. Made the green in between look about the size of a pizza—and you were going at the Mother Goose with a cold-jump two-iron.

The wind caused a lot of the big names to play like runover dogs. I was content to string together my 72s and 73s for 290, and I have nothing but admiration for the 282 that won it for Cheetah Farmer, giving the child star and his arrogant daddy their first professional major.

Only thing I wish is that Cheetah had been a little more gracious in his victory speech at the presentation ceremony.

There were twenty thousand fans listening to him when he said,

"As many of you know, I played this zoo once before in the British Amateur three years ago. It didn't do me no favors. One of your sheep-punks took me out in the second round. So I'm kind of happy today that I finally brought this rat track to its knees."

Not exactly Ben Hogan at Oakland Hills.

The Scottish crowd missed most of Cheetah's language, I'm pleased to report, as did the majority of the Royal & Ancient officials at the ceremony. I ventured the guess that the R&A chaps had already made their load in the clubhouse—where I'd once overheard an old Wing Commander say to an old Squadron Leader, "Quite right, a glass of port goes very well in the Big Room."

ALL THE British Open highlights that I knew of were duly reported in phone calls back to the States. I waited until after midnight Sunday to make the calls in an effort to catch the loved ones and chums around dinnertime their time.

I tried Cheryl first but no answer. I left a message saying I'd call her between flights tomorrow.

The first human I reached was Buddy Stark at his house in the Lake Austin hills. He was out of breath and I quickly learned that Cynthia was with him.

"Sorry to interrupt," I said. "I guess y'all were busy in the kitchen making fudge."

"Something like that," Buddy said.

I asked if they'd watched the tournament. All four days, Buddy said. Knut Thorssun, marquee name, had been on camera a lot till he missed the cut, and it had been a treat to see Knut suffering so much physically. Buddy asked, How sick was Knut? TV viewers were informed that he'd been fighting the flu.

"Nonnie Harrison took him hostage, is what happened," I said. "She turned up here. She could have ruined my week, not to mention my life. I tap-danced around it for two days, then Mitch came up with the idea to sic her on Knut, get her off my ass. I put Nonnie and Knut together at dinner on Wednesday night in the Old Course dining room. They were deeply in lust before I finished my shrimp cocktail."

Buddy said, "Woodrow must at least have a touch of the flu. I've never known him to be slowed down by a mattress tussle."

I said, "Nonnie don't play zone. She's man-for-man, full court press the whole game. Turn you into an emphysema case is what she can do."

"You can testify to that, as I recall."

"All part of growing up," I said. "Incidentally, I've been meaning to ask you about Emily, the scholar. I gather you've dusted her, what with the Cynthia thing going on. Did you let her off easy?"

"Emily let me off before Cynthia cropped up. She came over one day to tell me she was in love with her English professor. I know the guy. He has a beard, hangs around the joints on the lake. For a shit-kicker from Wichita Falls, he's done a good job of mastering a British accent."

"British accents do strange things to women," I said. "I've often wished for one."

"She says the best thing about him is, he has his own car."

I said, "Did you watch Cheetah do it?"

"Golf always needs new heroes," Buddy said. "It's a good thing Cheetah and his daddy are great Americans and wonderful human beings."

We talked about how tough the course played for a few minutes, then I got around to the real reason I called. Which was to pass on what I'd heard from Knut—that he was going to cough up the thirty million in the Tammy Wynette with Cynthia, but he didn't want her to know it yet.

"I won't tell her till we hang up," Buddy said.

I said that seemed fair to me and I'd let them go back to their fudge.

Next call I made was to Alleene Simmons. When she answered, I said, "I don't know why I'm calling you, but I have, and here you are, and I'm already feeling guilty about it. Do you have an explanation?"

"You're a leg man," she said. "You've always been a leg man."

"Not to mention spineless and weak-willed."

"You did okay today," Alleene said. "You were on TV twice, just briefly. Who was that Nigerian you were paired with?"

"I don't even know American lurkers," I said. "How am I supposed to know foreign lurkers?"

She said, "I played golf this morning. I watched it at Mira Vista. Cheryl was at the club having lunch with a couple. Clients. She was trying to sell them Versailles or the Kremlin, one of the two. My gosh, the houses they're building out there. Cheryl and I had a nice visit."

"You did?" Stunned deal.

"I like her," Alleene said. "She's nifty. You better throw a net over that lady pretty soon, Bobby, or you're going to lose her. We talked about going to the Ryder Cup."

"*Together?*" Stunned again.

"No, of course not."

"Good," I said, "because I was sort of thinking of taking Cheryl myself—and I don't think they allow the players to bring two wives."

"I'm going as a *fan*, Bobby. I want to see a Ryder Cup. I can take a long weekend off. You can handle a credential, right?"

"There's no prize money at the Ryder Cup, you know."

"I'll ignore that remark."

"Guess what I've done tonight?" I said. "I've figured out how much I've won this year, officially. It's almost a million, seven hundred thousand. The exact figure is one million, six hundred thousand, four hundred and sixty-six dollars and sixty-six cents. That would be Terri's count."

"That's wonderful. It really is. It's your best year by far."

"I know, but . . . I'm thinking about these other things. Like, for instance, twenty-two guys won that much last year, and five guys won over three million. But you know what? As much money as this is—

and it's a ton to you and me and most people—it's chicken feed compared to what a major league baseball player makes for scratching his nuts all summer."

"Or what a rock star makes for turning into a vampire."

"You know what else?" I said. "After I pay my agent his twenty percent, and pay Mitch his ten percent and bonuses, and pay the feds a third of it, and put what's left in my untouchable retirement fund, I can't buy a cheeseburger."

Alleene said, "It's disgusting. I honestly don't know how people live on less than a million-seven a year."

"I'm going to sleep now," I said. "I leave early in the morning. Listen, do me a favor, pard. Since you and Cheryl have become pals now, and since you might be talking to each other again before I come home, I'd appreciate it if you don't mention I called you tonight . . . that we had this little chat. It'll be better for me all the way around. You'll do this thing?"

"Who *is* this?" Alleene said. "Hello? . . . Hello?"

I laughed and we said good night.

I did have one more conversation before my head hit the pillow. I called Smokey Barwood in New York. He'd left three urgent messages for me. One message indicated he'd called at 3:15 in the afternoon, my time. I would have been on the golf course then. I wondered if Smokey had thought the hotel would send somebody out to the Principal's Nose to page me in the final round of the British Open.

"Great, you *finally* got back to me," Smokey said. "You don't check your messages regularly? God, I wish I could do that. Well, never mind. I have you now and we have decisions to make."

The most urgent decision was whether I wanted to sail back home on the *QE2*. It would involve killing a couple of days in London first and missing the International at Castle Pines in Colorado, but Salu Kinda had canceled and the cruise director needed another golf pro.

"I have a gun in their ribs," Smokey said. "You can have the same suite you had coming over, plus they'll pay fifty Grovers."

"Fifty Grovers," I said. "Is that more than five hundred Benjamins?"

"They're desperate. Yes or no?"

"Yes," I said. "I don't mind missing the International. I've never understood the format anyhow. Pars are Xerox . . . birdies are two . . ."

"Pine Valley," Smokey said.

"What about it?"

"After you come home, and before the PGA," Smokey said. "Strictly because you've made the Ryder Cup team—and because you have such a good agent—I can get you a two-day gig at Pine Valley. Two rounds of golf and two dinners with dot.comers. You stay right there at the club. Sixty Grovers."

"Done," I said. "I love Pine Valley. Grover, too."

"Okay," Smokey said. "I'm booking you in the Stafford Hotel in London for three nights. You'll have the same driver to take you to Southampton to board the ship. Oh! One more thing. What tournaments are you playing between the PGA and the Ryder Cup?"

"I've promised San Antonio," I said. "Other than that . . ."

"Bobby Joe, you have to play Firestone," the agent said. "Need I remind you it's only forty players, no cut, and you make thirty Grovers just for showing up?"

"Pencil me in."

"Have a good voyage."

"I will," I said. "I'll think about Grover all the way."

39

MEN GOLFERS WITH PONYTAILS. Frankly, I didn't know such things were allowed at Pine Valley—merely the greatest course in the world—but eighteen of them were there, and they were all mine.

These were my dot.comers, members of the stock option gang. Guys mostly from California in their late twenties and early thirties. Guys who'd said to the Wall Street crowd a decade ago, "You people just don't get it, do you?" and had gone about raking in fifty million and up for themselves, and had built all the mansions and bought all the trophy wives and other toys, and had thought there was nothing to it, like it was God's will.

But God and I had the last laugh at Pine Valley. When it came to trying to play golf, *they* didn't get it.

First of all, they didn't get Pine Valley. They'd only bought their way in there for an outing because they'd heard it was exclusive. Which meant I did a lot of explaining and gave a running history lecture during our two-day frat party.

We stayed together in two of the houses on the property, houses near the big white and green clubhouse but all of it tucked away in a New Jersey pine forest only thirty miles southeast of Philadelphia.

I called most of them Randy or Scotty, although I think there was a Skipper or two. Mainly, I looked for their golf balls—after they dumped them into the sprawling unraked waste areas and thick groves of trees and matted plantlife that make up most of the course. Pine Valley *does* have fairways and greens, but only the more accomplished or luckiest players can locate them.

The way I handled my Randys in the two-day outing was the way I'd learned from older pros who came before me. Might have been Dave Marr I heard it from first. In both rounds I played the first three holes with three of them. I waited on the fourth tee and played the next three holes with three more. And so on till I played the last three holes with the last threesome. That way, I played three holes of golf with everybody in the group. Or I should say I hunted for balls with everybody in the group. I laid some tips on them while we were out in the sand and weeds and scrub, but their awkward swings never showed much improvement. Most of them were as foreign to golf as I was to dot and com.

In the evenings we dined at Pine Valley on the club's glorified snapper soup and a man's menu of pork chops and steak and fish, no tulips or bath gel.

None of the group ever said anything the least bit interesting the whole two days I was around them. They could have made a whole city nod off with their wine talk.

Whether they were interested in me or not, I explained why Pine Valley was special and how it came about.

I talked about George Crump, the Philadelphia hotel man who'd had the brainstorm for it and purchased the land and desired to build the world's most unique golf course. He'd died before it was finished and opened in 1921. I talked about how Pine Valley could never host a major. The grounds were too confining. The club did host the 1936 and 1985 Walker Cup matches, knowing that roughly only two thousand amateur fans would attend.

Harry Colt, the Englishman, still gets most of the credit for the overall design—for Hell's Half Acre on No. 7, the Devil's Asshole at No. 10, all that. No two holes were parallel, I pointed out, in case they hadn't noticed, and it was the only golf course in the world where you could come close to remembering every single hole after you'd played it only once.

I told them you could make a strong argument that Harry Colt was the greatest golf architect the game had known. Pine Valley and Sunningdale alone might hand him the title. The Sunningdale outside London.

Harry Colt dated back to Vardon's day, was a member of the R&A, a fine amateur player himself, taught Alister Mackenzie much of what he knew, designed courses in fifteen different countries, was the first architect to use a drawing board, and the first to recommend planting trees. Some of the layouts Colt had reworked, and therefore improved, read like a partial history of golf in Great Britain and Ireland—Muirfield, Hoylake, Royal Lytham & St. Annes, Royal St. Georges, or what you call your Sandwich, Royal Portmarnock, and Royal Portrush, to name a half dozen.

The combination of Pine Valley's intimidations and my nightly conversation usually sent the Randys to bed early. But all of them seemed to leave the place happy. I know Grover did.

40

IT TOOK ME A BRACE OF SHOW-
ers for three days and a load of dry cleaning to recover from the month on the
road.

Cheryl welcomed me back like a school-
girl with a crush. We had a blissful and sex-
ually satisfying week. During all that
activity, and purely because I was so proud
of my innocence in the deal, I got around
to telling her about the dreaded Nonnie
Harrison turning up at St. Andrews.

I was more or less prepared for Cheryl
to explode and accuse me of nailing Nonnie again. But I would slowly explain how
Mitch and I had handled the matter so
craftily. And I would turn out the hero in
the deal.

But no explosion. Cheryl was amused and congratulated me on my inspired craftiness.

We were sitting at the breakfast table in my townhouse that morning. I'd eaten my three eggs basted and country sausage. Cheryl had eaten her Cheerios and was dressed for work.

"You buy it, just like that?" I said. "I don't have to bring in character witnesses?"

"No, I can tell," she said.

"You can tell what?"

"I can tell you didn't knock off Nonnie, or anyone else."

"You can tell?"

"Yes."

"That's bullshit."

"No, it isn't."

"Yeah, it is. You could have knocked off a dozen guys while I was gone and I'd never know it."

"That's true. Men can't tell. Women can."

"A woman can tell but a man can't?"

"Yes."

"All women can tell?"

"No. Smart women can."

"That's absurd. You didn't know about Nonnie at Pebble Beach until you talked to her."

"I knew you were acting guilty about *something*. I was going to let it slide, whatever it was, but then the slut called here."

"How could you tell I was acting guilty?"

I was thinking voice inflection . . . subject matter . . . overshow of affection . . . undershow of affection . . . too much aftershave . . .

"It can't be explained," she smiled. "It's a woman thing."

With that, she kissed me on the forehead and went off to sell a house.

The bliss wore off a day later. What did it was my announcing that I was leaving again and would be gone three weeks.

"Christ," Cheryl said, "I might as well be involved with a trapeze artist. There's always another circus."

I said, "Look at the bright side. My year will basically be over in a little while longer. We'll go to a movie."

"Great," she said. "Now I have something to cling to."

And she was off to work again.

As I sat around drinking coffee that day I gave some thought to the fact that in all our time together, over two years, Cheryl had never seriously mentioned marriage, and neither had I.

We'd joked about it. How it might screw up a perfectly good relationship. I'd quote Buddy Stark, who once said, "A man can't be happily married unless he always knows what time it is, and likes going out to dinner." And Cheryl would quote Jolene Frederick, who liked to say, "I wouldn't fucking darn socks for *Ben Affleck*."

But I'd always held to the notion that everybody really wanted to be married. Not young people. Young people were aliens. Young people didn't know what they wanted, other than lots of money and abortions and music that sounded like a disposal. Mature people, on the other hand, knew that being married was the best way to live.

I know I'd enjoyed all my marriages, even when they didn't work out.

So I asked myself, Was I possibly creeping up on asking Cheryl if she wanted to bust out of the single world and do this marriage thing?

I answered myself with a full-on maybe.

41

THE DAY BEFORE I LEFT FOR
the PGA I received a swell send-off courtesy of FedEx and Irv Klar.

Tees and Sympathy
By Bobby Joe Grooves
with Irving Klar

You must first allow me to rhap-
sodize on the beauty of the game of
golf before I begin my own story.
It is the only game that leads one
unrelentingly into the glories of nature. They are all around the golfer,
these sensuous charms. Fresh air to
breathe, the pungent solitude, the

velvet fairways, the finely textured greens, the dark looming forests, the shimmering sand, the blue ponds, the rippling streams, the sprawl of dazzling flowers. All of this thrusting you into an emerald cathedral each time you go out for a round to seek an examination of your own private skills. Ah, the eternal bounty of golf!

My thought this time: Irv Klar is a dead Jew.

42

THERE WERE NO DOT.COMERS AT
the PGA to listen to my history babble, so
I made do with lurkers. Most of your
lurkers are interested in anything a tournament winner has to say, believing him
to be smarter than atomic secrets.

After a practice round one day I was in
the clubhouse having a snack in the contestants' lounge, and I invited three lurkers to come sit at my table. Two Kevins
and a Chuck, or maybe it was two Chucks
and a Kevin.

Contestants' lounges are provided in
the clubhouses at the majors and most
other tournaments to afford us privacy.
Security guards are on the door to see to
it that nobody comes in but players.

This has always made me laugh because in every contestants' lounge I've ever frequented I've watched it overflow with family members of players, officials of the PGA of America, officials of the USGA, officials of the PGA Tour, network TV announcers, IMG agents, and equipment reps. Everybody but sportswriters.

If a sportswriter tries to enter, a SWAT team appears.

I mention this because a moment after the lurkers joined me in the lounge at Oakmont, a Pittsburgh writer I knew slipped past the security guard and came in and tried to ask Phil Mickelson a question, and I watched as the newspaper guy was quickly apprehended, cuffed, and led away.

Jim Tom Pinch, the magazine writer, once explained to me why such a harsh attitude exists toward sportswriters on the part of tournament officials and country club members. He said it's because the sportswriters are only needed to help sell tickets to the tournament by writing glowing stories about it before it begins.

"Once the tournament starts," Jim Tom explained, "we're a nuisance. All we do is take up parking spaces and write wise-mouth stories nobody likes but us."

I passed that info along to the lurkers while we munched on the fruit and cheese and lunch meat sandwiches from the players' buffet. Slices of lunch meat are often known as cold cuts outside of Fort Worth.

"I agree with Cheetah," one of the lurkers said. Kevin or Chuck. "Cheetah says newspapers ain't good for shit, except to read sometimes."

"Boy, you got that right," said another lurker. Chuck or Kevin.

I wondered if the lurkers realized how much history they were wading around in on these outskirts of Pittsburgh. One of them said Oakmont was the first course he'd ever played with a freeway running through it. I pointed out that the "freeway" that intersects the course, leaving the second through the eighth holes on one side of it, was actually the Pennsylvania Turnpike. It came slicing through the course in 1947 but didn't change the layout.

He said, "Pay deal. I guess that's why it don't look too busy down there on it. You see some trucks, but I'll tell you one thing. If it was in Houston or Atlanta, you'd be looking at NASCAR around the clock. Them bridges over it ever collapse?"

Not that I'd ever heard about, I said. Nothing in golf lore about it.

I noted their looks of surprise when I informed them that Oakmont had played host to more national championships than any club in the United States. The club had held seven U.S. Opens, four U.S. Amateurs, three PGA Championships, and one U.S. Women's Open. This PGA would make it a total of sixteen.

Oakmont's members could also brag that their course was the one and only course in history on which Bobby Jones, Ben Hogan, and Jack Nicklaus, the three greatest players of all time, had won majors—the '25 U.S. Amateur for Jones, the '53 U.S. Open for Hogan, the '62 U.S. Open for Nicklaus.

And the members might be eager to add that a few other fairly reputable players had won majors at Oakmont. Some fellows named Gene Sarazen, Tommy Armour, Sam Snead, Johnny Miller, and Ernie Els.

Oakmont deserved its distinction as a home of immortals, I said, because the man responsible for its existence, William C. Fownes, son of a steel baron, had set out in 1903 to design and build "the world's hardest golf course," and for more than fifty years it held the title.

Fownes was a golf nut and a fine player—he won the U.S. Amateur in 1910—and a fellow who devoted his whole life to the care and feeding of Oakmont. To its drainage ditches that are the only water hazards on the course, to the famed furrowed bunkers that are now gone, and to the greens that were once cut, shaved, and rolled into the fastest in the world, and are still among the speediest.

He invented the heavy three-foot-long metal rake with V-shaped teeth that was used to create the furrows in the bunkers. Those furrowed bunkers stood as the trademark of Oakmont's difficulty for half a century.

It was Jimmy Demaret who once said, "You could comb Africa with that rake."

Fownes invented the infamous device because he firmly believed, and relished saying, "A shot poorly played should be a shot irrevocably lost."

"Where is Ear Boaty?" a lurker asked.

"Where's what?" I said.

"You said something about Ear Boaty."

"I said *irrevocably*."

"Oh. Where's that?"

"Uh . . . yeah," I said, standing up. "Fownes was born in Irrevocably, then he moved to Pittsburgh. Nice visiting with you guys. I believe I'll have me some more of that salami and cheese."

ALTHOUGH THE PGA has a lusty history and is one of the game's four major championships, it suffers in terms of national publicity and in the mind of the public. Everybody knows this—I'm not giving away any inside information here.

The biggest reason it suffers is because it's last. The last major of the year. The Masters has April, the U.S. Open has June, and the British Open has July. This leaves August for the PGA, which means we generally play it in blast-furnace heat and dripping humidity no matter which city is the host.

Last is bad for another reason. The sportswriters who cover us regularly are tired of golf by then and ready for football and pennant races—unless Tiger Woods is working on the Grand Slam.

So the sportswriters, being tired—*and* hot, *and* humid—give the PGA of America a little bit of hell every year for not returning the championship to match play, for not taking it back to the good old days when it was won by Walter Hagen and Gene Sarazen and Byron Nelson and Ben Hogan and Sam Snead in head-to-head battles with other gladiators.

The PGA was conducted at match play for forty years, from the time it started in 1916 until 1958, the year it was switched to stroke play to get itself on TV. Television executives fear match play the way I fear esses. They don't want to run the risk of having two nobodies, two funny guys, in the final, afraid it will send viewers scrambling for their remotes.

The writers like to argue that the guys who might have won the PGA at match play couldn't have looked any funnier than some of the slugs who've won it at stroke play over the past thirty hot and humid years. If the PGA would smarten up and go back to match play, they insist, the year's last major would at least have its own look, and therefore might attract more interest and attention.

Personally, I would dearly love to have been one of the slugs who've won the PGA in the past. I would dearly loved to have won it this year, in fact, but Tiger Woods didn't give anybody else a Chinaman's chance, or even a slug's chance.

Oakmont still could have been trying to defend itself with its furrowed bunkers of old but Tiger wouldn't have seen any of them. Not off the tee. Not unless his ball looked *down* while he was airmailing them.

Tiger opened with a 64, a seven-under round that was six shots better than anybody else, and he put it on cruise control from there on. His 273 was eleven under and nobody else even broke par of 284. He won by twelve. A laugher.

Myself, I sat on 73 all week and hatched a 292. The total tied me for sixteenth and earned me $68,000. I wasn't so disappointed in my performance that I wanted to put the paycheck in a garage sale, but I did feel I had a valid excuse for not playing better.

It was finding out about our Ryder Cup uniforms.

I hadn't seen Larry Foster, our captain, since I'd qualified for the team. I'd received a note from him after the U.S. Open. His note said "Welcome" and "Beat Europe." But enclosed in the envelope was a copy of the brochure he'd had made up. It contained several pictures of him, scrappy little guy, smiling and swinging clubs, and it invited anyone who happened to have a loose $5,000 to "play a round of golf with Larry Foster, the U.S. Ryder Cup captain."

Most of the players laughed about our Ryder Cup captain becoming a crafty old fund-raiser—for himself.

The day before the first round I had a brief visit with Larry Foster and his wife, Jill, a half-blonde chunko, many pounds removed from her days as a *Playboy* centerfold. Jill owned a boutique in LaJolla, where they lived, but now she was Madam Captain, and hugely enjoying the role.

I was privileged to have a cup of tea with them in the U.S. Ryder Cup hospitality tent. The hospitality tent was overflowing with officials of the PGA of America in their blazers of the day. Red and blue candy-striped.

That's where I found out about the uniforms. Mrs. Larry Foster, Jill, Madam Captain, had taken it upon herself to design them.

This fact was dropped on me a moment after I said I was really looking forward to wearing the red, white, and blue.

They looked at each other, and Jill said, "Well . . . we're going in a slightly different direction this time. We—Larry and I—felt it was time our colors become more diversified."

"Diversified?" I said.

"Yes," she said.

"Does the United States know about this?" I asked.

They forced a smile.

Jill said, "I believe we, the United States of America, should stress our originality *and* our diversity. That is essentially what I've strived for. I've gone with a mixture of tan and yellow in two of the flowered shirts you'll wear on the course."

"Tan and yellow," I repeated, glancing at Larry. He didn't dare look like he was anything but pleased.

"The PGA has approved everything I've done," Jill said. "We will still wear red, white, and blue at times, of course, but they will be different from the red, white, and blue in our flag. For one thing, the red in one pair of the golf slacks and one of the golf shirts is more of a maroon."

"Maroon," I said. "We're the Texas Aggies."

No laughter that time.

I excused myself, thanked them for the uniform update, and told my captain that in whatever colors I wore when the competition started, he could count on me to leave it all on the field.

43

NO POINT IN DWELLING ON THE scintillating golf I played at Firestone and Oak Hills in San Antonio. Thinking most of the time about the Ryder Cup and Cheryl and marriage, all I did in Akron was finish last and collect my thirty Grovers. As for San Antonio, while it was good to see the old Tillinghast course again, I wasn't the birdie machine you need to be on that kind of layout. Old, short, sporty. I shot my 68 and 71 and did a Marlon Brando—got me "a one-way ticket to Palookaville."

Back home I worked hard on my game for ten days, hoping to sharpen it up for the Europeans. Our team was impressive at the top—Tiger and the others—but every point counts in the cup matches, and I wanted mine to count for the good old maroon, tan, and yellow.

The day before we left for Columbus, Ohio, I took Cheryl out for a romantic dinner of chicken fried steak and cream gravy at Rick's on the Bricks, a popular tavern-slash-restaurant not far from downtown.

We sat in the quiet dining room where we wouldn't be bothered by the noise from the bar—the booming discussions of good and evil as they related to TCU's football fortunes—and where we could read the big sign on the wall that said:

In Dallas they call it sushi—in Fort Worth we call it bait.

"I don't have enough makeup to live in Dallas," Cheryl said.

That was the night I asked Cheryl to join me in legal and maybe even holy matrimony, seeing as how I'd realized I couldn't live without her through another year on the tour.

"You'll empty the trash?" she said.

"Do my best."

"You'll unload the dishwasher?"

"If you'll show me where it is."

"You'll change lightbulbs?"

"I can learn how."

"You won't fuck Nonnies?"

"Never again . . . Alleene, maybe."

Cheryl startled me with a laugh. I'd expected a squint.

Then she said, "I won't have to worry too much about that. Alleene would rather be on the golf course."

"That's the truth," I said.

"Alleene is my buddy now," she said. "Your business partner, my new best friend."

"She is?"

Surprised deal.

Cheryl said, "We've gotten to know each other while you've been touring Western civilization. She's terrific. We have lunches. She wants to go to the Ryder Cup."

"Really?"

Even more surprised.

"I hope she does," Cheryl said. "You're going to be in a golf coma. I'll have somebody to fool around with. What is there to do in Columbus?"

"Not a whole lot," I said. "Mostly, everybody just walks around singing Ohio State fight songs."

"Well, that alone," she said.

Here was my plan, I said. We should get married—to one another—sometime after the Ryder Cup. Our wedding cake didn't necessarily have to be a stack of barbecue brisket. We could go on a honeymoon, if she wished. Anywhere but Mexico or Arizona. We should sell my townhouse and her garden home and move to Mira Vista. Buy Versailles or the Kremlin, whichever one she liked best. I preferred Versailles. More lawn for somebody to mow. And there was something else. In order for her to be free to travel with me as often as possible, I wanted her to have her own real estate agency, be the boss. I'd finance it. She could hire Bonnie Lasater and Jolene Frederick to work for her, take care of things when she was gone. They'd be a winning combination. When a couple came along and seemed interested in a house, they'd be good at closing the sale quickly. Bonnie could occupy the wife's time while Jolene fucked the husband.

"Sounds like a worthwhile plan," she beamed, clinking her glass of wine against my Junior. "Deal."

44

ALL YOU FOLKS OUT THERE WHO
watched the Ryder Cup in person or
on TV, you didn't see or hear much
of what I'm now going to report. I
want to try to tell it as clearly as I can.
Call it the inside story. Call it the flip side.
Just don't call it what Irv Klar wants to
call the chapter if we ever get around to
doing the book. Irv would call it "Little
Red Ryder Hood," may his typing fingers
be squashed by hefty people in hiking
boots.

Several things won't soon be forgotten
by some of us who were at the opening
ceremony. The opening ceremony took
place around the eighteenth green at

Muirfield Village, same as it had when Jack Nicklaus's club hosted the matches the first time back in '87.

The festivities began with the Ohio State band marching up the eighteenth fairway, having started back at the tee. The band played "Buckeye Battle Cry" and "Across the Field," the school's two rousing fight songs. Many in the hometown crowd teared up, as they normally do when they hear these tunes, but then some laughter broke out when the drum major in the tall fur hat tripped and fell.

The drum major scrambled up and continued to prance as if nothing happened, and the crowd applauded his effort.

"I hope that's not a bad omen for the U.S.," Cheryl said. At that moment, all twelve members of both teams along with their wives or fiancées and officials were waiting in the wings.

I said, "That's what they get for stealing Paschal High's fight song."

A little humor there.

The two teams huddled together and made small talk while we waited to march out. Cheryl couldn't resist playing around with Knut Thorssun, the only European team member without a wife or ladyfriend.

"Your wife isn't with you?" Cheryl said.

"No, we have taken our separate paths," Knut said. "I hope she is seeking medical advice. She is a sick woman in the mind."

"I'm sorry you're alone," Cheryl said.

I said, "You can bust me if he's alone."

Knut smiled. "Oh, ho, Bobby Joe. You know me too well. Yes, it is true. A lady awaits me back at the hotel. She did not wish to participate in the ceremonies."

I said, "She didn't want to wear anything but a garter belt and bra, but they wouldn't let her."

Cheryl said, "Well, that was rather small-minded of them."

Knut caught up with my remark. "*Har, har!*" he exploded. "Bobby Joe, you are always to be the funny one. But we must be serious about this competition, must we not?"

"Absolutely," I said.

With the exception of me, the rookie, I believed the USA had as strong a team as any in the past. Our marquee was loaded with experience and "names"—Tiger Woods, Phil Mickelson, Davis Love, David Duval, Justin Leonard, Cheetah Farmer, Rickey Padgett, Hal Sutton, Jim Furyk, and the two wild cards, Fred Couples and Paul Azinger.

I was well acquainted with most of the members of the European squad, the ones who played our tour often or occasionally—Knut, of course, and Colin Montgomerie, Sergio Garcia, Jesper Parnevik, José Maria Olazabal, Paul Lawrie, Lee Westwood, Darren Clarke, François Despeaux, and Romeo Nadi.

Although I knew Karl Hein by name, I'd never met the European captain until that week. He'd been one of Germany's early golf stars, and was called in to lead the team after Tony Jacklin and Seve Ballesteros both refused to come out of retirement.

Karl Hein was already operating under a cloud of criticism from the British press by the time he arrived in Columbus. The Brits were outraged at his two wild card selections that rounded out the European team. The captain had passed up such veterans as Nick Faldo and Ian Woosnam to go with two of his fellow countrymen, Gottfried Kunz and Otto Schwarzmann.

Defending his choices, the Europeans' captain had been quoted saying, "We need up-and-comers, not disappearers."

The Europeans—players, officials, and wives—marched into the public ceremony first, and if it seemed that they received more lasting applause and exuberant shouts than we did, I lay the blame directly on the doorstep of Jill Foster, Madam Captain.

The Europeans wore three-piece navy blue suits, white shirts, and red ties, and their wives wore tasteful red, white, and blue ensembles. They looked like the Americans usually look.

We, on the other hand, were dressed like athletes from a Third World country marching into an Olympic stadium. We were wearing maroon suits, blue shirts, yellow ties, and maroon fedoras. Hats, yeah.

Some of us turned our hat brims up all the way around, and some of us turned them all the way down. Cheetah Farmer and Rickey Padgett wore the dark glasses they were being paid to endorse.

I sincerely thought you could see better-dressed people at a bank robbery, but I didn't tell Madam Captain that.

Our ladies weren't let off any easier. They were wearing yellow pants suits, red turtlenecks, and brown golf visors.

The band played all of the anthems. I was like most people, I think. Only three of them sounded familiar to me—England, France, and Germany. Spain's was the longest. We could have played two rubbers of bridge before it was over, and we weren't even sure it was over when it was over.

Cheryl whispered to me that in her official outfit, she was happy she hadn't been run up the flagpole when they played the Spanish anthem.

I'd heard somewhere that in the Ryder Cup flag raising, which accompanies the anthems, the flags of at least two foreign countries invariably seem to get themselves hung upside down and fly that way the whole weekend. The Italian flag flew upside down at Muirfield Village and Sweden's flag turned out to be Denmark's, but you had to read *Golf Digest* later to find this out.

Cheryl and I scanned the crowd while the speeches droned on, seeing if we could spot any of our pals. I'd obtained credentials for Alleene, Buddy Stark and Cynthia, and Jerry Grimes. All of them were supposed to have arrived that morning. We didn't see them anywhere, but there were more than fifteen thousand people on hand, including three thousand rowdies from Europe.

Cheryl planned to make contact with Alleene as soon as possible. Our pals were all staying in another hotel. I said I sure hoped I would be present when Knut saw Cynthia with Buddy for the first time.

A week earlier I'd asked Buddy on the phone, "What does Woodrow know, and when did he know it?"

Buddy said, "As far as we can tell, he doesn't know about us yet, but the divorce is final, so who cares?"

Irv Klar and Smokey Barwood had both called to say I didn't need to worry about credentials for them—they weren't going to make it as they'd intended. Bad timing.

Irv said, "My sports editor is a black guy. He's making me cover the UCLA–San Diego State football game Saturday. He says the Ryder Cup's an event for Republicans. It's not, is it?"

I said, "What have you heard from the resumes you sent out? Anything promising?"

"I got laughed at by *SI* and the *New York Times*," he said. "I haven't heard back from the others. I'm not giving up on your book, Bobby Joe. Your voice isn't easy. I'm thinking hard about it. I know it's somewhere in the ballpark of, let's say, professional golfer from Texas has a head-on collision with the English language."

I said, "Keep thinking hard, Irv. Thinking hard is good for the mind."

My agent passed on the Ryder Cup at the last minute because of another client's problems.

Smokey was busy trying to do damage control on all of Mucus Benson's endorsement contracts because of the latest incident involving the all-pro linebacker, who only last March had been acquitted of the axe murder of LaToya Boyette, his girlfriend, the Olympic hurdler.

Mucus had now been arrested at a party in a Dallas apartment house and charged with murdering his new girlfriend, a fifteen-year-old high school student named Samantha. He beat her to death with a tire tool. He was also charged with raping Samantha's older sister, Teresa, a sixteen-year-old, by forcing her into a bathroom on her hands and knees. But there was more. Apparently he was in possession of a full Ziploc bag of cocaine and was said to have permanently crippled one of the arresting officers, a female, by hurling her down two flights of stairs. Eyewitnesses saw all of it.

"It's going to be a tough one," Smokey said, "but I've had calls from six criminal attorneys in six different states who think they can beat it—they say public opinion will be on Mucus's side."

I said, "One of the calls wasn't from a chick in Fort Worth representing a lawyer named Red Taggert, was it?"

Smokey said, "Yes, do you know him?"

45

WE HELD A PRIVATE TEAM DIN-
ner meeting on Thursday night before the
matches started the next morning. This
was where Captain Foster reminded us
that there would be foursomes, or
alternate shots, Friday morning and
four-balls in the afternoon, and the order
would be reversed on Saturday, and
there would be twelve singles matches
Sunday.

Like we weren't able to read the pro-
gram.

The captain also reminded us that
we should conduct ourselves in a sports-
manlike manner at all times because
we represented the United States of
America.

Rickey Padgett, striving for a joke, said, "It says USA on my bag—is that the same thing?"

Cheetah Farmer said, "We don't need no pep talks, Larry. These guys aren't in our class. What are they? Bunch of frogs ... wops, spicks? They ought to be *caddying* for us."

I said, "I know a way to sabotage their team."

Everybody looked at me.

"Put a bar of soap in their rooms." I grinned.

Everybody was still looking at me.

"That's funny," I said, "y'all are supposed to be laughing."

"Why?" Larry Foster asked.

I said, "Have you ever found a bar of soap in Europe?"

"Oh," he said.

The captain called me aside after the meeting broke up. He informed me that he was going with experience in the morning. I would be sitting out the morning foursomes. I said fine. But he really wanted to ask a favor.

"Will you take Cheetah for a partner?" he said.

"If you want me to," I replied.

"Good," he said, looking relieved. "Nobody will play with him. I've asked everybody else. They all say keep that cocky prick and his dickhead daddy away from me."

"Or words to that effect," I said.

"More or less."

"I'll take Cheetah," I said. "He's a hell of a talent, mouth and all."

THE MUIRFIELD Village course was in gorgeous condition, better than I'd ever seen it, and I'd played in eight or nine Memorial Tournaments. I almost hated to take a divot out of the velvet fairways, and I wouldn't have minded licking food off the bent greens.

Jack had designed and built the course in the early '70s and it immediately took its place among the Top Ten in the country, but he'd never stopped jacking with it, proving himself as much of a perfectionist as an architect as he was as a player. The layout meets the "memorability" test with ease, and the fourteenth hole, the short but dangerous par four with water on the right, seems to make somebody's All-Time Best 18 every year.

Nicklaus named the club after Muirfield in Scotland, where he won his first British Open in '66. But there's a story that a British golf writer once complained to Jack before the club opened that the name Muirfield Village was a big mistake.

Jack should name it something else, the British writer told him. Bear Creek, Golden Bear, something personal, more suitable. The word "muir," he informed Jack, meant "village" in Scottish, thus Jack surely didn't want to name his club Villagefield Village.

As the story goes, Jack's response was "Well, this is Ohio, not Scotland, and the stationery's already been printed."

That story didn't do much for Cheetah Farmer.

Cheetah was more interested in moving the conversation back to his favorite topic, himself. We were waiting around on the seventeenth tee of our four-ball match Friday afternoon. We were one up on our foes Otto Schwarzmann and Romeo Nadi.

All day long, between making birdies for us, Cheetah had talked about leaving IMG to go with WhapServ, a new firm whose agents were wooing him. The agents had been telling Cheetah they could do far better for him than the fifty million IMG made for him a year ago.

"It's a dilemma," I'd said to him more than once.

I couldn't help wondering how many people in America weren't sleeping well lately, having to worry about a twenty-two-year-old golfer who'd only made fifty million dollars last year.

I mentioned that to my pals who'd been in the gallery all day walking along together—Cheryl, Alleene, and Jerry Grimes. The shouts of "Go USA!" had mostly come from Alleene Simmons, golf fan.

Buddy and Cynthia were in town, but the lovebirds had yet to emerge from their hotel room.

When all four of us reached the seventeenth green in regulation, Captain Foster came driving up in his golf cart. He walked out on the green to tell Cheetah and I how desperately we needed this point.

The morning foursomes had split 2-2, Tiger and Duval had won the first four-ball in the afternoon, but the European pairs of Knut-Jesper and Garcia-Olazabal were winning their matches handily. Our match, therefore, was critical. It would clinch us a 4-4 tie for the first day.

We were all looking at birdie putts ranging from twenty-five to eighteen feet. The Europeans were both inside of us. I left my putt six inches short, right in the throat. I slapped the Armour and said, "Way to go, Doris." I tapped in for the par four.

Cheetah's daddy, the arrogant caddy, said, "Time to go into our two-minute offense, kid."

"No prob-lemmo," Cheetah said.

Cheetah addressed his ball, but glanced at me before he putted.

"Watch this," he said. "This is gonna look like a BB rollin' into a washtub . . . send these dudes home in a hearse."

The putt didn't even come close. Cheetah yelled, "Fuck me!" He kicked his ball off the green. His daddy picked it up.

Our foes both missed their birdie tries. Better still for us, they left themselves very difficult putts for pars. Breaking putts of five or six feet.

I went over to stand by Otto Schwarzmann, the German, while Romeo Nadi, the Italian, studied his putt from all angles. He would putt first. One of them had to make the putt or the match was over.

Speaking softly, I said, "Otto, what did your granddaddy do in the war? You hear any stories growing up?"

"No, this subject was never discussed," he said. "Why do you ask at a moment like this?"

"It's only a game," I shrugged. "I've heard half a dozen people say golf is the real winner here this week."

"Games are serious," he said.

I said, "I know what *my* granddaddy did in the war, Otto. He flew

B-17 raids over Germany. Hey, you know what? I'll bet my grand-daddy bombed the shit out of your granddaddy. What do you think?"

Otto was glaring at me in an insane way as Romeo Nadi barely missed his putt. The ball rolled around the cup and stopped on the lip. Margarita with a slice of lime.

Otto had no chance, then. Not with the whole match riding on his putt. Not while thinking about his granddad buried in all that rubble. He blew the putt by a foot to the right.

I sauntered over to the ropes where my friends were whooping and applauding. Behind me, still on the green, Otto Schwarzmann and Romeo Nadi were pointing in all directions and barking furiously at each other in German and Italian.

46

SATURDAY OF THE RYDER CUP
was the first time I'd been benched
since high school—when I missed three
straight J's and Coach Baldy Toler threw
a chair at me.

What Captain Larry Foster did was, he
decided to go with his more experienced
players, his brand names. This put Cheetah Farmer and me on the sidelines along
with Jim Furyk and Rickey Padgett. I
joined the cheering section out on the
course, as did Rickey and Jim. Cheetah,
that staunch patriot, chose to hit practice
balls and talk to his IMG agent all day.

We'll never know whether Larry made
the right decision. We do know that our

big names at least fought their way to another 4–4 tie in the four-balls and foursomes. Which meant that after two days of fierce competition the score was USA 8, Europe 8.

It would all come down to Sunday's twelve singles matches. We needed to win seven of those to nab the cup. Or they did.

By late Saturday afternoon every player was aware of who his singles opponent would be. It works like this: the two captains, as the rules call for, secretly list their players 1 through 12 in whatever order they prefer. They are then revealed and announced. USA No. 1 plays Europe No. 1, USA No. 2 plays Europe No. 2, and so forth on down to USA No. 12 duking it out with Europe No. 12. Luck of the draw on who you play.

It's a captain's guessing game and it's always been debated as to the best way to arrange your lineup. Put strength at the top and strength at the bottom, or throw all your strength in the middle.

Larry Foster went with strength at the top and strength at the bottom. That's why Tiger led off and Mickelson brought up the rear. A hoss to get us out of the starting blocks with a win, hopefully, and Phil back there in case things tightened up and we needed a hoss who could handle the pressure of a decisive match.

That was the logic. If you've ever explored Ryder Cup history, you know that's always been the USA's logic. It's successful about 50 percent of the time.

The captain tried to hide me, putting me ninth, but as fate and destiny conspired to have it, that was where Europe slotted Knut Thorssun.

I was as elated about the matchup as my captain was depressed.

Larry's look and body language told me he'd already conceded a point to the enemy. Knut had been Europe's stud-bubba-muffin for two days. He and Parnevik had won all four of their partnership matches, Knut doing most of the damage.

Then, of course, my performance at the Saturday night press conference didn't make my captain feel any better about things. If it had been a football game, I'd have been accused of providing bulletin board fodder for the other team.

When the twelve Europeans were seated behind the microphones in the press room to discuss their singles opponents and offer their thoughts in general, they made every effort to be nice and complimentary.

Our guys did the same thing when it was our turn, even Cheetah.

Well, everybody but me.

The thing a writer said to me was "Bobby Joe, you seem to have drawn a pretty tough assignment tomorrow. How do you feel about having to play Knut Thorssun?"

I made the impulsive mistake of saying, "Knut's real tough, especially when he's got the zebras going for him."

"What do you mean?" the writer followed up.

"Knut gets his share of favorable rulings," I said.

All it takes is a sniff of controversy for the media to be on you like alligators on marshmallows. Hands went up all over the room. The PGA officer who was sitting up there with us and running the interview pointed at a guy in the crowd.

The guy stood up and said, "What rulings are you talking about?"

I said, "Well, for starters, go back and check out how he won at San Diego, Colonial, and Winged Foot this year."

"Are you accusing Knut Thorssun of cheating?" somebody yelled.

"I don't really know what constitutes cheating anymore," I said. "You tell me. Is it cheating to take advantage of a ruling when the dumbass official is obviously making a big mistake, but it helps you win a tournament? Knut did it three times. Bobby Jones would never have done it, and I don't think most of the guys on our tour would have done it."

The writer said, "San Diego, Colonial, and Winged Foot—are those the three worst things Knut Thorssun's ever done, in your opinion?"

"No," I laughed. "He's done three worse things than that."

"What, what?" The shouts came from different areas.

I started to respond but a Rally Killer interrupted.

"Bobby Joe!" he screeched. "Bobby Joe! Over here!"

I nodded to him.

"What year did you start using Hogan irons?" the Rally Killer asked.

He was roundly booed and hooted into the rear of the room.

"Tell us the three worst things Knut Thorssun ever did," a writer yelled. "What were they?"

"Yeah, what?" somebody else shouted.

"That's easy," I said. "He got born . . . came to America . . . stayed."

There was some laughter. Most of the writers scribbled on their notepads. My captain held his head in his hands.

AS THE eight matches ahead of us were sent out to do combat, Knut and I hit balls on the range, a good distance apart. Mitch either liked my action or he was only trying to build up my confidence.

"I believe I see grease drippin' off them irons," he said.

Translated, that meant I was in a clubface mode.

The surprise I'd planned for Knut worked out well on the first tee. Buddy and Cynthia arrived early enough to secure a place to stand right up against the ropes, parallel with the tee markers. Stationed next to them on both sides were Cheryl, Alleene, and Jerry Grimes.

Even if Knut hadn't spotted Cynthia himself, I was going to make certain he did before we teed off.

He exclaimed, "My God, it is the she-bitch I see! Look!"

"I see her," I said. "She's with Buddy Stark, isn't she? I wonder how long that's been going on?"

Knut went over to the ropes. I followed him.

"What is this nonsense of you being here?" Knut said to Cynthia.

"I just came to root against you," Cynthia said.

"You have made enough trouble for me," Knut said.

Somewhat giggly, Cynthia moved her arms and hips back and forth, and quietly chanted, "Bobby Joe, Bobby Joe, he's our man . . . if he can't do it, Tiger can!" Cheerleader deal.

I glanced at Buddy as if to ask if it might be a little early in the day for Cynthia to be into the white wine. Buddy shrugged.

Knut said to Buddy, "You are selecting to be with this crazy woman?"

Buddy pulled Cynthia close to him and said, "Love's got hold of us, Knut. We can't hardly help ourselves."

Knut shook his head in what was supposed to be disbelief and faked a laugh, *har-har*, and walked away to take the driver out of his bag.

I grinned at my pals. "Well, I've got my ankles taped. Guess I'm ready to go."

"Fairways and greens, Bobby," Alleene said.

"Tell me that helps," I said.

THINGS CHANGE quickly on the last day of the Ryder Cup matches. Always do. You can't take anything for granted. A good example is The Country Club in '99. That's where Olazabal was four up on Justin Leonard with only seven holes to play, but Justin rallied and sank that putt from Boston to Providence and the USA swooped the deal, broke the little European hearts.

All I could do was try to concentrate on my own match with Knut. I'd learn from murmurs in the crowd, or by perusing the occasional scoreboard, or from my captain appearing out of the trees, that Tiger and Davis and Couples were winning, but then I'd hear later they weren't.

One thing I did with Knut was wait until we were on the fourth tee to examine his bag, make sure he was carrying only fourteen clubs. The fact is, I only did it to annoy him. Even Knut wasn't dumb enough to have too many clubs in his bag at the Ryder Cup.

Actually, I did it to remind Knut that I was aware he'd once been caught by Jerry Grimes with a fifteenth club in his bag. It was in the first round at Harbour Town four years ago, on about the sixth hole, and Jerry had been generous enough, or stupid enough, to stand by while Knut instructed his caddy to take the extra club, a third wedge, into a portable toilet and ditch it. Knut ended up winning the tournament thanks to Jerry's silence.

"Just checking," I said to Knut on the fourth tee as I peeked around in his bag. "Some of us remember Harbour Town."

Knut looked injured. "I have heard such vicious rumors these years, and I must tell you I am greatly offended beyond description."

I said, "Knut . . . ? Play golf."

Knut and I wound up in what you call your melee.

I was playing as good as I knew how, shooting three under par—Mitch rewarding one of my shots from time to time with a "Hello, golf." And Knut was cheating quite well on the greens. I was aware of it but I was waiting for the right moment to call him on it.

The right moment came at the seventeenth hole. We were all square there and we'd inherited most of the gallery—not to mention all the teammates, sweethearts, wives, and mothers on both sides.

By then I was aware that we'd won six matches and Europe had won five, which meant the whole Mother Goose was riding on our match.

Time to play my ace.

I played it after we'd both steer-jobbed the fairway and hit the green in regulation at seventeen, and after I'd two-putted for a par, and Knut had missed his twenty-foot birdie putt that slid two feet past the cup.

As Knut walked to his ball, I stopped him on the green and said, "Nukester, you're not gonna mark *this* ball the way you've been doing it all year. It's fucking cheating. You know it and I know it."

Knut looked flustered. "You are saying what?"

"What I'm saying is, I'm gonna lie down on my stomach and watch you mark this ball unless you do it with two fingers and very daintily."

That came out real slow, real clear.

Knut had been cheating when he marked his ball on short putts on good bent greens. I don't know where he learned it. From some old guy on the Senior Tour, I guess. It's an old trick, going back to the '50s and maybe even longer.

Knut would put the coin down behind the ball, but in the seconds before he'd lift the ball, he'd mash it down and rub it forward just hard enough to make a slight groove in the green. Then, when it came his turn to putt, he'd replace the ball precisely back in the slight groove before he putted.

What the slight groove can do, it can make the two-footer race straight for the cup regardless of any break that might be there. Knut had been deadly on short putts, two-footers, for months.

I stood right over him while he marked his ball daintily, properly.

"Knock it in," I smiled, stepping away.

He pulled the putt to the left.

There were gasps and then the gasps were drowned out by raucous cheers as the ball didn't even get a piece of the cup.

All Knut could do was stare down at the ball as if he couldn't figure out where in the hell that ace of clubs came from.

I didn't realize we'd won the Ryder Cup in that moment. Not until Mitch was picking me up and whirling me around and everybody came rushing onto the green to pick me up and whirl me around.

There was another hole to play, and it hadn't occurred to me that Knut's bogey had put me one up with only one to play. I'd cinched a half-point for us, which was all we needed.

Captain Larry Foster, fine sportsman that he is, gave the last hole to Knut. In the permanent record book this would show that Knut and I halved the match individually, but this didn't matter to me. All that mattered to me was the final score of the Ryder Cup.

USA 14½, Europe 13½.

After all the handshakes and backslaps and hugs from good pals and total strangers, and while a massive celebration involving hundreds of American fans was forming up near the clubhouse, I was left with Cheryl and Alleene.

Cheryl embraced me and we kissed, long and hard.

"Can I kiss this guy, too?" Alleene asked Cheryl.

"Of course," Cheryl said.

Alleene put her arms around my neck and I put my hands on her waist and we slowly kissed on the mouth.

"Careful," said Cheryl.

Alleene and I broke off the kiss, laughing.

The three of us then walked arm in arm toward the clubhouse.

"Hello, golf," Cheryl said with a grin.

THE BASIC END